A Burning Lie

Clai

Book 3 –

Books in series:

Perfect Lie
A Silent Child
A Burning Lie

Stories that inspire emotions!
www.rubyfiction.com

Published 2022 by Ruby Fiction

Penrose House, Crawley Drive, Camberley, Surrey GU15 2AB, UK
www.rubyficiton.com

A CIP catalogue record for this book is available
from the British Library

EPUB ISBN: 978-1-912550-70-8
PRINT ISBN: 978-1-912550-75-3

PRINTED AND BOUND BY AMAZON

To all those who keep us safe:

Especially Nottinghamshire Fire and Rescue and station 23

East Midlands Ambulance Service and the Hazardous Area Response Team

Nottingham University NHS Hospitals

East Midlands Special Operations Unit

Acknowledgements

Thank you to my work colleagues old and new – some of whom I've not seen properly in over a year. Bonds, renewals, new and old clients, Open Cover, Covid, processing and everything else in between: YOU'VE GOT THIS.

My Choc Lit family, and the original Ruby Newbies, who I am yet to meet in real life, but who are all happy to support and cheer me on, despite Ikea kitchen nightmares, bookmark making and random questions!
My editor, who has more patience with me than I have with myself.
The Choc Lit Tasting Panel who continue supporting me, and especially the readers who said yes to this manuscript and made publication possible: Siobhan Bray, Julie Lilly, Jenny Mitchell, Lorna Baker, Fran Stevens, Sharon Walsh, Jo Osborne and Lynda Adcock.

Multiple Sclerosis is such a big part of my life, and a lot of research for this book has come from speaking to the inspirational ladies who form part of the muMS Facebook group.

My amazing consultant, Dr Evangelou, who is never too busy to answer my questions/humour me.

Mike Gale, for his first-hand experience of being a serving police detective with MS.

The Creatives@Cogs: a group of amazing local authors who I am only just getting to know.

Helen Keeley and the team at Ulverscroft who continue to bring my characters to life in audio format. Each time I listen back to a book, you always manage to bring happy tears to my eyes.

Sharon Smith, who helped raise an astonishing amount for Child in Read. I hope I've done Selina's character justice.

Lesley Burge, Lucy Mitchell, Cathryn Northfield and all the other bloggers and authors out there who continue to cheer me and this series on.

Jimmy Eat World – whenever I have struggled with this book, I have put your albums on and things have magically made sense. Though I doubt you'll ever know what you do for me and countless others, this is my thanks to you.

All those people I spoke to about working in entertainment venues. There are so many supportive Facebook groups when it comes to loneliness of being an author: The Fiction Café Book Club, The UK Crime Book Club and Crime Fiction Addict to name a few.
My extended family, who sell my books, talk through plot problems with me and generally cheer me on, thank you. X

Alex and Melanie for always keeping me sane – at least you can finally go as yourselves for World Book Day!

Andrew, who has continued to keep me on track by telling me "That would never happen in a fire".

Prologue

'Come on, Gabe.' Dean raced up the stairs towards where the band were playing.

'Slow down! I'm coming, I'm coming.' Light emanated from the stage as the lead singer of the young support band sang. 'See, I told you there was no need to rush. The support band's still playing,' Gabe said as he caught up with Dean, who was now standing in the doorway and looking excitedly into the packed hall.

'I just want to make sure we can get to our usual spot,' Dean replied, grabbing Gabe's hand. They made their way through the packed room, where everyone was standing shoulder to shoulder and any space they could find would come at a premium. As they continued to squeeze their way past people, Gabe suddenly noticed a strange smell.

'Can you smell that?' he shouted towards Dean, who was too preoccupied in trying to get them a prime spot. *It's probably just someone's perfume*, he thought, as Dean continued to pull him along, but it didn't really smell like perfume exactly. It was sort of citrusy though …

'Sorry, sorry, excuse me.' Dean stopped, turned and looked at him. 'Here we go.'

'Dean, I can't move, let alone breathe!' Gabe protested, looking around at all the people they had displaced just to get into the middle of the room.

'Once the support band comes off, there'll be plenty of space. Everyone heads to the bar, remember?'

Gabe hoped so, but this was a sold-out concert. He couldn't help but feel uneasy, although he had no idea why; there seemed to be strange atmosphere tonight, and he didn't think it was *just* to do with the other revellers Dean had annoyed in his quest to get to their spot.

'Who's ready for the McDermitts?' the support band singer shouted, causing people to scream with excitement and surge forward, pushing Gabe and Dean as they did.

Gabe *really* hoped that Dean was right about the crowd thinning out. Right now, he was starting to feel a little bit trapped …

Chapter One

DI Chris Jackson
Thursday night

'Good evening, Inspector.' Chris scrunched his eyes closed and opened them again as he listened to the voice on the other end of the phone. 'I'm phoning to tell you that there have been reports of a series of explosions in the centre of Nottingham. We've been instructed to call your team in.'

'Where are we needed?' Chris jumped up from his sofa and then regretted it as the room immediately started spinning. He was forced to sit down again as a sense of dread descended over him.

'Detective Inspector Shufflebotham is on the scene as SIO and has asked that you make your way to the main entrance of the university.'

'All received. I'll be there.' Chris got up more slowly from the sofa. It didn't help that he now felt sick from the thought of what he might be facing once he got into Nottingham. He'd seen the aftermath of enough fires to know what could await him, and what was worse was it was likely to be young people involved this time.

He had spent the previous afternoon in a MRI scanner at the Queen's Medical Centre, having his brain and spinal cord assessed for signs of what was causing the symptoms that were now part of his daily existence. It was becoming a regular occurrence: he'd previously been rushed in for an emergency MRI scan after going to see his doctor with rising concerns about dizziness and headaches. Six months on, he was still haunted by the grainy image of the white mass that had appeared on the original scans. As a result, he was now under investigation for a potentially life-altering disease that could change everything about his current existence. Both him and his consultant knew what was coming, but the reality of it all was too scary to think about ...

Leaving his cat a plate of food, Chris grabbed his backpack and rushed out of his flat. As he drove his car out of the underground car park and towards Nottingham, he turned on his radio in hope there would be some information about what was happening on the local news broadcasts – though it didn't seem to have filtered through just yet. He joined the almost empty A52 and made his way into the city to meet the team, where they'd hopefully all find out what the hell was going on. His medical worries would just have to wait, just like they had already been waiting for the past two years.

Jen Garner

Jen had to force her eyes to stay open as she attempted to locate where the ringing noise was coming from before it woke anyone else up – the kids being her main concern. She felt completely shattered, having completed her first day back at work with Nottingham's Special Ops team under DI Chris Jackson. She'd previously worked a case with Chris and her old team, which had become the catalyst for getting her back into full time policing.

'Detective Garner, it's control. Sorry to disturb you this early.'

'What's going on?' *Is it normal to be called in the early hours on the second day of a new job?*

'I'm afraid there's been a serious incident in Nottingham and your assistance has been requested at the university. DI Jackson will meet you there.'

'Okay, I'll head in now,' Jen said as she got out of bed and stretched. *Well, this is what I signed up for, what I wanted ... isn't it?*

'James,' she whispered.

'Eh?' came the typical half-asleep response.

'I've got to go into work. Something's kicked off and we've all been called in. Will you make sure the kids get to school? I'll get back as soon as I can.' Not bothering to wait for a reply, she leant over and kissed him. 'Love you.'

Jen rushed down the stairs as the adrenaline hit. She hadn't been expecting anything big to happen here in Nottingham; her new boss had already warned her that this was "local-level policing" and not what she had been used to in the past. She threw on her jacket and then was out of the door, into the car and on her way to the city and whatever awaited her there.

Chapter Two

DI Chris Jackson

Chris parked his car at the office, where the air was alarmingly thick with the smell of burning wood and sulphur. He headed up the hill towards one of Nottingham's two universities, which was situated in the middle of the city, making it very popular with students keen to experience their studies and Nottingham nightlife hand in hand. Chris could see the glow of the fire lighting up the sky, and as he neared the outer cordon, he noticed Officer Nikki Haywood speaking to a group of bystanders.

'Sir,' she greeted him as she excused herself from the locals.

'Morning, Nikki. What's going on?'

'It's not looking good, boss. It's Carbon, the nightclub. A series of explosions were reported late Thursday night, and from what the first responders have said, there's going to be quite a few casualties.'

'Is DI Shufflebotham expecting me?'

'Yes, she's at the university. They've set up Gold Command there.'

'Okay, thanks,' Chris called back as he ducked under the tape.

The university was situated half a mile away from Carbon, so it was close enough for easy access between the two venues and also ensured the teams could communicate with a chain of command about what was going on further up the road. Carbon was Nottingham's premier music venue, and Chris couldn't help but feel sick to his stomach at the idea that something awful had happened there during a packed-out concert.

Chris made his way past fire engines and ambulances, all lined up and doing their bit to bring the fire under control and take any injured to hospital. The closer he got to the university, the fewer people were around … and then it turned into a different type of chaos.

'I'm here to meet DI Shufflebotham,' Chris said, holding up his ID to the officer on the door. As he walked into the main entrance, he saw some of his team were already waiting for him. 'Morning, all.'

'Morning, boss,' they echoed in response.

'What do we know so far?' he asked.

'The McDermitts were just finishing their encore when the explosion happened, according to witnesses,' DS Julie Ryan replied.

'Do we have any idea of numbers of survivors and deceased?'

'Not yet, boss, but I've seen some walking wounded … hopefully that's a positive?'

'I am *so* sorry.' Jen rushed over towards them. 'I got here as fast as I could.'

'Not to worry, Detective. I've only just arrived myself.' Chris gave her a small smile.

'Do you think you could have waited a couple of weeks before telling all the criminals you were working Special Ops, Jen? You know, at least settle in a bit first?' DC Colin Goodwin joked, clearly trying to ease the tension that they were all starting to feel.

'I'll try my best next time,' Jen quipped as she turned and looked at Chris, awaiting instructions.

'I'm going to find the DI and see where she wants us. If you guys want to hang around and see what more you can find out, I'll come back for you all when I know where we're needed.'

Chris left his team, headed in the general direction the officer at the door had pointed him in, and found the DI surrounded by incident command.

'Excuse me, I'm sorry to interrupt. DI Chris Jackson here. I got a call earlier … it was mentioned you needed my team's help?'

'Ah, Inspector Jackson,' the DI said, holding out her hand. 'Nice to finally meet you. I've heard so much about you and your team.'

'All good, I hope.' Chris shook her hand.

'I'm sorry to drag you all out of bed, but I think we're going to need all hands on deck with this.'

'What have you got for us?'

'At this moment in time, from talking to the fire service, we believe the explosions reported happened at the back of the main floor area of the venue. They're now working on getting the fire under control, which is proving difficult given the age of the building. There are also some concerns about the underground car park, where there are several cars and a tour bus belonging to the band performing tonight.'

'And where are we with casualties?' Chris was almost afraid to ask.

'We do have some lucky people who got out relatively unhurt, but …' The DI paused as Chris found himself thinking about those who obviously hadn't been so lucky. 'But the reports coming in from the fire service suggest a lot of serious casualties.'

Chris closed his eyes momentarily. 'I'm guessing all gas canisters have been removed?'

'You'd need to speak to fire command, but I think we can assume so.'

'What do you need my guys to do?'

'All the walking wounded have been triaged and are now either on their way to the hospital or receiving medical care at the hotel situated at the back of the university building we're standing in. If you could send someone to help there – collect names and information, that sort of thing – I'm sure the officers would be grateful for that. We also have uniformed officers up at the hospital and, again, they'll need all the help they can get.'

'Do we know if all the band members and their road crew got out?'

'Yes, they've all been accounted for and have already gone back to their hotel. I've got a member of uniform with them now.'

'I'm guessing we aren't in the position to be removing any of the deceased?'

'From what I'm understanding, the fire service have asked for no one to be removed till the fire investigation team arrive.'

'I just hope they're not left lying in there for too long …'

'The duty manager and the staff have all been taken to the Knight Hotel. They've got a uniformed officer with them, but if you could send one of your team over there too it would be much appreciated.'

'The venue owner?'

'They're trying to contact him as we speak.'

'Anything I can do to help?' Chris asked, wanting to ensure it didn't look like he was trying to take over the DI's command post.

'I could also do with someone taking a walk around the building who knows what they're looking for – any signs of suspicious activity that the fire investigation teams need to be made aware of, that sort of thing.'

'Okay, not a problem. I'll grab one of the team.'

'If you could take an earpiece and radio, I can communicate with you from there.'

'I'll pick one up before I go.'

'Thank you, Inspector.'

Chris walked quickly away from the DI as someone else moved over to speak to her. Grabbing a radio and earpiece, he made sure he was on the right frequency before he returned to his team.

'Okay guys, this is where you're needed …' He explained the situation and assigned roles. 'DI Shufflebotham wants me to do a perimeter check of the venue. Jen, you okay with that?' Chris asked as they all began dispersing to carry out their duties.

'Everything seems pretty quiet around this side of the building,' Chris commented as he and Jen walked around the back of the nightclub a little while later on. They had passed and acknowledged the odd firefighter on the way. 'I think the underground car park entrance is around the other side.'

'That might explain why there isn't a large presence this side then, if they're worried about outbreaks of fire under there,' Jen responded, taking in what was going on in front of them.

They continued to walk, but then suddenly a fire door in front of them was flung open.

'Help! Help!' the young man shouted between coughs and gasps as he ran towards them. 'You've got to help me. My boyfriend is in there, he's hurt … I can't get him out.'

'We're here to help.' Chris rushed towards the boy. 'But I need you to try and slow your breathing down.'

'I can't leave him trapped in there … I told him I'd find him some help … I said I'd be back,' the boy choked out as he continued to cough, wincing in pain.

'Can you tell us where he is?' Jen asked gently.

'I can take you … I can take you back to him.'

'We need to get you away from here, get the fire service in there. They'll have all the equipment to make sure he gets out.'

'No! It'll take too long. He needs help now!'

Chris already knew what Jen would be thinking before she spoke again. 'Okay, well, you tell me where he is and I'll go in there and get him out.' *There it is.*

'No, no, you'll never find him. He's in a bad way.' Chris knew how much trouble they would be in if he didn't radio for help, never mind letting Jen enter the building.

'What if we leave you here to direct the fire teams, and I'll go in with my partner and look for him?' Chris asked, knowing that there would be no point arguing with Jen or trying to stop her, plus he wasn't about to let her go in on her own.

'No … I need to show you … I need to know he's going to be okay.'

Chris had a moment to decide what to do, but he knew in his heart that Jen and the boy wouldn't take no for an answer.

'This is Inspector Jackson,' he spoke into the radio. 'I'm located around the back of Carbon. Myself and Detective Garner have just come across a survivor from the explosion. He says that there are people trapped inside the building that need urgent medical attention. Detective Garner and I are entering the building. Please send medical services to our location.'

God, he'd be in so much trouble when … or if … he got out.

Chapter Three

DI Chris Jackson

Chris wasn't sure what to expect when he and Jen entered the still burning nightclub. Neither of them were dressed appropriately – if anything came down on them, they'd be in serious amounts of trouble. He coughed as he tried to clear his throat and the acrid taste in his month.

'You doing okay there, boss?' Jen turned to ask.

'Just trying to get rid of the taste in my mouth.'

'You'll get used to it.'

Chris found himself wanting to ask her all sorts of questions. *Has she been in a situation like this before?* But he needed to concentrate on finding survivors … if there even could be any. He was aware of the danger all around him as he walked through the blackened corridor.

'Inspector, please wait for backup. I'm sending assistance now,' came the message over the radio. *Bit late for that*, he thought grimly as he continued to follow Jen and the young man.

They battled through crates of bottled alcohol and all manner of random items before getting any closer. Then, suddenly, the boy rushed forward.

'He's over there. Gabriel! Gabe!' he shouted.

'Whereabouts are you?' Jen called into the darkness.

They all heard a moan as the boy rushed over to where he had left his partner.

'I got out! I found someone to help,' he told the other young man who was laid out on the floor.

'Gabriel, I'm Detective Jen Garner and this is my partner, Chris Jackson.' Jen immediately addressed the situation, seemingly automatically switching into crisis mode. 'I need you to talk me through your injuries,'

'I … I don't know. I'm bleeding … my legs are really hurting.'

'Okay, let's take a look,' Jen said, kneeling by Gabriel's side and shining her phone over his crumpled body. 'Chris, I need your shirt.'

Chris didn't ask questions as he stripped off. Jen knew what she was doing … *right?*

'Gabriel—'

‘Please, it’s Gabe,’ the boy gasped which took Chris by surprise, considering how much pain he seemed to be in.

‘Okay, Gabe,’ Jen said as she ripped Chris’ shirt. ‘I’m just going to make a tourniquet and tie your legs together.’ Gabe didn’t answer as Jen went to work pulling the shirt apart.

‘How are you doing?’ Chris asked, turning to the other boy.

‘Yeah, I’m fine. Please just concentrate on Gabe.’

‘My partner is looking after him. Let me look after you, okay?’

‘Yeah, yeah, I’m fine … just struggling to breathe,’ the lad said before promptly crumpling to the floor in front of him. Chris instinctively dropped to his knees as he tried to find his pulse. ‘Jen, I need you to come and help with CPR,’ he shouted.

Jen had seconds to react as she moved towards Chris. ‘Gabe, I need to help your friend.’

‘Oh my god, Dean … Dean!’ Gabe cried, trying to sit up.

‘Look, the only way you can help Dean is if you stay perfectly still, but keep talking to me. Where are you both from? Where did you meet?’ Jen reeled off questions as she started chest compressions while Chris continued mouth to mouth, trying desperately to bring Dean back.

‘We need urgent help.’ Chris spoke quickly into his radio. ‘We’ve one male in possible cardiac arrest and a second unable to move.’

‘God damn it,’ Jen shouted into the empty space.

‘Do you need to swap?’ Chris paused to ask, aware of how physically demanding compressions were.

‘Where the hell’s backup?’ Just as she said it, Dean spluttered back to life. ‘You’re okay, Dean. I need you to stay exactly where you are,’ Jen reassured the boy as Chris rocked back on his knees. Then they heard a rumbling noise. ‘God, that doesn’t sound good.’

‘Where the hell’s the fire service?’ muttered Chris, feeling like they’d been in the building for a lifetime. In reality, it had probably only been five minutes, but so much has happened in that short space of time. Just as he was beginning to give up hope, he saw the search light. He stood up and waved, directing them to where they were.

‘Inspector Jackson?’ A firefighter called out.

‘Over here! We’ve got two young males – one is injured and the second we’ve had to perform CPR on, but he’s currently responsive.

‘I need help,’ Jen shouted. ‘He’s going again.’ A firefighter immediately rushed over and placed an oxygen mask on the boy’s face.

‘We’ve got it from here, Detective,’ he told her as she stepped back. ‘I need you both to go with my colleague and get yourselves out of here before the building comes down.’

‘What about the other boy?’ Jen asked frantically.

‘Detective, I need you to leave *now*,’ he barked back at her.

‘Come on, Detectives. Let’s get you out of here,’ said the other firefighter, putting a hand on Jen’s shoulder.

As they broke out into the cool night, Chris’ nostrils filled with the smell of burning rubber and sulphur. Taking a gasp of air, he promptly lost his balance, wobbled and hit the floor.

It seemed that coming out of a burning building, passing out and then practically vomiting over someone’s shiny shoes wasn’t the done thing. Chris now found himself partially clothed, having lost his shirt for Gabe’s tourniquet, with blankets wrapped around him as he sat in a medical tent that had previously been set up to triage all the walking wounded. He had heard the words “chemical” and “decontamination” repeatedly as they took his temperature and tried to draw blood while medics buzzed around him. He knew what these words meant, and he also knew why he’d lost his balance and vision – and it was nothing to do with a dirty bomb – but if he said something then the medics would know, and then it would become like a great big game of Chinese whispers, but instead people would be playing “Guess what’s wrong with the DI?”

‘Excuse me, is there any way I can speak to someone in confidence?’ Chris asked, removing the oxygen mask again as the latest medic got ready to stick something in his ear.

‘Is there anything I can help with?’ the young medic questioned.

‘I need to make a medical disclosure.’

‘A medical disclosure?’ The medic looked confused, clearly unsure what the bloke in front of him was talking about.

‘Look, can I speak to your boss?’ Chris hated pulling rank, but there was hardly any point in him sitting in here when he could be out there doing something to help.

‘I’ll go and see if I can find them. We’re super busy right now.’

No shit, Sherlock, Chris thought as the young medic disappeared and returned moments later with someone from the Hazardous Response team.

‘Inspector, my colleague informs me you want to make a medical disclosure?’

‘Yes, I need to speak to someone in confidence … about what happened earlier.’ The officer turned and said a few words to the young medic, who promptly disappeared.

‘Kyle Lee, Hazardous Response team. How can I help, Inspector?’ Kyle asked, holding out his hand.

‘Chris Jackson,’ he said, taking the other man’s hand and shaking it. ‘I’m really sorry about what happened earlier, with me losing my balance and whoever’s shoes got covered in the process.’ Kyle visibly suppressed a smile as he nodded at him. ‘I need to tell you something about a medical issue that you have to keep in the strictest confidence.’

‘Okay, I’m listening,’

‘I’m suffering from a range of symptoms, some of which I experienced when I left Carbon earlier with my colleague.’

‘Okay ...’ All trace of humour had left Kyle’s face.

‘I’m under investigation at the hospital because of them.’

‘Can you tell me any more?’

‘I’m really not comfortable disclosing anything further, but with all the talk of a chemical attack —’

‘I’m not sure where that has come from if I’m honest with you, Inspector. But are you able to tell me which doctor you’re being investigated by?’

‘Dr Evangelou. He’s part of the neurology team at the Queen’s Medical Centre.’

‘And you’re not experiencing any of these symptoms now?’

‘No. That’s what’s so complicated about them …’ Chris was going to continue but decided not to confuse matters any further.

‘Right, I’m going to make some enquiries and I’ll be back with you.’ Kyle turned to leave the tent.

‘I’m fine. There’s nothing to worry about!’ Chris called after him.

‘Okay, Inspector. Leave it with me.’ Kyle continued walking, leaving Chris alone with his oxygen mask and his thoughts once again.

Chapter Four

Jen Garner

Friday

Jen's hands were dirty, her clothes were stained with blood and all sorts of black marks, and she didn't dare think about what the wet patch was. She looked at herself in the mirror of the women's changing rooms in the police station, wondering how she had ever believed that local policing would be quiet and relatively easy compared to the team she used to work with. All she wanted to do was go home, jump into a hot shower and soak all the stresses of the morning away. Fat chance of that happening anytime soon, but she felt she'd already done her bit with their successful rescue mission.

Her thoughts were distracted when she heard the opening of the changing room door. 'Jen! You in here, hun?' Julie shouted.

'Yeah, just be a minute,' she shouted back.

'I'm just dropping off some clothes and toiletries so you can get out of whatever you're wearing and grab a shower.' Jen breathed out a sigh of relief – at least she wasn't going to be stuck in her damaged clothes until she finally made it home.

'Thanks, Julie. You're a lifesaver,' Jen said as she made her way to collect what Julie had left before diving into one of the station's showers. It wasn't as luxurious as home, but at least she could get the smell and marks of that morning off her and hopefully start afresh.

'Hey,' Jen said into the phone as she dialled home later, hoping to catch the kids before they went to school.

'Everything okay?' James asked with a distinct sound of a panic in his voice. 'I saw it all on the morning news. The boss has told us all to work from home.'

'The kids still there?' she asked, desperately wanting to hear their voices.

'Yeah, I'm going to take them in in about ten minutes. Want me to put them on?'

'Please, James. I'm sorry. I'll tell you more about it all later.'

'Mummy!' Alex screeched down the phone.

'Hey you.'

'Where are you? Daddy said you had to go to work.'

'I'm in Nottingham, sweetie.'

'Is everything okay?'

'It is now that I'm getting to speak to you,' she lied. Alex didn't need to hear the ins and outs of what she'd just experienced – no seven-year-old needed to know about that. 'You have a good day at school, okay? And I'll see you later.'

'Okay, Mum. Love you.'

'Love you too,' Jen said quietly as she heard Alex shouting for his sister.

'Mum, Mum! Is it true what they're saying on the news?' Melanie asked, after having clearly wrestled the receiver from her brother.

'There's been a … fire in Nottingham, yes, but it's nothing to worry about.'

'Were you there, Mum?'

'Not quite, sweetie.' Jen sighed inwardly. How could she explain to a ten-year-old she had gone running into a burning building to rescue people? 'You have a good day at school and I'll see you when I get home.'

'Okay. Do you want Daddy back?'

'Just tell him I'll speak to him later, okay?'

'Bye, Mum. Love you.'

After the call, Jen felt relatively more human. There was no way she could have told James everything over the phone – she didn't really fully understand it all herself yet. Hopefully by the time she saw him later she'd have made sense of it all. Plus she knew he wouldn't have been too impressed with her running into the building to rescue those boys. Maybe she'd keep that bit from him, for now anyway …

DI Chris Jackson

After being discharged from the medical tent Chris half expected a call from his neurologist, which would no doubt signal the gossip machine whirring into life. He made his way up to his office, prepared himself a coffee, and was about to switch on his computer when his boss, Superintendent Gil Gray, appeared at his door.

'Good morning, Chris. Everything go okay at the hospital yesterday?'

'Yes, sir. Everything is fine, thank you,' he lied, wondering how much his boss knew about what had happened earlier that morning.

‘There’s an incident command meeting in the conference room shortly that I suggest you attend.’

‘Just excuse me for a moment, sir,’ Chris said as his desk phoned started to ring. ‘Detective Inspector Jackson,’ he answered.

‘Chris, it’s your dad.’

‘Give me a second,’ he muttered into the receiver. ‘I’ll see you down there, sir,’ he said quickly to the Superintendent. ‘Dad, is everything okay with Mum?’ Chris asked, returning his attention to his caller.

‘Yeah, yeah, she’s fine. We’re both fine. We’ve just been worried about you, especially when you weren’t replying to messages or answering your mobile. You know what your mum’s like ...’ Chris realised he’d manage to leave his mobile phone somewhere between Carbon and the office; that would be something else he’d no doubt get into trouble for later.

‘Yeah, sorry, Dad. I had to hand it in when I went searching for survivors last night and forgot to pick it up again.’

‘It’s okay, son. I’m sorry – look, will you talk to your mum, tell her to stop worrying and everything?’

‘Of course. Put her on.’ Chris waited for his dad to pass the phone over so he could quickly explain everything that had happened to his mum.

‘Mum, I’m sorry, I’ve got to go. I’ve got a meeting in five … Yes, I promise I’ll come over and visit as soon as I can … and yes, I’ll bring my lady friend for you to meet … Okay, love you too, Mum.’ Chris sighed as he finally put his phone down, collected his things together and headed to the meeting.

He walked into the room and took a seat. Looking around, he realised that he didn’t recognise many of the faces around the table.

‘Sorry I’m late.’ A man whose voice Chris instantly recognised entered the room. ‘I couldn’t get away from things at the scene.’

‘Not to worry. Take a seat, Kyle,’ Gil told the late arrival. ‘Now, if we can set the ball rolling, ladies and gentleman. I suggest we introduce ourselves as we go. I think most of us will have worked together previously.’ The Superintendent shuffled the papers in front of him and continued. ‘I’d like to start off by saying thank you for all the hard work that has already been put into this major incident. I would also like to thank your teams personally for all they have done since the alarm was raised late last night. I know some of them have families left waiting at home for their safe return. I just hope that we can offer some reassurance to those who have been out all night that their job for now is complete – they can go and get well-earned rest.' There was a moment of silence around the room. 'Okay, Graham. Do you want to start us off with your teams at Nottinghamshire Fire and Rescue?

'Thank you, sir. I'm Graham Styles, Watch Manager, and I was the Incident Command Manager last night. I'm relieved to say that we're now in the position to start reducing the number of pumps on the scene. Working alongside the station managers and their crews, we're also looking to reduce the number of crew on site, making sure that we're still able to operate safely and provide cover for the rest of Nottinghamshire.'

'And could you just give us an overview of your plans going forward?'

'The crews we have at the site are currently dampening down and tackling hot spots. We'll continue to reduce the officers on scene and assist the structural engineers and fire investigation.'

'Thank you, Graham. Lyndsey?'

'DI Lyndsey Shufflebotham. I was the Senior Investigating Officer at the incident. At around ten-thirty last night, control received several distressed calls from members of the public reporting that they'd heard explosions coming from the city centre. We were then alerted that there had been a major explosion at the nightclub and music venue, Carbon, and officers were dispatched to assist the fire service with the Hazardous Response team also being alerted. I personally arrived on scene at approximately ten-forty-five and assumed the role of SIO.'

'I'd like to add that over fifty uniformed officers have been dispatched to help at the scene,' the Superintendent added.

'They've all been put to use across the investigation.'

'I've asked DI Jackson if his team can work alongside your guys, Lyndsey.'

'That would be great. Thank you, sir.'

Chris nodded his agreement.

'Okay. Kyle?'

'Morning all. Kyle Lee, Hazardous Area Response team. We arrived at the scene and immediately set out attending to the walking wounded until we could get access to the venue to search for further survivors. Working closely with the ambulance service, we sent up a triage, so those who were seriously in need of medical help were seen quickly and efficiently.'

'How is the hospital holding up with the influx of patients, Selina?'

'Morning. I'm Selina Smith, the Emergency Response Coordinator for the Nottingham hospitals. There are always various plans and strategies in place for such events, and I'm happy to report that the NHS is holding its own despite the influx of patients and their critical needs.'

'Selina, I know we still have worried parents looking for their missing children out there. Do you have everyone who is in the hospitals identified and next of kin informed?'

'We've been working with the lists received from the ticket sales and the triage during the early hours of the incident, and I'm happy to report that everyone who is currently in hospital has been identified.'

'Great news. At least those parents can rest easy,' Gil responded thoughtfully, then his face took on a grave expression. 'The remaining names are now listed as missing.' There was a moment of silence around the table as everyone took in what that meant.

'We managed to secure a space to act as a temporary morgue this morning, and when I left bodies were being respectfully moved into that space,' Lyndsey spoke up, breaking the silence. 'Detective Portis is helping coordinate the removal and identification of the deceased.'

'Do you think we are likely to have everyone identified by the end of the day?'

'I can't comment, boss … but I would like to think so.'

'Most of them had ID on them. Those that didn't, we're looking at alternative ways to identify them,' Selina chipped in.

'The structural engineers were about to assess the scene as I left, so hopefully they'll give clearance for the removal of any further bodies,' Graham confirmed.

'What is the likelihood of us finding someone alive in there now, would you say?' Selina asked.

'In my personal opinion, very unlikely.' Graham looked sombre.

'Can I inform the crash teams at the hospitals that we're probably not expecting any further survivors?'

'I think that makes sense,' Kyle said, his expression also grim.

'I know we have a lot of other companies in the area who have opted to tell their staff to work from home, but do we know when utilities such as electric and gas are likely to be restored?' the Superintendent continued.

'Work is being undertaken as we speak, and we hope to get those surrounding areas back on in the next hour,' Kyle responded.

'Okay. Thank you, everyone. Chris and I will be working with Felicity later today with the aim of holding a press conference at 4 p.m.—' *Hang on a minute*! Chris almost said out loud '—to try and address the many concerns that people are no doubt having right now. So, if you can all make yourselves available to answer any further questions from us, that would be great.'

Chris wondered how he'd suddenly been volunteered to front a press conference; he was sure he wasn't usually the first choice. *Lots of bright and flashing lights are* really *going to help my symptoms*, he thought sardonically. What if he had to get out? Wouldn't it be better if one of the more good-looking detectives were presented to the media anyway?

'I'm in close contact with the anti-terrorism team in London, who have offered their assistance if we start to suspect this could be terror related,' Gil told the team. 'Also, whilst I remember, it's already been arranged that tomorrow morning there'll be a memorial service with a two minutes' silence held for those who have lost their lives. If you could all make yourselves available for that too, that would be great.' There were murmurs of agreement heard around the room. 'I think we can bring this meeting to a close, unless anyone has any questions? Thank you very much, everyone.'

Though Chris nodded along with the rest of them, he couldn't help but feel he'd rather be on the ground investigating than in and out of meetings with the chain of command. He got up from his seat as everyone else did, keen to make a quick exit towards coffee and whichever pill he was due to take.

'DI Jackson,' Kyle said as he moved over to talk to him. 'Just to let you know that your phone is in your team's office. You left it in the medical tent earlier and I wasn't sure how best to get it back to you.'

'Thanks, Kyle. I'll pick it up shortly.'

'Not a problem.' As Kyle turned to walk away, Chris wondered if he should say something about his situation.

With all the issues going on with his health, he couldn't help but worry that his future would always be office and meeting-bound before too long. No more roaming the streets and bringing the bad guys in. He wondered vaguely whether that was why, in part, he had been so keen for Jen to join his team. She could probably do half this stuff with her eyes closed.

Chapter Five

DI Chris Jackson

'If I could have your attention, please,' Chris said as he and Lyndsey walked into his team's office. 'This is DI Shufflebotham. She was the SIO at last night's incident.'

'Afternoon,' Lyndsey addressed them as they all turned to look at Chris. 'I just want to say a quick thank you to you all for your help at the scene this morning. I'm looking forward to working with you on this case.' Chris studied the room while she spoke, wondering where he was going to squeeze in the new staff members who would shortly be joining them. 'Before anyone asks, I didn't think about the implications of taking my wife's name when we married and have regretted it ever since.' A short burst of laughter rippled around the room, which seemed to break the tension around the thoughts of what was currently going on outside the city centre police station, if only for a moment.

'Lyndsey and I have had a short meeting and worked out how we're going to progress the investigation, so if everyone wants to grab their notebooks and coffees, we'll meet in the incident room in, what, say five?' There was a low murmur in the room as everyone came to life and started preparing for action.

'Boss, someone dropped your phone off,' Greg said, handing Chris his mobile.

Chris thanked him, turned it on and was quickly greeted with several bleeps as he made his way to the incident room, which was quickly becoming the most used room in the station. As he walked in, he was relieved to see that, for once, the board was completely clear. Being the first one there, he quickly wrote *Carbon Music Venue* at the top of the board and busied himself with making a few notes. Then he remembered the messages that had come through since he'd turned his phone back on and decided he'd better check they were nothing important.

Hope you're okay? Heard the news. Let me know if you need anything, love Hannah.

Chris' insides contracted. There was that L word again. He had no doubt used it too, but with the way his health was, and the pending diagnosis, he wondered if he had better stop – just in case his life was about to take a different trajectory. One that perhaps didn't involve Hannah …

'You okay, Chris?' Julie asked as she entered the incident room ahead of the others.

'Yeah, just thinking about the case, that's all. Everyone else on their way?'

'Think so. Greg was just in the middle of one of his "back in the day" stories with Lyndsey.'

'Ah, we've got a good ten minutes before the troops arrive then.' Chris chuckled.

'Boss, tell me to mind my own business if you want, but was everything okay at the hospital?'

'Yeah, just a check-up after last year.'

'You've just been a bit … distant recently.'

He obviously hadn't been *that* good at hiding his concern for his health. 'No, I'm all good. Thanks though, Julie.'

'If you ever need to chat, you know where I am, okay?'

'Probably knee-deep wading through a case? But thank you – really.'

Just then, the unmistakable sound of Greg's laughter filled the corridors, and the rest of his team entered the room alongside the DI.

'I've just sent a message to my team members and asked for them to meet me here when they can get away from the scene,' Lyndsey informed Chris.

'I'm looking forward to meeting them. But excuse me just for a second.' Chris pulled out his phone to send Hannah a quick message.

All good so far, and no mention of Lisa Carter, yet …

The last big cases Chris had worked on had direct links to Lisa, and he hoped this one might break the cycle at last.

'Can I have your attention, please?' Chris called as he focused on the matter at hand once again. A few more people had entered the room, who he assumed were members of Lyndsey's team. He waited for them to be seated before he began. 'Carbon was filled to capacity last night with approximately two thousand five hundred concert goers, plus staff members, band members and roadies. I personally suspect we've approximately three thousand people to trace. Lyndsey?'

'Explosions were heard across Nottingham at ten-thirty last night. Emergency services were on the scene shortly after and were greeted with what can only be described as chaos: walking wounded, those who had managed to escape unharmed but were visibly distressed, as well as the critically injured.'

'Lyndsey and I spoke after the incident command meeting this morning and have agreed that her team are going to be focusing on the investigation around the venue. My team and I will be focusing on the criminal investigation. Though we're two separate teams, we need to remember that we're all members of the Nottinghamshire police force, so we're going to have to work together to bring this investigation to a close,' Chris summed up. 'Any questions?'

'Do we know how many dead we've got so far?' a voice that Chris didn't recognise asked.

'When I left the scene, they were talking in the tens.' Lyndsey stepped forward. 'In all honesty, I sadly suspect this is likely to rise once everyone has been accounted for.'

'I know we're at the very beginning of this, but do we have any suspects so far?' Jen cut to the chase, as usual. 'Chris and I saw the damage that had been caused by the fire first hand. Personally, I don't think this is an accident …'

'In short no, Detective Garner,' Lyndsey answered.

'But if this is, God forbid, terror related, don't we need to call in the terrorism team?'

'I don't think it's a good idea for us to get blindsided until the fire investigation team have had time to investigate.'

'Okay, Jen,' Chris interrupted before a disagreement could break out between his newest recruit and Lyndsey. 'I want you and Greg to interview the band. I know Greg spent some time with them last night, so I'm sending a friendly face with you.'

'They were all pretty subdued, so it'll be interesting to see if there's been any change in the dynamics,' Greg chipped in.

'Trudie, could you and Colin work together and look at collecting all CCTV in the area? Let's see if we can pick anything of interest up. I know Carbon is surrounded by businesses and student accommodation, so pull in what you can and we'll take it from there.'

'Boss.'

'Julie and I will head out and speak to the venue management, and hopefully get a list of staff members and others who were on site. Lyndsey?'

'If my guys could just continue with their assigned jobs.'

'The Sup has organised a press conference for 4 p.m., so let's try and find something I can give the media.' Chris slowly stood up as he spoke, painfully reminded that days of bouncing up and going were long gone.

Though the time was now getting close to midday, everyone's mind was focused on the case. If they'd yet to eat they would grab something on the way out, or go without. For some of them, this could be their biggest case yet.

'Thank you for seeing us at such short notice,' Chris said as he shook the hand of Carbon's manager, Karl Jenkins. Julie and Chris had taken the short walk across the city to the Lace Market area where the offices of the Carbon nightclub were based.

'It was the least I can do, given the situation. Can I get any of you a drink?' Karl asked before clearing his throat.

'A coffee would be great. But the most important thing is getting a list of those staff members who were working last night.'

'Ah yes, someone from your office rang ahead. I think it would be best if I direct you to our box office manager. She should be able to give you everything you're looking for,' Karl replied.

'Have all your staff been accounted for?' Julie asked.

'We've five members of staff who are in hospital, but other than that everyone else was accounted for,' Karl said, slipping his hands into his pockets.

'Well, that's something positive at least.' Julie smiled.

'Yeah, I guess … I'll go and grab some drinks and get Cindy to start sorting the lists. All being well, they'll be ready once our meeting is over,' Karl said as he moved towards his office door. 'What was it again, a coffee and …?' He looked expectantly in Julie's direction.

'Just a water, please.'

'If you both want to make yourself comfy, I'll be back shortly.'

Chris stood up and looked around the large office, which was easily twice as big as his. The shelves were host to awards and photos of Karl and various bands.

'How many of these have you seen live then, Julie?' he asked, turning to look at his partner

'I'd say at least half. You?'

'I don't want to comment if you've seen at least half.'

'More or less?'

'Less … a lot less.' Chris moved away from the cabinet and sat himself back down in front of the large Ikea desk. 'Do you think he put the desk up himself?' Chris asked as he inspected it from his seated position. It took a moment for Julie to register as she looked over at him. 'It's an Ikea desk,' he commented, waiting for Julie to catch his drift.

'How do you know? No, hang on, don't tell me.'

'It's the bachelor lifestyle, you know? Spending weekends in Ikea shopping for flat-pack furniture in hope it'll fill that hole in my life.'

Julie laughed at him. 'And Hannah?' she questioned when she had regained her composure.

'Back in London, I assume. I had a message from her this morning, so unless she's on her way to steam roll into the case …' Chris shrugged.

'How are things between you two? Her reaction when you got taken into hospital was enough to show how much she cares about you. I've never seen anyone drop everything so quickly just to be by someone's side.'

'Yeah, well. She's the boss up there now, so she's busy … and I'm ...'

'Avoiding answering the question.' Julie finished his sentence. Just then Karl returned, balancing two cups, bottled water and a decanter on a tray. Julie jumped up to assist him before he dropped everything.

'I'm sorry that took a bit longer than I expected. Cindy is … let's say, still a bit fragile over what happened. As soon as I mentioned the list, the water works started again.' Karl shook his head. 'Even at a time like this she has to be centre of attention,' he muttered.

'You said you had five members of staff who were in the hospital?'

'Yes, a few floor staff and a member of the bar staff.'

'Do you know how they're doing?'

'I'm not sure, if I'm honest with you. I just had the messages passed on when I finally got back to the office this morning.'

'If you can let me know their names, I can look them up when I get back,' Julie offered.

'That would be great, thank you,' Karl responded as he plunged the coffee strainer and poured himself and Chris a drink. Then he handed Julie the water after retrieving a glass from the cabinet Chris had just been admiring. 'Okay,' Karl said, finally returning to his chair and lacing his fingers behind his head. 'How can I help you guys?'

‘Do you want to talk us through what happened yesterday. Let’s say from when you arrived at work?’ Chris asked, half expecting Karl to put his feet up on the desk.

‘Can I ask why this is relevant? Shouldn’t you be concentrating on who blew up my club?’

‘We just want to get a feel for how a normal gig night comes together from when you get in.’

‘Well, the box office opens around 10 a.m. at the venue, and the band tend to arrive just after lunch. So I met the McDermitts on their arrival at, I would say, 2 p.m.’

‘How did they seem?’

‘Like anyone who had spent the night on a tour bus. We also tend to get a lot of fans hanging around the venue waiting for bands to arrive, so there’s always the quick rush to get the bus into the underground car park and away from the wannabe groupies.’

‘Did you have any trouble with fans yesterday?’

‘A couple of the band members got off the bus and greeted them, but the bus was directed into the underground car park, then their roadies followed and the chaos of setting up a gig began.’

‘Is it usually chaos?’

‘Oh, always – equipment coming in, my guys working with their guys, but it all comes together.’

‘And where were the band during all of this?’

‘Mostly on their tour bus. Sometimes they go out into Nottingham and explore, but given how popular the McDermitts have become, they stayed at the venue in their bus or hung around the stage.’

‘So nothing out of the ordinary?’

‘No, I mostly stayed at the venue, had a couple of drinks with the band and handed over to the duty manager before heading home.’

‘You didn’t stay to watch the gig?’

‘I’ve seen it all before. If I’m honest with you, these days once you’ve seen one band play, you’ve seen them all.’

‘So you didn’t hang around?’ Julie clarified.

‘Yeah, don’t get me wrong. If it’s the greats, I’ll stay and party all night with them, but these are still young lads, still pretty new on the scene.’

'Okay.' Chris was unsure how to respond. Karl's attitude seemed a bit strange given the circumstances. 'We're going to need the contact details for the duty manager last night.'

'Yeah, it was Clarissa Oates. Let me get her number for you,' Karl said as he typed away on his computer.

'Any idea where Clarissa might be now?'

'No, we briefly spoke this morning and I told her to stay at home and get over the shock. I'll meet up with her tomorrow.'

'Can you talk me through your security arrangements?' Chris continued once Karl had finished on the computer.

'Can you be more specific?'

'Well, with all due respect, someone clearly managed to get some form of explosive device into your venue and basically blow it up.'

'As you may know, Detective, I have six fully qualified and registered door men. Any bags brought into the venue are searched, and the owners are advised to put them into the cloakroom.'

'Do many of them?' Julie asked. 'Put their bags in the cloakroom, I mean?'

'I'm not sure.'

'Okay, and during the day?' Chris prompted.

'The box office is open and the main doors into the venue are open, but we've got security cameras, so if anyone gained access I'm pretty sure they'd not get very far.'

'And the underground car park, with the tour bus and all the other stuff the band bring along with them?'

'Again, CCTV and barriers. There are always plenty of people milling around down there. So if anyone got in, they would've been spotted and removed.'

'But someone *did* get something into your venue, and we need to investigate how and why.'

'I understand, Detective, but I honestly can't see how they did it. With all the added security … especially with the McDermitts playing.'

'Do the band bring their own security teams?'

'Yes, but you'll have to speak to them about that.'

'Okay, so we'll need all your CCTV footage from last night. Is that stored here?'

'It's all kept at the venue.'

'Which has been blown up?'

'Afraid so. I haven't been able to get access yet. Truth be known, I've not been able to enter the venue since I got here, seeing as it's as good as burned to the ground this morning.'

'So who's down on-site at the moment?'

'One of my general managers. I was waiting to hear from the fire investigation team about when it was safe for me to return to see what I can salvage.'

Chris had taken an instant disliking to this man. Shouldn't he be at his venue waiting to get access to assess the damage, instead of leaving someone else to pick up his mess for him? 'And those who have lost their lives …?' Chris questioned to no response.

'Can I just ask,' Karl went on, 'after the fire investigation team have finished, what happens then?'

'The site then becomes part of my criminal investigation,' Chris responded as politely as he could.

'So … no chance of getting the insurers in and getting it back up and running?'

Chris couldn't believe what he was hearing. 'No one else is going anywhere near my crime scene until I say so.'

'And do you have any idea of length of time?'

'Could be months, could be years …' Chris said, in jest more than anything else as this guy was really starting to wind him up. They were already painfully aware that people had died, Karl's own staff members were in hospital, and all he seemed concerned about was insurance pay outs. God only knew how much structural damage there was for a start, and Chris knew that no one, not even hot shot venue owners like this guy, had insurers on the end of the phone who would come out and get a burnt-out building approved for a rebuild that fast.

'So had I better get my team phoning around cancelling gigs, or looking for somewhere else to host them?'

'Might be a good idea,' Chris answered sarcastically.

'Has anyone made any threats to you or the company recently that you think we need to be aware of?' Julie asked quickly, clearly noticing that Karl had riled Chris.

'Difficult to say. There's always someone who's upset because they've been refused entry or kicked out.'

'But no direct threats? Just annoyed customers?'

'Yes … I mean no. Most customers are happy with the experience.'

'What about former staff members?'

'A place like this has a big staff turnover, but I can't think of anyone who'd go this far.'

'The five members of staff who you said had been injured – have you ever had any issues with any of them?'

'I don't think so … I'd have to check who they were.'

Really! Chris was glad he'd let Julie take control of the interview because he was seriously pissed off now. He left Julie and Karl to talk while he wondered vaguely about karma.

'Well, thank you very much for seeing us both,' Chris heard Julie say and snapped out of his daydream. But then, being so keen to get out of there, he stood up too quickly and immediately felt dizzy. *Not what I need right now.*

'We'll be in touch if we have any further questions,' he said, holding out his hand and going into autopilot, as he had learnt to do in these situations.

'Here, take my card,' Karl offered. Chris didn't know if he could trust himself to not let on that his vision wasn't exactly clear. He had taught himself some coping mechanisms, but he hadn't been prepared for this one.

'Thank you.' He held out his hand, hoping Karl would just give it to him anyway.

As Chris stood outside the Carbon offices waiting for Julie, who had popped in to meet the box office manager, he thought about the dizzy spells and hoped after the scans the previous day that his neuro would be able to give him something to help stop them; over everything else, they were the thing making his job ten times harder.

'What a cock,' he commented to Julie as she reappeared and they started walking back to the station. 'I don't feel the slightest bit sorry for him. Five of his staff members are in hospital and he has no idea who they are!'

'I could tell he'd annoyed you.'

'He seemed more concerned about getting the insurers in to assess the damage than about those who lost their lives in *his* nightclub.' Chris sighed.

'Yes, I did notice he didn't once ask about the deaths,' Julie agreed, looking thoughtful.

‘When did Cindy say she’d get the lists over to us?’ Chris changed the subject, not wanting to think about Karl Jenkins any more.

‘In an hour or so … but she was a bit tearful.’

‘With a boss like Karl, who doesn’t seem to be offering any support at all, I’m not surprised.’

‘Might be an idea to get hold of Greg and Jen and ask them to speak to the band about their security arrangements. The explosives obviously got in there somehow.’

Chapter Six

Jen Garner

Jen and Greg decided to take the short walk from the police station across town to meet the McDermitts, the Scottish band who had apparently been making waves on the alternative music scene. According to Jen's research, they'd had several number ones and were at the beginning of their UK tour, which had been due to end in a sell-out hometown gig in Glasgow at the end of the year – though this had now all been cancelled out of respect for the victims of the previous evening.

They took the lift to the top floor and the penthouse suite that was accommodating the band during their unexpected stopover in Nottingham.

'You seen these guys live?' Jen turned and asked Greg.

'I'm too old for gigs now. I'm not like you young'uns. To tell you the truth, I didn't know they even existed before I met them last night,' he replied.

'Ah, come on, Greg. You're not that old! They're pretty good, actually. I've heard them on the radio a couple of times, and I think James has their CD in his car.'

'He'll be jealous when you get home and tell him you've met them.'

Jen laughed as they both reached the door to the penthouse and knocked. They could clearly hear voices coming from inside.

'Detectives Garner and Sanders,' Greg said as they both showed their ID to the exhausted-looking but well-dressed young man who answered the door.

'Come in. We've been expecting you guys. The boys are keen to get back home to their families.'

'Are they not staying for the memorial tomorrow?' Jen asked.

'I think the consensus is they all just want to get home, if I'm honest.'

Jen was slightly surprised but part of her also understood. She'd probably feel the same way in the circumstances. 'We'll try and get this over as quickly as we can so they can be on their way.'

'Thank you. I'm Troy, by the way. I think we met briefly when you were here last night.' Greg nodded his acknowledgement. 'I look after the boys when they're on tour,' Troy explained, holding out his hand as he backed away from the door and led the officers into the large open-plan area complete with a big-screen television and huge sofa. 'Boys,' Troy called. 'Detectives Garner and Sanders are here to speak to us about last night.'

The band members were scattered around the room, each doing their own thing, strumming on guitars or playing on their phones. They all looked completely drained.

'Take a seat, Detectives. Can I get either of you a drink?' Troy asked, leading them over to the seating area.

'Just a water, please,' Jen responded, having already got through countless cups of tea at the office and on site earlier.

'Same please,' Greg responded.

Jen watched Troy head to the bar area and pull several bottles of chilled water from the fridge just as the band members joined them.

'Where's Ronnie?' Troy asked on his return.

'Not sure. Probably out somewhere. Who knows?' one of them responded – Jen thought she recognised him as the lead singer, Alistair.

'Sorry, our drummer Ronnie is a bit of a wild one. I'll get on the phone and find out where the hell he is,' Troy apologised ruefully as he walked away with his phone pressed to his ear.

'Thank you for seeing us both.' Jen turned to the band. 'I'm Detective Jennifer Garner and this is my colleague, Greg Sanders, who you briefly met last night. We've just come here to speak to you about what happened – if you are okay talking about it. I know it must've been a shock, watching it all happen right in front of you.'

'Yeah, I keep getting these flashbacks,' Alistair began. He squeezed his eyes shut and opened them again, as if trying to blink away the memories. 'We were just finishing our encore, then there was this almighty bang and the balcony area sort of … fell down in front of my eyes. Then the screaming started … and I just sort of turned and ran for the exit.'

Jen nodded as she started to scribble down notes into her notebook. 'I'm sorry, my colleague isn't really into popular culture. Can I just check? You're Alistair, correct?' Jen apologised, using Greg's age as an excuse to get everyone's names noted down. She was also hoping that the interruption would help lift the sombre mood that had clearly descended upon the band members.

'Yes, sorry. I'm Alistair and this Anders, Lachie, Will …' Alistair introduced the band members.

'And you said Ronnie was MIA?' Greg asked, giving Jen time to catch up on her notes.

'Yeah,' Alistair replied. 'He's always going off somewhere for whatever reason.'

'So he does this a lot?'

'We joke he's like a junkie or something sometimes, but I think he just doesn't like being stuck in one place for two long. Cabin fever, don't they call it?'

Greg nodded his response.

'Did any of you or your crew suffer any injuries in the crush to leave?' Jen asked.

'No ...' Alistair seemed to pause for a moment. 'There's an exit behind the stage area, so we were able to get out before the crush.'

'As a band, have you had any threats made against you in recent weeks?'

'Detectives, I hope you understand that we didn't have any choice. We saw what was happening in front of us and just ran for an exit,' Anders suddenly said, as if he'd been holding it in before.

'We do,' Jen reassured him, although in truth she wasn't sure if she did.

'Not that we know of. Wait, do you think whoever did this was targeting us?' Alistair looked horrified. 'We do get some weird messages sometimes, but what happened last night is on a whole other level.'

'Has there been an official word yet on the dead?' Lachie interrupted.

'No, still estimates at the moment. Until we've got everyone accounted for, I don't think we can give out any numbers,' Greg responded.

'God, we should have stayed and helped,' muttered Anders, holding his head in his hands.

'I know you guys were all busy doing your thing on stage, but did you notice anything strange happening?' Jen picked the thread back up.

'It all seemed like a normal gig night. We did the meet and greet in the green room and then we all moved into our dressing room. We sort of high-fived the support act, did our little ritual thing and went on,' Alistair answered, whilst the others just stared into space, clearly lost in thoughts of what had happened the night before.

'Anything odd happen during the meet and greet? Anyone acting strangely?'

'No, they were all on top form … once they got over the excitement and everything.'

'Are the support band staying local as well?'

'I'm not sure. They were the local winners of some battle of the bands the venue held, and the prize was to support us for the Nottingham gig. I'm sure Troy will have their contact details or the venue certainly will.'

Suddenly there was a banging of doors and shouting came from the hallway.

'That'll be Ronnie.' Alistair sighed.

'Sounds like he's found a drink as well.' Lachie grimaced, standing up as the drummer crashed through the door followed by two giggling girls who couldn't have been much older than sixteen.

'I've found these two hanging around downstairs,' Ronnie slurred. 'They said they'd come and help us drown our sorrows.'

'Dude, the police are here to talk to us about last night,' Lachie said as he made his way over to where Ronnie was now swaying

'Quick, girls. Better get your ID out.' Ronnie put his arm round the pair, whose facial expressions visibly changed when they realised the police were there.

Jen and Greg both remained sitting down and let the scenario play out in front of them, not wanting to get involved with band politics. The girls might have been a little young to be hanging out with drunken drummers, but no obvious crime was being committed.

'Come on, mate, you knew the police were coming to talk to us about last night. Why go out and get in this state?' Alistair hissed.

'Well, in that case, the girls and I are going to my room.'

'I don't think that's a good idea, Ron, mate.' Alistair was clearly making an effort to calm the situation down. 'You maybe, but I bet you two have got somewhere else you need to be. What time are you due back in school?'

The girls looked at each other, slightly embarrassed but also clearly in awe that the lead singer of the McDermitts was talking to them.

'Oh, come on, Alistair. You're not the innocent one here. How old was that girl when we were in Texas?' Ronnie continued to argue his point.

'Tell you what, ladies, I'll personally escort you back to wherever you need to be and give you a bunch of signed stuff,' Alistair offered, smiling at them and also obviously trying to change the subject.

‘Over my dead body. You get all the girls,’ came Ronnie’s reply.

Jen wondered if she or Greg should stand up and try to intervene when Troy made an appearance again.

‘Ronnie, you twat, I told you not to go off on your own. Excuse me, ladies,’ Troy said as he put his arm round Ronnie and moved him away from the girls so that Alistair could swoop in and usher them out.

‘I’m sorry, Officers, but I think I need to phone for a car and get these young ladies home.’ The girls were now back to the giggling mess they’d been when they’d first arrived.

‘It’s okay,’ Lachie said as he returned to the sofa, having done his bit to stop a fight breaking out. ‘We can answer any further questions the detectives have.’

‘Righty, I’ll be back soon,’ Alistair said as he left the room.

‘I am so sorry, Detectives.’ Lachie looked sheepish.

‘Does this happen often?’ Greg asked.

‘Ronnie bringing back young girls?’ Lachie sounded a bit defensive now. ‘I can assure you, Officers, most of us are all in relationships. Alistair’s even got kids, for crying out loud. We wouldn’t let anything untoward happen to our fans.’

‘Good to hear,’ Greg responded, just as his phone began to ring. ‘Excuse me,’ he said, standing up.

‘Like Alistair said before Ronnie came crashing in, he can’t cope with being stuck in one place. Most times he goes out and comes back fine, sober as a priest with no girls in tow,’ Lachie continued.

‘So nothing strange happened at the gig and none of you noticed anything suspicious?’ Jen asked, trying to rein the questioning back in again after the interruption.

‘No, nothing.’

‘So what next? Can we go home now?’ Anders spoke up again.

‘I don’t see why not. It’s not like you’re going very far. We’ll still be able to get hold of you if we’ve any further questions.’

‘If you let Troy know when things are settled, we’ll arrange to come and see the fans who got injured … maybe play a benefit gig or something,’ Lachie offered.

‘Okay, thank you. I’m sure everyone will appreciate that.’

‘I am so sorry, Officers,’ Troy said as he came rushing back into the room, clearly having left Ronnie somewhere to sober up. ‘I told him not to go anywhere, and I certainly didn’t think he’d bring anyone back.’

'Boss, the detectives were asking if any threats had been made against us or anything?' Anders turned to him.

'Not that I'm aware of. I take the safety of the band members very seriously.'

'Except when it comes to Ronnie,' one of the other lads said in a low voice that Jen most certainly heard. She was unsure whether Troy was supposed to hear or just chose to ignore it.

'I'm keen to get everyone back to Scotland, Officer. Will there be anything else you'll be requiring from us?' Troy asked.

'I was just telling the guys that I think we're done for now, but if you have any concerns about what happened last night or any of you remember something, no matter how small or unimportant you think it is, please *do* get in touch,' Jen summed up.

'Thank you, Officer, and again please accept my apologies for Ronnie's behaviour. I'll be having a harsh word with him when he sobers up.'

'Not a problem,' Jen said, just as Greg returned.

'Sorry, that was the boss. We've a couple more questions regarding the security at the venue last night and wondered if you'd be able to answer?' He turned to Troy.

'Yeah, sure, if you'd like to follow me into my temporary office space.' Troy led the detectives to a side room away from the band. 'I've been using this as my office for the last twelve hours,' he explained as he walked over towards the small desk where he had his laptop open and various papers piled up. 'I usually have a space on the bus, but what with everything ...' He trailed off.

Jen surveyed the room, wondering where they were going to sit.

'I'm sorry I can't offer you guys a better seat,' Troy said, seeming to notice Jen's indecision.

'It's fine, we can stand. It's just a couple of quick questions,' Greg replied.

'What can I help with?' Troy asked as he settled into his own chair.

'We were just interested in the security while you were at the venue. We understand the bus was in the underground car park?'

'One of the crew stays with it at all times – stops any of the fans trying to sneak on and hide.'

'Has that happened before?'

‘Oh yeah, the band members have come back to find fans in their beds.’

‘What about the band? I’m guessing they all stayed at and around the venue?’

‘Yes, I think even Ronnie stayed put last night.’ Troy laughed weakly.

‘So there were no security issues regarding the band or venue?’

‘No, I was pretty happy with how things rolled. Our guys and their guys just seemed to click.’

‘I know you provided me with your staff listing last night. I just wanted to check you hadn’t forgotten anyone?’

‘Not that I can think of, though I wish I could offer more help.’

‘If I leave you with my contact details, you know where you can get in touch if you think of anything else.’ Greg held out his card.

‘Thank you.’ Troy stood up and led the detectives back to the front door of the penthouse suite. ‘They’re all good lads, you know? Despite what you might think, having seen Ronnie’s performance,’ he said, clearly trying to reassure them.

‘We’ll be in touch if we need anything else,’ Jen said as she headed towards the lift with Greg not far behind her.

They both stood in silence as they waited for the lift and, once safely inside, Jen let out a sigh. ‘I really thought there was going to be a proper fight with Ronnie and Alistair,’ she said, turning to Greg.

‘Ah, these young rock stars can’t handle the beer like we could back in the old days.’

‘There was certainly some tension there … and those girls, they couldn’t have been more than sixteen if that.’

‘Yes, I did notice. I felt all fatherly – their skirts were far too short for this weather.’

Jen laughed at Greg’s response before she continued. ‘I think I’m going to Google the band when we’re back in the office, see if there have been any other incidents we should be aware of that might be connected to the case.’

‘Chris seemed pretty concerned about the venue’s security when I spoke to him on the phone.’

‘Be interesting to hear what they found out at the venue,’ Jen commented, falling into step with Greg as they headed back towards the office.

Chapter Seven

DI Chris Jackson

Chris' motivation was in tatters. He was fed up with everything and everyone. Yet here he was, back in the same old incident room, with its same smell of fast food, whiteboard markers and the lingering scent of whatever air freshener had last been sprayed in there.

'Everyone ready to start?' Lyndsey shouted to bring the room to attention. 'DI Jackson?'

'Ready when you are.' Chris snapped back to reality.

'You okay, boss?' Greg asked as he wandered past.

'Yeah,' Chris said, smiling back. He was getting used to playing this game. 'After this meeting I have a press conference to plan for with the Sup, so let's make this as productive as possible. I want to make sure I've actually got something to report back,' he instructed the room. There was a mutual sound of agreement from everyone congregated. 'So ... any good news?'

'All two thousand five hundred attendees have been accounted for.' Luiza, one of Lyndsey's detectives, offered.

'Thank you, Luiza. Have our deceased all been reunited with their next of kin?' Chris asked.

'Yes, sir. All the next of kin are waiting to see their loved ones, and we are in the process of moving bodies to a suitable location. With twenty-two dead, sir, it's a logistical nightmare for our hospital mortuaries, but hopefully by tomorrow morning we should be able to start reuniting people.'

'Thank you, Luiza, for your hard work on this.' Chris nodded towards her. 'Do you want to fill us in on your meeting with the band?'

Jen looked over to Greg, who nodded for her to lead. 'Okay, well, the McDermitts are five lads from Scotland who were playing at Carbon when the explosion happened. They didn't see anything suspicious and were as shocked as the rest of us when the incident occurred. Ronnie, their drummer, seems to be a bit of a wild one to put it politely. He wasn't there at the beginning of the interview but returned with two – very young looking – fans part way through.'

'We were a bit concerned that a fight was about to break out, but it seemed to calm down as quickly as it started,' Greg added.

'Do we have a safeguarding issue?' Chris asked.

'I'd like to have a further look into the band, boss. We were led to believe that Alistair was going to organise getting the two girls home. Which they seemed *very* happy about.'

'Taken home by their favourite lead singer?' Lyndsey mused.

'Well, to be fair, he was probably only phoning for a car. I don't think anything untoward would have happened.'

'As for security, their tour manager had no concerns. Tour bus is occupied at all times and there haven't been any threats to the band over social media,' Greg finished.

'So, other than safeguarding, no major issues,' Chris summed up.

'Do we know anything about the staff members who were injured last night?' Lyndsey asked.

'Well, they aren't dead,' Luiza offered.

'Luiza, would you be able to double check on them?'

'Of course, boss.'

'So, Chris, Julie – the venue manager?'

'A complete cock,' Julie said immediately.

'That's putting it politely,' Chris added.

'I don't really know how to put it – he was so full of himself! He wasn't even at the venue and had left his duty manager in charge. He had no interested in socialising with the band before or after the incident.'

'The best bit was when he said he didn't even know who the injured members of staff were.' Chris was still seething about the man's attitude.

'A manager who really cares about his staff then.' Lyndsey raised her eyebrows.

'My question is whether he blew up his own venue?' Julie finally voiced what she and Chris had no doubt both been thinking. 'The talk of getting the insurers in so he can get his business back on the ground, the fact he wasn't at the venue when it happened …'

'All very suspicious,' Lyndsey concluded. 'But let's keep an open mind for now.'

'Did you have any luck with the CCTV?' Chris asked.

'The guys on the site weren't confident but promised to look first thing,' Lyndsey answered.

'Just so everyone is aware, there is currently no CCTV footage from the venue as the footage isn't backed up elsewhere,' Chris explained.

'So … we've got nothing?' Trudie looked incredulous.

'It seems that way.'

'One positive: the final lists have come through from the box office manager of the staff who were working last night,' Julie interrupted the sighs over lack of video evidence.

'Might be worth grabbing a couple of uniformed officers and asking them to start ringing round,' Lyndsey suggested.

'I'll go and see who I can round up in the canteen,' Julie said, looking thoughtful.

'Curtis and Haywood might be your best bet,' Chris butted in.

'If they've not been snapped up elsewhere.'

'How did you and Colin get on, Trudie?' Lyndsey asked, taking back control of the meeting.

'With the help of your detectives, we had the chance to look through the CCTV footage from the businesses around the venue and didn't really notice anything suspicious. We were hoping that there would be footage from the venue we could work with.'

'Anything on social media?'

'We didn't get a chance to look over it properly, boss, but we'll start our search when this meeting is finished.'

'Great work, you guys, especially considering the limited resources. Let's hope we can make further progress,' Lyndsey told them. 'Okay, so finally, I don't really have anything to report from the crime scene. There's still a lot of concern for the structure of the building, so they're not letting anyone on site who doesn't need to be there.'

'Thank you, everyone,' Chris said as he stood up, ready to go to the next job on his list. 'All being well, I won't be too long at this press conference. I'll catch up with you all afterwards.'

'So we'll all walk in together. Sir, if you go on the left, and Chris you sit in the centre. I'll sit on the right,' Felicity, the press officer, instructed them as they prepared to face the media gathered in the conference room. They'd just spent the last hour coming up with a game plan: what they were going to say, what questions they would be willing to answer and what they wanted to keep to themselves for now.

'Are there many of them in there?' Chris asked.

'Quite a few. I've made sure the local media are sitting at the front, so we can prioritise questions from them over anyone else.'

Chris could feel his stomach doing flips and the bile rising in his throat. His vision was fucked, and he'd struggled to focus on anything in front of him throughout the briefing with the Superintendent and Felicity. How on earth he was going to be able to read a press statement out was anyone's guess.

'Have I got time to just pop back into my office to get something?' He realised that now was the last time he'd have the opportunity.

'Of course, but don't go wandering off anywhere. We'll be needing your input, Inspector,' Gil replied.

'Will be five minutes, tops.' Chris stood up, hoping his balance wouldn't let him down in front of the boss and headed downstairs towards his office.

'You're back quick. All okay, boss?' Greg called as Chris passed the team's office.

'All good here, Greg. Just collecting something from my office before I greet the world's media. How are things going down on the ground?'

'It's a mess, boss. I really don't know how Nottingham is going to recover from this loss. It feels like the whole city is grieving.'

'I can see the streets being quiet on a Friday and Saturday nights for a while.'

'What channel do we need to tune into to see you on the telly in a bit? Or can we stream it live?'

'Ha!' Chris didn't respond as he moved out of the doorway and headed towards his own office.

Chris knew they would be easy to find. He had thrown them into his drawer as soon as he had brought them back from the opticians. He didn't need glasses – he could see just fine – but maybe, just maybe, they would help when facing the media and the bright flashing lights.

'Bingo,' he said as he put his hands on the case. He wasn't even sure if they really did suit him, or whether that optician had just been on commission; he hadn't really been in the mood to spend hours looking at glasses at the time. Putting them on, he was amazed at how much clearer things suddenly looked. Maybe he really did need them at the ripe old age of thirty-four …

As he walked through the station and back up the stairs towards the Sup's office, he couldn't help but feel self-conscious of his new facial appearance. No doubt they'd all have a laugh about him later behind his back.

'Sorry, sir,' Chris said as arrived back in the office.

'Not a problem,' the Sup said, pausing as he noticed Chris' new attire. 'Nice glasses.'

'Thank you, sir. Thought this would be the right occasion to wear them … you know, helps to see who you're talking to.'

For perhaps the first time ever, the Sup let out a short chuckle and then returned his attention to the computer screen in front of him. 'I hope they aren't going to want to put make-up on us, Chris,' he commented. 'Because when they have before, it's played hell with my skin for weeks after.'

They walked into the conference room like they were in a procession. Felicity led the way, followed by the Superintendent and Chris. He tried to look upbeat and positive about the investigation, though he felt neither. Felicity showed them to their seats and took the chair next to him as the cameras started to flash away and Chris began to feel that familiar sinking feeling. He wanted to close his eyes but could imagine the headlines the next day: *Has the DI been staying up way past his bedtime?* Instead, he focused on a spot at the back and prayed that the room wouldn't start spinning.

'Good afternoon, and thank you for attending. I'm going to hand over to Superintendent Gray, and then Detective Inspector Christopher Jackson will be making a statement. If I could ask that all questions are left till the end.' As Felicity introduced them, Chris surveyed the room; his Sunday name had been used so this meant business.

'Thank you for coming,' the Superintendent began. As Chris continued to look around the packed room, he wondered where all these people came from. He recognised some faces from the local outlets, all sitting there with their pens and notebooks. What hadn't escaped Chris' notice though was the selection of microphones that were attached to the table in front of them, making sure they got every single word, and no doubt the photographers would catch every single bead of sweat and every instance of strange body language. *Welcome to the world of police press conferences*, he thought grimly.

'Detective Inspector Christopher Jackson will now read out a statement about the ongoing investigation and the help we need from members of the public …'

Show time. Look straight ahead and smile.

'Good afternoon. I can confirm that the explosion at Carbon on the night of Thursday 7th June during the McDermitts' concert is being treated as a criminal investigation. The fire services were able to bring the fire under control and those who needed emergency care were taken to the Nottingham University Hospitals. I can confirm that the death toll currently stands at twenty-two, but it's possible this will rise. I would like to take this opportunity to thank our fire and rescue service for their continued efforts to extinguish the blaze, and also to our medically trained professionals who worked long into the night to make sure everyone who needed medical assistance was looked after.' Chris took a breath as the cameras continued to click.

'I can confirm that, at this point, we are not treating the incident as a terrorist attack. We are asking if any members of the public with video footage or photos from the night of the incident at Carbon could send them, free of charge, to the phone number or email address which are shown on the screen to my left. There is also a phone number for those who are concerned about missing loved ones. If anyone has any information about the shocking events and wants to speak to someone anonymously, the Crimestoppers will be happy to take your calls. Thank you.'

Chris was glad that bit was over, but now the onslaught would begin.

'I'd just like to confirm that all this information will also be available in your press packs. Any questions?' Felicity asked as the camera clicking went into overdrive and everyone started shouting their questions at once. As agreed, Felicity took the lead and chose who would get to ask the first question.

'Carly Saunders from *Nottingham Post*. There has been speculation that APEX was used in some form of homemade device. I'm wondering how you can be so sure that this isn't terror related?'

'Good afternoon, Carly. I'm afraid I'm unable to comment on the type of explosives used at Carbon or the reason why the attack happened, but as soon as the fire investigation team have finished at the site and I have their report, I'll be able to answer this question more fully,' Chris answered. 'I'd like to reassure the public that we're working closely with the anti-terror squad, and would ask people not to panic and make assumptions based on hearsay.'

'John Royal, BBC Nottingham. Anyone taken responsibility for the explosion?'

'We've had no group take responsibility, which backs up the idea that this isn't terror related,' the Superintendent cut in.

'Judith Smart, *Notts News*. Are our entertainment venues safe to be open? Is there any reassurance you'd like to give members of the public intending on going out tonight?'

'Good afternoon, Judith. The incident at Carbon was unexpected, and I'm also aware that a lot of entertainment venues aren't planning to open tonight in respect for those who have lost their lives,' Chris replied.

'So you're expecting there to be a second attack?'

'I didn't say that. If you're planning on going out, make sure you're aware of your surroundings and stay alert for anything suspicious—'

'Are you telling me that my pub could be next and there's no way of knowing?' A large, muscular man started to make his way from the back of the room, jabbing his finger towards the assembled officers.

'Please, sir, could you take a seat?' Felicity was the definition of calm and controlled.

'We're already losing bookings from bands because of what has happened at Carbon.' He continued to point his finger at Chris.

'If you could take a seat, sir, I'm sure Inspector Jackson will be more than happy to address your concerns,' Felicity soothed, but the guy wasn't having any of it and the cameras in the room were lapping it up.

'Please, sir, if you take a seat—' Chris began.

'But you can't protect us?'

'There will be extra officers on the streets tonight in order to alleviate anyone's concerns. I'm aware that entertainment venues in Nottingham are linked up to Pub Link and share information with each other and the emergency services if there's an issue.'

'But my pub could be next!'

'I think we've answered your question,' Felicity butted in, clearly not wanting Chris to put his foot in it.

'So you've got no clue, no evidence about who could have caused these explosions?' a shout came from the back of the room.

'Are the emergency services struggling? I heard that two police officers had to enter Carbon to assist an injured reveller.'

'Will nobody be able to get into work tomorrow again because another venue has been targeted over night?'

The press conference descended into chaos as the three officers sat at the front of the room, being bombarded with a mix of shouting, accusations and conspiracy theories from clearly very overactive imaginations.

'I think we'll leave it there,' Felicity said, standing up. Chris sensed that even the unflappable press officer felt they'd lost control of the situation. 'If anyone has any questions that we've not answered, then please feel free to contact the press office and I'll do my utmost to answer them,' she finished as Chris and the Superintendent stood up and hurriedly made their way out of conference room.

'Well, that went well …' Chris attempted to joke as Felicity held the door open for them.

'Who the fuck leaked that you and Detective Garner went into the building on your little unofficial search and rescue mission?'

'Sir, I have no idea,' Felicity shouted as she chased after the Superintendent and Chris along the corridor. 'Lots of people could have witnessed Chris and Jen leaving the building along with the boys and the fire service. It could have been anyone … our own included.'

'If it's someone within the department, I want their badge on my desk by the end of play today. I've got enough problems with the fire service breathing down my neck about disciplining them both without the press twisting it all into a story too.'

'With all due respect, sir,' Chris spoke up as they neared his office door, 'we had no choice but to enter. Those two lads were in dire need of medical help.'

'Then you should have sought appropriate assistance.'

'The young man, Dean, wasn't going to sit around and wait for that to arrive. I took the decision that it was best for Detective Garner and myself to enter the building and offer whatever assistance we could.'

'I know Jennifer Garner is a highly trained officer, but I warned her when we first discussed her move to Nottingham that I didn't want any heroics – that's not how it's done at local-level policing.'

'Sir, Officer Garner was purely following my instruction. In her defence, without her help, Dean wouldn't have made it out alive and his partner might still be awaiting rescue.' The three of them piled into Chris' office with the Superintendent slamming the door behind him, which was almost immediately followed by someone knocking on it. 'What?' Chris's voice boomed.

'Sorry, sirs, Felicity … I just thought you might all be in need of these,' Julie said as the door of the small office was opened again.

'Thank you, Detective Ryan, that was very thoughtful of you,' Felicity said as she helped Julie with the tray of drinks.

'Sir, all the team are back in the office awaiting further instruction.'

'Thank you, Detective, I'll be with you all in five,' Chris replied, glad of the cooling down time it gave the Sup from his rant; though once Julie had closed the door, he was off on one again.

'Thank heavens they didn't catch you vomiting everywhere,' the Superintendent continued. 'If you aren't match fit, Inspector, I don't want you anywhere near this investigation. Understand?'

'Sir.'

'And as for Detective Garner, I'll personally issue her with a warning and some choice words reminding her what we agreed when she started working for the Special Ops team.'

'It's fine, sir. Being her superior, I'd rather speak to Detective Garner myself.'

'I'm not sure that's a good idea, Inspector. You're both guilty parties in all of this. Just make sure you remind her of her place here and that she can quite happily go back to her old team if she's missing the action.'

'I will do, sir,' Chris agreed.

'Felicity? Please tell us we managed to achieve something positive from that mess?'

'You and the Inspector were on point, sir. I would like to think before our gatecrasher arrived everything was going as well as could be expected.'

'Good to hear. I'll be very interested to know who this gentleman was and what his connection to all of this is.'

'I think he said he owned a pub near the venue, sir,' Felicity clarified.

'So how the hell did he find his way into our press conference?'

'I'll get one of my team to investigate that as soon as I have finished here, sir,' Chris offered.

'Fine. Preferably before he ends up on the front pages tomorrow, please. I'm going up to my office to see what damage control I can implement. You both know where I am and I expect to be kept up to date.'

'Sir,' both Chris and Felicity responded in unison and stood up as the Superintendent made his way to the door.

'And Chris – no more heroics.'

'Certainly, sir.'

Once the Superintendent was out of the office and down the corridor, both Felicity and Chris slumped down in their seats.

'Well, that could have gone better.' Felicity sighed as she reached for one of the mugs of coffee on the tray.

'You're more than welcome to hide out in here for a bit,' Chris offered.

'No, I better go and start returning some of the calls that will no doubt be waiting.' She downed her drink and put it back on the tray. 'Thanks for the offer though. On a more personal note, you do look rather hot in those new glasses of yours.'

'Er … thanks?' Chris responded, not sure what response he should give. He had more or less forgotten he was wearing them. 'Let's just hope the world's media sees it that way and goes easy on me!'

Jen Garner

'Hey, I'm home,' Jen shouted as she walked into the house. She had no idea what time it was, other than it was late and she was exhausted. But as soon as she closed the front door and walked into the hallway, Melanie and Alex came running to meet her. Both were dressed in their PJs and dressing gowns, and Alex was clinging onto his teddy, which was a sure sign he was tired.

'You two all ready for bed then?'

'Yeah, Daddy said we could stay up till you got home,' Alex replied sleepily.

'I don't think he realised what time it would be though,' Melanie offered, as it slowly dawned on Jen they were both up way past their bedtimes. 'But we promised we'd be on our best behaviour tomorrow and not cause any trouble.'

'Well, you two better get yourselves to bed then. I'll come and tuck you in once I've said hello to Dad.'

'Okay,' Alex said as he began to climb the stairs.

'Mum ...' Melanie started. 'Are you investigating the explosion at the nightclub?'

'I might be. But, wait, Daddy made me promise I wasn't going to bring my work home so I can't talk about it … or I'd have to tickle you,' Jen said as she grabbed Melanie into an embrace and tickled her until her husband made an appearance in the doorway.

‘Come on, you two. Bedtime.’ He laughed as he moved closer to Jen and kissed her on the cheek. ‘Good day?’

‘Yeah …’ There was no more that needed saying. James knew exactly where she had been all day and what she’d been investigating.

‘I’ll go and run you a bath while you kiss the kids goodnight.’

‘That’s the best thing anyone has said to me all day.’ Jen smiled as she slipped her heels off, stood on her tiptoes and kissed her husband. ‘Come on, Melanie, up those stairs.’ Jen turned towards her daughter, scooting her up to her bedroom.

Later, Jen lowered herself into the warm bath and felt every muscle in her body relax into the water. She relived the last twenty-four hours in her head: it was only her second day on the job and she hadn’t properly seen the kids since they went to bed the night before. Had she really made the right decision to return to the service?

When Jen had shared with James that she had been thinking about going back into policing, they’d both spent many late nights talking it through, having heart to hearts about what it meant for the family. Jen knew there was no way she could go back to undercover work and her old job in the Met so she’d decided to explore the possibility of working locally. She knew DI Jackson and the team in the Nottingham office well, having worked closely with them six months ago on a case involving a little boy who had turned up in Nottingham, asking for Lisa Carter: Jen’s old alter ego from her undercover days.

In an effort to still her racing thoughts, she closed her eyes; it would only be for a minute, just to relax, then she’d wash and make her way down for the dinner that James had made …

Chapter Eight

DI Chris Jackson

Saturday

Chris had stayed late after he'd sent everyone home, Julie included. He just wanted some silence. He knew he'd get it if he went home, but that was at least a thirty-minute drive away and he'd needed to find the energy before he could make that trip. He felt he should be motivated with a renewed sense of purpose because of the new case, but this all felt different. He didn't know if it was because of Lyndsey and her team, his impending diagnosis … or something else. Even the thought of seeing Hannah didn't excite him like it used to. Yes, she was still amazing in every way. The more time he'd spent with her, the more he noticed her break away from the vixen she'd always portrayed herself to be. He was getting closer to the core of Hannah herself – her past, her life experiences outside working for the service – but he was scared to dig much deeper if it was about to all coming crashing down.

Now, donning a hard hat and the appropriate high-vis jackets, Chris and Lyndsey made their way towards the structure that had once been Carbon.

'This is so heartbreaking,' Chris murmured as he walked past the collection of flowers, cards and teddies that were lined up at the side of the cordon, taking a moment to glance at them and pay his respects. Then he took a final mouthful of his fresh coffee with his selection of pills, which would hopefully work their magic soon, and placed the cup in one of the litter bins which had been set up near the cordon.

'Graham said he'd meet us here, so hopefully he'll be able to walk us through the venue layout.' Lyndsey explained as they stopped just outside what used to be the main entrance of the club. Though the fire service has entered through those doors with their equipment, and water could be seen pooling on the floor, the shell of the venue still looked the same as it had days earlier.

'God, this is a mess,' he said out loud. He wondered if the venue manager had made an appearance yet, or whether he was still leaving it up to others to pick up the pieces.

'The structural guys say that this whole place is going to need to be knocked down and built back up from the ground,' a voice he didn't recognise said from behind him.

'Have they said when the demolition work can begin?' a second voice asked.

'Soon, I hope.'

Chris laughed to himself at the response. Nothing would be happening on *his* site till the criminal investigation was over.

'Good, because I don't need Mr Jenkins on my back any more than he already is.'

Chris decided to turn and see whose conversation he was eavesdropping on. 'Detective Inspector Jackson.' He held his hand out to the two men who were standing behind him.

'Lloyd Hansen.'

'Jed Floyd.'

'I heard you say that they're going to have to demolish the site?'

'Yeah, I've not broken the news to the venue manager yet,' Lloyd said with a sigh.

'I would have thought he'd be on site.' Chris raised his eyebrows.

'Fat chance of that when he has others to do his dirty work,' Lloyd muttered.

'You guys work here, I take it?'

'Worked,' Jed corrected him.

'It'll be back up and running in no time,' Lloyd reassured him. 'Jed here is the bar manager and I'm duty manager.'

'Nice to meet you both. Were you the duty manager when all of this happened?'

'Oh no, I was fast asleep before the explosions woke me up.'

'You live nearby?'

'Canning Circus.'

'Pretty close then.'

'As soon as I heard the sirens, I knew it was something really bad.'

Chris noticed Lyndsey was chatting away to Graham, who'd just arrived, and thought he'd better find out what was happening. 'If you'll excuse me, I think my colleague might want me shortly. Please take my card; if you can think of anything that might help with the investigation, you know where to contact me.'

He quickly re-joined Lyndsey. 'Sorry.'

'Anyone interesting?'

'Lloyd and Jed, duty manager and bar manager, apparently.'

'The fire investigation team think they've found ground zero, if you'd both like to follow me,' Graham cut in as he turned to walk through the structure and into what Chris knew was the stage area. He studied the area; it looked like a war zone with stray clothing and other personal items left abandoned, either damaged by the fire or soaked by the water from the hoses. He doubted that these things would ever be returned to their rightful owners, or if they'd even want them back. *Or if they're alive to take them back*, Chris thought grimly.

'Okay, so, as I'm sure you're both aware, this used to be the main room. The stage was on your right, which seems to have only suffered moderate blast and fire damage. If you look up, you can see the leftovers of the balcony level.'

'So are you going to tell us that the blast came from behind us?' Lyndsey asked as she looked round.

'Correct.'

'It's safe to say that the band weren't the target.'

'Why do you say that?' Chris questioned.

'Well, you'd have thought whoever set it off would've done it in front of the stage if they were targeting the band instead of back here with the crowd,' Lyndsey explained.

'That's right,' Graham confirmed.

Chris surveyed the empty shell of the room, noticing pieces of litter stuck under blocks of rubble. He could almost make out where the bar used to be, and as he looked upwards to where the lighting rig would have been, he noticed it had been replaced by a gaping hole.

'We also know that this must have been the blast site, rather than the stage, due to the number of dead victims we found. Behind the stage is still pretty much intact,' Graham continued.

'Any news on what they used to pull this off?' Chris questioned.

'The fire investigation team have taken some evidence away with them to get it looked at more closely. Between us three, we think it was some form of IED.'

Chris's stomach immediately dropped.

'Improvised explosive device,' Lyndsey said it out loud. 'The terrorist's favourite.' There was a moment's silence. 'Okay, do we need to start looking at the terrorism angle?' Lyndsey asked, sighing. Chris knew full well how much she'd brushed off the idea previously.

'I'm afraid I don't have the answer to that one,' Graham responded 'But I think we can say, without a doubt, it wasn't a suicide bomber. We've found no forensic evidence of one.' He looked thoughtful. 'I don't know what else your guys can collect from here that hasn't already been picked up, but if you want to have a look around yourself, you're more than welcome to. I'm told the building – or what's left of it – is stable, but you'll need to keep your hard hats on at all times.'

'Did the underground parking area sustain much damage?' Chris asked as Lyndsey began looking around.

'No, they were lucky there, but all vehicles are being kept until the investigation team can check them over.'

'Does that include the tour bus and band equipment?'

'I'm afraid so, yes.'

'I don't suppose you've located where the CCTV might have been recorded?' Chris asked as Lyndsey continued to inspect.

'Yes, we've located the office, but I'm afraid it's not good news ...'

'Water damaged,' Chris finished for him.

'You guessed it. I'm not sure if your tech guys will be able to get anything from the server, but they're more than welcome to try. I just hope they've got it all backed up somewhere.'

Chris let out a laugh, knowing full well this was the only place the CCTV had been stored. 'Thanks. I'll get someone down to look at it. Hopefully something can be rescued ...'

Jen Garner

'Can I get either of you a drink?' Clarissa asked as Jen and Greg pulled a stool out from under her breakfast bar.

'I'm good, thank you,' Jen responded as she looked around Clarissa's vast Mapperley apartment. 'We were told that you were the duty manager at Carbon on Thursday night?'

'Yeah ...' she replied with a sigh.

We were wondering if you could take us through what happened at the McDermitts' gig?'

‘I think that’s pretty obvious,’ Clarissa responded as she walked over towards her large fridge and poured herself some water from the contraption in the door.

‘Okay … well, talk me through your day. What time did you start?’ Jen prompted.

‘Well, as it was a gig night, I started later than I normally would,’ Clarissa said as she sat down on one of the stools, crossing her legs. ‘I went to the office to check in with Karl and get my briefing for the evening. Then I walked across to the venue to meet up with my staff, and the band, of course.’

‘Did you notice anything out of place or anyone acting suspiciously?’

‘No more than normal. Everything was happening as it usually did.’

‘What were the McDermitts like? Did you have any issues with them?’

‘No, the leader singer guy … Alistair? Isn’t it?’ Jen nodded. ‘He seemed to have nominated himself as spokesman for the band, so a lot of my communication was with him.’

‘Not the tour manager, Troy?’

‘Oh no, he was too busy running around after the drummer; right little family drama they had going on.’

‘Oh?’ Jen prompted. Even though she already knew of Ronnie’s personality from what she had witnessed at the hotel, she was keen to hear someone else’s take on it.

‘There was a lot of drama about where Ronnie was and what was he doing.’

‘Did you see anything that caused you concern?’

‘No, not really, the bloke just needed space. I’ve seen enough strung-out musicians in all my years working gigs at Carbon to realise that.’ Clarissa laughed.

‘Do you think Ronnie was on some form of illegal drug?’ Greg asked, having been silent up until then.

‘It’s possible, yes. They’re all taking something, aren’t they? Either that or he needs to seriously get some help.’

Jen looked over towards Greg. At least Clarissa was backing up some of what they’d previously been told. ‘Talk us through what happens on a normal concert night,’ she went on.

‘Before we open, I have a meeting with the team leaders – so door staff, bar and backstage crew – to make sure we all know what’s going to happen during the night. All door staff are issued with their earpieces and the team leaders have them too. It can get very noisy when a band is playing, and I need to be in contact with my guys at all times.'

'So you're in your office, everything is going great, when did things start to change?' Greg asked.

'As soon as we heard the loud bang and screams of terror.' Greg nodded and waited for Clarissa to continue. 'The screams were like someone running their nails down a blackboard.' Clarissa shivered. 'As I was duty manager, it was my responsibility to get everyone out and safe.'

'So you single-handedly evacuated two thousand plus people?'

'Well, I ran towards the danger … first aid kit in hand.'

'Did anyone else assist?'

'The door staff followed and did what they could, but we couldn't get very far into the main room because of the rubble, fire and,' she paused for a moment, 'and I guess … the bodies.'

'I think it was a very honourable thing to do, to run towards the danger,' Greg reassured her.

'And I get rewarded with a day off. Woo, go me. I bet I won't get paid for it though.' She laughed bitterly.

'Sorry?' Jen questioned.

'It's nothing.' Clarissa tried to brush off what she'd just said, but the cat was out of the bag. 'Anyway, in situations like this my team leaders are responsible for their staff and anybody around them.'

'The explosions happen. Everyone gets evacuated, then what?' Greg took over the questions again.

'According to procedure, I'm then supposed to go and instruct the emergency services, but I couldn't leave those poor people there suffering, so the rule book went out of the window. It was pretty obvious that something serious had happened, so I stayed and did what I could until the emergency services took over. Then, like a fool, I moved on to the next person who needed help.'

'So all that's done, the emergency services take over and you leave the building?'

'Yeah, I was in a mess, so I phoned hubby, spoke to Karl at the scene, then went home and, in all honesty, downed a bottle of wine.'

'Did you do some sort of debrief with Karl?'

'Nah, that was supposed to be today, but he isn't interested in the details. In fact, he told me to write it up and email it to him last night.'

'Nice.'

'Yup, he's a chauvinistic pig at the best of times. All he's concerned about is the bottom line and the money coming into the venue and into his pocket.' Jen nodded as she looked down at her notepad. 'Do you know how many are dead so far? I know I saw on the news it said twenty-two … but there were just so many bodies everywhere.' Clarissa fell silent.

'Those are the official figure, but they're expecting it to rise,' Greg said sombrely.

'Any news on my colleagues? I asked Karl yesterday but, unsurprisingly, he didn't have a clue. Don't think he even cared.'

'We can find out for you as soon as we get back to the office.'

'Someone's got to take interest in them and it might as well be me. To be honest, I'm not even sure who they were yet. I mean, I know they're bar staff and a floor staff, but I never got to see all my staff in the same place after the incident to notice who was missing.'

'Can I just ask, Clarissa, how many duty managers are there that work at Carbon?'

'There are five of us who work concerts on a rota basis, and then Lloyd Hansen works in the day.'

'Brilliant, thank you. You've been an amazing help.'

'Do they know why or how it happened? For an explosion that size—'

'We're not sure at the moment, I'm afraid, but I know our teams are at the venue now looking into the cause.'

'The news is saying it was some sort of bomb, but everywhere was secure before the event started. We bag check everyone that comes in.'

'I'm afraid I really don't know at this point,' Jen lied. *Of course it was a bomb of some sort, to have caused such carnage*, she thought.

'Thank you for talking to us, Clarissa.' Greg stood up.

'Not a problem. You'll be in touch though, about my colleagues?'

'I'll get one of our officers to contact you as soon as I'm back in the office,' Greg reassured her.

'Thanks,' Clarissa got up herself. 'I best make use of my free day off,' she said as she led Jen and Greg towards the door of her apartment.

'Thanks again, Clarissa,' Jen said, feeling like she should have said more, but what was there she could say? *I've been through what you have.*

As the lift door opened and closed, Jen sighed.

'What's up?' Greg questioned.

'There's something about this Karl bloke … he doesn't seem to be the most caring boss.'

'I guess we're just lucky with Chris.' Greg laughed. 'We could have it so much worse.'

Chapter Nine

DI Chris Jackson

'Shall we all feed back before we head over to memorial?' Chris asked the busy incident room as he made his way to the whiteboard. He prayed that all the furniture was where it normally was and that no one had left a chair or table out of place. As he felt the now familiar spinning sensation and his vision blurred, he knew he needed to retain control and pretend like nothing was happening. Making it safely to the front of the room, he turned round, smiled at the team and began the meeting.

'Shall we start with the venue?'

'Sorry, sorry …' Lyndsey said as she rushed into the incident room with large sheets of A3 paper before proceeding to stick them to the walls. 'Venue layout,' she explained as she continued sticking.

'Lyndsey and I went up to visit the venue this morning and spent some time with Incident Command Officer Graham Styles. Lyndsey, do you want to take it from here?'

'Okay, so,' she said, moving over towards her printing, 'Graham believes that ground zero was here.' She pointed to the location.

'Not a high impact area,' Jen commented. 'If they'd wanted to do the maximum damage, they'd have done it in front of the stage, or in the centre of the crowd.'

'It brought down the upper balcony area though, and was near the main exit.'

'Caused more panic as people wouldn't have been able to get out the way they came in and would have had to rely on other fire exits. Let's be honest, how many of us go to a gig and study exit routes?' Trudie commented.

'Plus, however this thing was set off, the person who did it had an escape route.'

'Are we ruling out suicide bomber?' Jen asked.

'There's been nothing in witness reports that have suggested one,' one of Lyndsey's team replied.

'From talking to the forensic team, they haven't found any evidence of a suicide bomber either,' Lyndsey clarified.

'Do they know what was used?' Jen questioned.

'Graham has his suspicions, but this doesn't leave here.' Lyndsey looked around meaningfully at everyone. 'He suspects they used some form of IED.'

'Fuck,' could be heard echoing around the room as each detective realised exactly what that meant.

'The Superintendent is in close contact with the anti-terror squad, who have said they can be on hand if we have any major concerns,' Chris added.

'Greg and I went to visit Clarissa, who was the duty manager at the gig, this morning,' Jen offered as the room settled. 'Clarissa confirmed the possible tensions within the band that Greg and I noticed. She also raised the issue of Ronnie, the drummer, and backed up the concerns about his health. His band mates just passed it off as "cabin fever".' She moved over to the sheets Lyndsey had printed. 'We asked her to run through what she does on a usual gig night. During the gig, she was sitting in the office, which is situated here,' Jen explained as she marked the venue layout.

'Completely out of the way of ground zero,' Chris remarked.

'Yes, but give her her dues, she did run into the danger after the explosion and helped where she could with first aid.'

'Which doesn't give her a free pass for not being a suspect,' Chris said quietly.

'She doesn't speak highly of her boss and was very sarcastic about being given the day off.' Jen ignored Chris' remarks.

'I spoke to Lloyd after Chris left the venue and his thoughts about Karl Jenkins also echo what everyone else is saying about him,' Lyndsey added.

'Clarissa talked us through the pre-event checks before they let the general public in, and I hate to say it, but it *must* have been a member of the public who brought the explosives in; the area was clear beforehand,' Jen finished.

'So how did the guys on the door miss it during the bag checks?' Chris questioned, as Julie moved to the front of the room and started writing things on the board before he'd even thought to attempt it.

'There were some concerns about the band's behaviour and safeguarding, if I remember rightly. Did we find out anything further?' Lyndsey asked.

'I searched through various internet forums and websites and couldn't find anything about rumours of fans sleeping with the band members.

Though I *did* find an article about the lengths these fans go to meet their idols,' Jen offered. 'Either way, I think it might be worth getting a couple of uniform officers to go and speak to the girls concerned about skipping school.'

'If we send someone from the safeguarding team, we can see if they have any concerns after meeting the girls,' Chris suggested.

'How have you been getting on with the witness reports?' Lyndsey asked.

'Thanks to the Superintendent's provision of extra officers, we've been working our way through those who are now home from the hospital and also those who made it out with no issues,' Lyndsey's detective, Preston, responded. 'I've also been contacting staff members, and have now been able to identify the injured members of staff,' Preston continued as he swung back on his chair.

'Give me the edited highlights,' Lyndsey instructed.

'None of attendees noticed anything, but given they were all watching the band and standing around ground zero, it's perhaps not surprising. It just seemed like a normal gig night to them.'

'And the staff?'

'The staff tell a different story. Some report seeing a flash before the explosion, but no one reports seeing anything suspicious. The team leaders told me that their area was clear of anything prior to the gig.'

'Any news from the injured members of staff?'

'One member of the floor staff is still critical, so we weren't able to speak to her. The other four say that they're okay, but we're sending officers over there to speak to them first thing tomorrow,' Preston concluded, finally rocking back onto all four legs of his chair.

'Thank you, Preston.' Lyndsey turned her attention back to everyone else. 'I think we can conclude that whatever caused the explosion was brought into the venue during the gig,' she summed up.

'Preston, I know your team are working their way through attendees. I think we need to consider that someone on that list is our suspect.' The response to Chris's suggestion was a silent room, until the door swung open and Luiza rushed in.

'I'm so sorry I'm late. I couldn't get away from the identification process.'

'Not a problem Luiza. How's it going?' Lyndsey said, clearly noticing the harassed look on Luiza's face.

'As expected, I guess…' she replied in a sombre tone.

'I was just summing up. Is there anything you'd like to add to the meeting?' Lyndsey asked.

'No, boss, nothing to report. Just that we're trying our best to reunite the victims with their families so they can start making funeral arrangements.' Luiza sat down heavily on a spare chair. 'Have you heard anything regarding when the coroner will be releasing the bodies?'

'I haven't heard anything yet, but I can ask the Sup. He might know more,' Lyndsey replied.

'I just don't want to give these families false hope that they can start organising funerals tomorrow …'

'I know this is a silly question, Luiza, but is there anyone who you've been struggling to find a next of kin for?' Chris decided to jump in.

'Not that I am aware of, sir. Why?'

'I was just thinking about our bomber, wondering if he's or she's perhaps among the dead.' Chris sighed. It was probably wishful thinking on his part; the forensics team had already told them they probably weren't dealing with a suicide bomber.

'Trudie, you and Colin were looking at CCTV?'

'Yeah, nothing major to report there,' Colin responded.

'There's nothing out of the ordinary. Everyone we've picked up around the area is just going about their business,' Trudie followed on.

'Did the CCTV from the venue get to the tech team?' Chris asked.

'They said it wasn't looking good but would send over what they could rescue first thing tomorrow,' Lyndsey replied.

'For those of you who aren't aware, the CCTV footage may not have survived the fire, mainly because of the water from the fire hoses,' Chris explained.

'I know the additional officers are working their way through, but there are still hundreds of images and videos to look at sent in by attendees. So hopefully we might get something.'

'Yes, I was just about to ask how the appeal for footage was going, Colin?'

'Last I heard, boss, there had been a lot sent in, so fingers crossed.'

'Does anyone have anything else to offer?' Lyndsey asked.

'We know where ground zero is, we know what caused the explosion; we just don't know why, who and how,' Jen summed up what everyone was thinking. 'A dead end.'

The team would have seemed defeated to anyone looking in at them, as they all tried to think of avenues that they could explore.

'I'm going to speak to the pathologists again and see what they can tell me about the types of injuries people sustained,' Trudie spoke out first.

'Okay, great. Might be worth speaking to Amanda, although she could be snowed under,' Chris replied.

'I know we're all super busy, but did anyone get anywhere in identifying our press conference gatecrasher?' Lyndsey asked.

'I do have an answer on that one, boss,' Colin spoke up, sounding pretty proud of himself.

'Do tell …'

'A Mr Matthew Dale, boss of the Dale's pub. It's a family-owned pub and entertainment venue that hosts various unsigned bands. Sometimes they strike lucky with the odd band who goes on to make it big; in this instance, the McDermitts.'

'I thought they were a Scottish band?' Chris questioned.

'They are. They just so happened to be doing a tour of the UK and played at Dale's before they were signed. In fact, back in my university days—'

'In your days of sex, drugs and rock-and-roll. Yes, Colin?' Chris cut in before Colin could start reminiscing.

'Well ... me and the lads used to go there quite a bit. Nice venue, if I'm honest with you. I think it was run by Dale Senior at that point though. No doubt needs some work doing there now …'

Chris rolled his eyes. This wasn't the time for a trip down memory lane. 'As you're all aware, we have a memorial service we're all expected to be in attendance at today. Obviously, we all want to pay our respects, but I suggest that my team try and make a quick getaway at the end so we can continue our investigations,' Chris reminded them all.

'Makes sense,' Lyndsey responded. 'If my guys want to be on hand to crowd spot and see if they notice anything out of the ordinary?'

'Colin, will you take Julie and go and speak to Matthew Dale? Offer a bit of lip service, reassure him we're doing everything possible and all that. Hopefully he'll make an appearance at this service later so he shouldn't require much hunting down.'

'Will do, boss.'

'By the time you get back, we should have some news from the tech team.'

'Okay, boss.'

'Jen, will you and Greg go and see our Mr Jenkins and see what he has to say for himself?'

'On it.'

'Lyndsey and I have an incident command meeting to attend. If we all report back here, say about 6 p.m.?' Everyone nodded their agreement and the volume in the room started to increase. 'Jen, sorry. Before you go, can I have a chat with you in my office?' Chris jumped in before she could leave.

'Of course, boss. I'll just speak to Greg and be right with you.'

Jen Garner

'Come in, Jen. Take a seat.' Chris directed her.

'Is everything okay, boss?' Jen questioned, a little bit puzzled about why she'd been called in.

'If anyone asks, I'm giving you a warning – but between me and you, it's just a chat.' Jen looked over at Chris in confusion. 'As you may know, if you saw yesterday's press conference, someone leaked our rescue mission to the press.'

'I did hear something.'

'Well, the Sup wants me to have a word. Our little rescue attempt hasn't exactly gone down very well with those in charge.'

'I did wonder …'

'So he wants me to remind you that you're working in local community policing and that the heroics you may have got away with in London are not appreciated or needed in Nottingham.'

Jen didn't have a response. Even if she hadn't worked all those undercover cases previously and wasn't as street savvy, she still would have gone in to rescue those lads.

Chris was still talking. 'If I can be honest with you, Jen, I personally think we did the right thing in the situation we found ourselves in. Dean wouldn't have waited for backup to arrive. He was more concerned about his partner, and if we hadn't followed …'

'Neither of them would've got out alive.'

'Exactly. So talk over. Carry on with what you're doing.'

‘Thanks, boss.’

Jen left Chris’ office, still a little mystified as to why she was getting into trouble for what they’d done – they might have saved two lives, after all. No doubt this telling off was coming from higher up. The fire service had told everyone to stay away from the building as it burned out of control, there had been clear instructions of the job she and Chris were expected to carry out – and those instructions definitely hadn’t included running into a bomb site. God, it was at times like this she missed her old life. Lisa wouldn’t have stood for any of this; she’d have run into the fire, sod anyone else, and pulled both boys out before backup even arrived …

But this was her life now, she reminded herself. She’d chosen this path for her family.

Chapter Ten

DI Chris Jackson

'Here, let me help you,' Julie said as she moved over towards Chris to help him with his tie.

'When I got it out of the wardrobe this morning, I panicked about whether it would fit or not,' Chris joked as he let Julie take over. As the rest of his team weren't standing at the front, permitted to just mingle in the crowd, they hadn't been forced to wear full policing uniform. Chris didn't wear his very often; in fact, the last time was when he had been awarded that medal for bravery the previous year, and then he'd sent it to the dry cleaners straight after wearing it. He wasn't sure how this whole thing was going to go down; he just knew the boss wanted him and Lyndsey front and centre. It was her who appeared at his door now, equally suited and booted.

'Ready?' she asked, looking at him expectantly.

They took the short walk from the police station across to the market square where the crowds were beginning to gather for the memorial service. The only other time Chris had seen this many people congregated in the square was when the royals had last visited Nottingham. He'd asked his team to spread themselves within the crowds of people; not only to be on hand to comfort anybody that needed support, but also to be his eyes and ears on anything suspicious or out of the ordinary.

Chris held his hand out to help Lyndsey climb onto the small stage, which had been erected in the market square, and pondered briefly if it should be him who was being assisted up the steps. Admittedly, the team at the council had done a good job in setting the whole thing up with less than twenty-four hours' notice. Chris remembered the sea of photos, flowers, candles and teddies that had appeared close to Carbon when he and Lyndsey had first visited and wondered vaguely if the plan was to transfer them here.

The crowds of people were oddly silent, though every now and again Chris heard the odd whimper from someone, who would immediately be comforted by someone else who was close by – whether they knew them or not, it seemed. Nottingham appeared to be coming together to remember those who had lost their short lives in a way the city had never seen before.

Jen stood in the crowd, wondering whether she'd see Gabe or Dean at the service. She wasn't sure whether either of them had been discharged from the hospital, but her brief, strange meeting with Chris had reminded her to look them both up when she got back to the office.

The large screens that had been placed around the market square flickered into life. Jen had never seen this much grief on display in the same place since 7/7; she'd been working for the service then but remembered the panic and the anguish like it was yesterday.

'Good morning,' a voice boomed out from the direction of the stage as the screen lit up. It was then that she noticed Chris and Lyndsey, all suited and booted, sitting at the back of the stage. Suddenly, she felt a warm hand slip into hers.

'Hey,' James said as she looked up at him. 'Have I missed anything?'

'No! What are you doing here? Where are the kids?' she asked.

'I got a call from the boss; some network problem that was stopping him working. So I asked next door if she'd watch them for a while.'

'On a Saturday? What's he doing working on a Saturday?' Jen questioned. 'Thanks for coming to find me though.'

'I fixed the problem and decided I'd come and pay my respects,' James answered as he gazed around at the crowd surrounding them.

'We come together today to remember those who lost their lives in the tragic incident at Carbon. Though they are not here with us, they will be forever in our hearts,' they heard the Lord Mayor say over the PA.

Jen noticed a woman next to her quietly sobbing. She seemed to be standing there alone, holding a single rose. Jen slipped her hand from James' and moved over towards her, passing her a tissue. She smiled and gently put her arm around the woman. It seemed like she'd automatically clicked into mother mood and, though James had come down from his office to support her, she'd immediately recognised somebody who needed her more. The large screens started to display pictures of those who had died at Carbon as the Mayor read out their names … *Percy Reynolds, Lilly Dorrian, Sophie Bray, Natalie Westwell, Kayleigh Herbert, Bethany Gall, Joseph Pierre, Charles Parish, Toby Egan …*

DI Chris Jackson

Chris looked over the crowds of people who had gathered in front of the stage and beyond. He had the perfect vantage point as he was able to see who was there and who wasn't. He noticed several of the staff from Carbon were near the front of the stage, but there was no sign of Karl himself, unsurprisingly. He also quickly noticed the gatecrasher from the press conference standing next to an older, shorter, pot-bellied man, who Chris could only assume was his father – they both shared such similar features. He almost wished he had an earpiece in so he could contact his team and tell them that the Dales were there. He wondered who else he'd be able to see as he continued to survey the crowds.

'No matter our faiths or what we believe in, let us all come together and stand in two minutes' silence for those young people who lost their lives …'

Chris closed his eyes and bowed his head. The silence of the crowd was palpable, but Chris could still sense the grief dripping off the mourners in front of him.

'Thank you, Mayor Gordon.' The Superintendent stood up to speak once the silence had ended. 'I know this is a difficult time for our city, but I have to ask you to please speak out. My officers are here to listen to your concerns and to offer comfort in this dark time. Don't be afraid to approach any of my officers; whether they are in uniform or in plain clothes, they are here for you. We will get through this, Nottingham, and we will bring those at fault to justice.'

DC Colin Goodwin

'That was a bit intense.' Colin sighed as he got into the pool car next to Julie.

'So much grief … I'm not even sure how I held it together.'

'Didn't spot anyone of interest though,' he commented thoughtfully.

'Yeah, you'd have thought at least the venue owner might have turned up,' Julie agreed.

'From what you and Chris both said about him, I don't think I'm surprised, to be fair.'

'We're in for a treat though. Dale Senior has invited us for a chat over at his place,' Julie said as they pulled out of the station car park.

'Thought we were just going to visit the pub.'

'The Dales were at the memorial, so I went over and introduced myself and asked if we could have a chat. He practically fell over himself to invite me to his place in Bilborough.' Julie laughed as Colin fiddled with the radio station, trying to find something he liked. 'Did nobody teach you that whoever drives chooses the radio station?' she growled.

'Oh God, you're one of those, aren't you?' Julie took her eyes off the road momentarily to give him an evil look. 'Lizzie is the same. She's always complaining about me playing with the radio in her car.'

'My kind of girl. What did you find out about the Dales' company before we left?'

'The company accounts are late, which means they could be very close to insolvency … or someone is just filing late.'

'When I looked at the company accounts I could find, they didn't look very healthy, but what motivation would either of them have for blowing Carbon up, never mind targeting Mr Jenkins?' Julie questioned.

'The only thing I can think of is he's trying to get rid of the competition. Remember what he said when he stormed into the press conference? Without Carbon, where will bands play?'

'Birmingham, probably.' Julie indicated into a quiet cul-de-sac, where they were met with iron gates and what looked like a long driveway to a house beyond the trees.

'Some money round here.' Colin whistled as he looked around. The Dales' house seemed to be the only one hidden behind gates. Julie lent out of the car and pressed the buzzer next to the gate, holding her ID up to the camera. Moments later, the gates automatically opened and she started the car up again. 'I think they might have been expecting us.'

After they'd driven down the driveway, they were both met at the car by what could only be described as a butler, who welcomed them and led them into the house where they were greeted with an expansive hallway, complete with bare oak panel walls and marble flooring.

'Someone will be with you shortly,' they were told as they were left to admire their surroundings.

'This is not what I was expecting,' Colin said quietly, turning to Julie.

'Me neither. Well, there's no way Senior made all his money from a pub in the centre of Nottingham.'

'Detectives.' Dale Senior startled them, appearing from a door just out of their line of sight.

‘Thank you for agreeing to see us at such short notice.’ Julie pulled herself together quickly and reached for her ID.

‘No need, Detective,’ Dale Senior said. ‘Nottingham’s finest are always welcome here. Detectives Goodwin and Ryan, I take it?’

Julie and Colin both nodded their response as Dale Senior beckoned to them. ‘If you’d like to follow me, I’ll take you into the boardroom.’

Julie and Colin swapped looks of confusion as they followed him along the corridor and into a large, bright room where other members of the Dale household were already gathered.

‘Detectives, I know you’ve already met my son, Matthew Dale Junior, or Matt as he prefers to be known.’ Colin moved over towards Junior to shake his hand. ‘But let me introduce my daughter, Danielle, and my wife, Darla.’

‘Nice to meet you all,’ Julie said as she followed Colin in greeting everyone.

‘Can I get you detectives any refreshments?’ Darla asked as she moved to the side of the room where a tray of drinks and French fancies seemed to be waiting just for them.

‘Tea, if you don’t mind,’ Julie said.

‘Detective Goodwin?’ Darla asked.

‘Water would be great, please.’

‘Help yourself to the decanters on the table.’

Once the drinks were all distributed, Colin and Julie were shown to their seats at the meeting table.

‘Forgive the formality of all this, Detectives. It’s just when we spoke at the service earlier and you said you wanted to talk about the business, I thought it best to assemble the entire family. Danielle is here as my legal representative. My lovely wife is the company secretary and, as you know, Matt and I currently both run Dale’s.’

‘Thank you, Mr Dale. This really was just an informal chat, but it’s nice to meet the whole family,’ Julie responded. Colin noticed that both Darla and Danielle were taking notes so he decided to pull his notebook out to make things look more official, although he had to admit, he was momentarily blindsided by Danielle; she was nothing short of a super model – tall, blonde and stunning.

‘We wanted to come and speak to you about the incident at Carbon. I know your son attended our press conference a couple of days ago …’

'Yes, that wasn't the wisest thing to do. I have had words with Dale Junior and he knows how disappointed I am in him. Things could have been addressed very differently,' Dale Senior butted in as his son started to pick at the skin around his nails, visibly uncomfortable.

'I know Dale's is a very popular bar in the centre of Nottingham. Are there any specific concerns that you would like to address with us after the incident at Carbon?'

'No. Dale Junior here was just overreacting. How is the investigation progressing anyway?' Colin noticed that Matt seemed to have suddenly found something very interesting to look at on the table in front of him.

'Pretty much early days, but clean up at the site has begun.'

'How is that ponce taking it all?'

'I'm sorry?' Colin asked, unsure whether what he'd heard was correct.

'That ponce, Karl Jenkins.'

'Daddy!' That was Danielle's voice. 'You can't say things like that to the police. They'll take it the wrong way.'

'Darling, the detectives aren't here as barristers. They're not questioning me in the court room!'

'But still! Please rephrase your question.'

'I'm sorry, Detectives. Please ignore my daughter. She takes this legal representation thing a bit too far sometimes. Seems to forget, for some reason, that we are in my home and not in the court of law.' Colin watched as Danielle then proceeded to stick her tongue out at her dad once his head was turned back. *Clearly not that much of a professional.*

'Do you know Mr Jenkins?' Colin ignored the weird family politics going on and continued his line of questioning.

'Oh yes, back before he took off on his own, he used to be my bar manager. In fact, I could quite possibly say I taught him everything he knows.'

'I take it you parted on good terms?'

'Yes, he came into some money, brought the wreck that was once Carbon … though if you think of it another way, it's now been returned to its original state.'

'Da—'

'Danielle,' Dale Senior shot back

'So … you're running the place now, Matt?' Julie asked in a bright tone, clearly trying to steer the conversation away from any further objections from Danielle.

'Yes, I've been running it for five years now. Haven't I, Father?' He received a nod in response. 'My father is currently going through the process of handing the business over completely to me.'

'How are you finding it, stepping into your dad's shoes?'

'It hasn't been easy and now, with events at Carbon, there's the cancellation of gigs by worried performers who seem to think just because Carbon went up, we will too—'

'We've been through worse and adapted,' Dale Senior butted in again.

'My husband's health isn't what it used to be, Detectives, so we decided together it was time for him to step away from the business.' Darla spoke up for the first time since the whole conversation began.

'You have no interest in going into the entertainment industry, Danielle?' Colin asked.

'As I'm sure you've guessed, Detective, Danielle is training to be a barrister and is currently working with one of the top law firms in London.'

'She'll be representing the rich and powerful in no time.'

As Julie spoke, Colin wondered if it was the same law firm they'd had dealings with previously; the one that refused to come and represent Harry Greenidge when they'd brought him in after he'd sold drugs to two undercover officers – who just so happened to be Chris and Hannah. 'Are there any concerns you'd like to address with us regarding the safety of the business?' Colin asked, realising his mind had drifted away from the matter in hand.

'I feel you've had a wasted journey, Detective, if I'm honest with you,' Senior answered. 'I was as outraged, as I'm sure your inspector was, when my son gatecrashed the press conference.' Colin glanced over to where Dale Junior was sitting with his head bowed, still staring at the table.

'I'm sorry for wasting your time, but thank you for coming out to see us,' Dale Junior now responded in a sulky voice. He was acting like a small child who had just been shouted at.

'Thank you for the tea,' Julie said politely as she got her things together.

'I'm so sorry, how rude of me. I should've offered you both a cake,' Darla said suddenly, obviously remembering she hadn't offered out the tray of French fancies.

‘Oh, go on then,’ Colin said, reaching towards the plate. He’d been eyeing them since he’d come in, if he was honest.

‘Will you take one for the journey back to the station, Detective?’ Darla asked now, holding the plate towards Julie.

‘No, thank you. It’ll spoil my diet.’

‘Don’t be silly, take one.’ Darla said, pushing the plate closer towards Julie.

‘Thank you for your time,’ Julie said as she reached out and took a cake. Colin suspected she’d give it to him in the car.

‘If you have any further concerns, please contact me directly,’ Colin said, reaching for his business card with the cake free hand.

‘I will. Thank you, Detectives. I’ll get someone to show you out.’

Chapter Eleven

Jen Garner

'Everything okay with the boss?' Greg asked as they walked the short distance between the station and the Lace Market.

'Yeah, he wanted a word about our little rescue mission.'

'Do you think he's getting grief from above?'

'I guess so,' Jen said as she looked out for the Carbon offices.

'I wouldn't worry too much then. If you think about it, you might've dodged a bullet there.'

Jen was silent for a while as they walked along the main road, thinking over what Greg had just said. The Superintendent had warned her on her first day about any heroics, and almost right away she'd gone running into a burning building, but, whether she'd been in her 'Lisa Carter' persona or not, she'd have still done the same.

Greg held open the door and Jen entered the vast marble reception area.

'Good afternoon. We're here to see Mr Jenkins. Is he available?' Jen asked as she held up her ID to the receptionist, who seemed to be busy typing away and didn't bother even looking up to acknowledge them.

'If you'd like to take a seat, I'll see if he's in,' she said as she picked up the phone with her other hand.

Jen and Greg made their way over to the plastic seats on the other side of the reception desk.

'What time did you make it home last night?' Greg asked.

'It was more like this morning. My dinner had been plated up and put in the microwave for me.'

'How's the family taken to the career change?'

'The kids have seen more of my neighbour than me, James is reverting back to microwave meals, and, what, we're on day three?'

Greg laughed as a young woman approached them with a lanyard hanging from the left pocket of her jeans.

"Detectives?' she questioned.

'Detective Sanders and Detective Garner,' Greg said as they held up their IDs.

'Cindy, box office manager,' she said, stepping forward to shake both of their hands. 'I'm afraid you've had a wasted journey. Karl is yet to arrive.'

'Do you know what time he's due in?' Greg questioned.

'I am afraid I don't know. Come up to the office and I'll try his mobile.'

'Thank you.'

Greg and Jen followed Cindy out of the entrance hall and through a set of double doors, then they waited for a lift.

'What time does he usually get in?' Jen questioned.

'It varies, if I'm honest with you. A lot of it depends on what's happening at Carbon – which we know is very little at this moment in time – but he always checks into the office first thing, even if it's only via a phone call,' she replied as they got into the lift.

'And no one's heard anything from him yet today?'

'Not that I'm aware of. We usually get a list of instructions from him if he's going to be at the venue itself for the day,' Cindy explained. They stood in silence for a while as the lift took them to the correct floor.

'If you'd like to follow me over to my desk, I'll give Karl a ring,' Cindy said, once they were out of the lift. She led them across the busy open-plan office. 'Take a seat. My colleague doesn't work Saturdays so that desk is free.' She looked around for a second chair.

'It's not a problem. Detective Garner?' Greg said, pulling the chair from under the desk and motioning for Jen to sit down.

As Cindy held the phone to her ear, Jen surveyed the office. There seemed to be two separate rooms at either end, and Jen assumed that one was likely to be Karl's office, and the second probably some form of meeting room.

'I'm sorry, Officers. It rings for a while before going straight through to answerphone.'

'Does Karl live alone or have a family at all?' Jen asked.

'Alone, I think. We don't really socialise with him outside of work. He isn't one for drinks after work or inviting staff to after show parties with rock bands.'

'Always best to keep your work life and social life separate, if you ask me,' Greg commented, as Jen found herself thinking about her old friend, Chloe, and what would have happened if she'd followed that advice. Back when she'd joined the service, Chloe had been her saviour after a busy day – they'd both worked hard but played even harder. Which was pretty much how she'd ended up falling in love and restarting her life as Jen Garner, the perfect wife and mum. A part which she'd played so well, for so long…

'Right,' Cindy said, ripping off a heart-shaped post-it, handing it to Jen and breaking her out of her thoughts. 'I'm afraid he doesn't live locally, Officers. He commutes in from Hinkley.'

'It's not a problem. We can get a local force to check in on him if need be. A colleague mentioned that the venue also has five duty managers. Are you aware if any of them have heard from him today?' Greg asked whilst Jen's mind temporarily wandered off once again.

'I can send out a WhatsApp message to them if it'll help.'

'That would be great. Thank you, Cindy.'

'Can I ask if there have been any developments?'

'I'm afraid everything is very early days at the moment.'

'It's just one of our colleagues were seriously injured, and I was just wondering—'

'Would you mind just trying Karl's number again?' Jen asked as she broke out of her daydream to see Cindy looking at her expectingly.

'Yes, yes, of course.' She dialled the number again and waited. 'I'm sorry, there's still no answer.'

'Not to worry. Thank you for your time,' Jen said as she stood up. 'I hope your colleagues make a speedy recovery.'

'Thank you,' Cindy replied, suddenly falling quiet like she had forgotten for a moment all about her injured workmates.

'Take my card. If you hear anything from your colleagues about Karl's whereabouts, will you let us know?'

'Of course. I'm sorry, Detectives. It's just …'

'Not to worry, love. We understand.' Greg put a reassuring hand on Cindy's shoulder as she stood up to show them out of the office.

'As soon as I hear back from the others, I'll let you know,' Cindy reassured them as she pressed the call button for the lift.

'That would be great, thank you. And if the man himself arrives, could you ask him to contact us also?'

'Of course.'

The lift door opened and they stepped inside. Jen selected the ground floor.

'Thank you for your time today, Cindy,' she called just as the doors closed. She looked at the screwed-up post-it in her hand and was suddenly transported back to meeting Sam for the first time, when she'd returned to the service briefly to help in the search for Chloe's killer. She was initially annoyed by the PA's sunny persona and her vast collection of colourful stationery. Maybe Cindy and Sam were alike. Her mind drifted again as she wondered how everyone in the London office was …

Greg quickly broke her out of her reverie. 'What did you make of all that?'

'Well, our venue manager seems to have disappeared. I'm not expecting him to be at Carbon, unless he's persuaded Chris to release the site so he can get the insurers in – and I doubt that's happened.'

'Might be worth contacting the station and asking them to do a check on that address to see who comes up on the electoral roll.'

'On it.' Jen strode out of the lift and retrieved her mobile phone from her back pocket. Nottingham city centre seemed quiet and there was still the faint smell of burning in the air. Jen hadn't ever seen the area this deserted and quiet, with shoppers no doubt deciding to stay well clear for fear of being caught up in another incident.

'According to the office, the only person registered at that address is Karl himself,' Jen confirmed as she ended the call.

'Okay, shall we head towards Carbon and see if he's hiding out there?' Greg asked.

'No time like the present.' They walked across the market square, where people were still milling around after the memorial, and up towards where the ruins of Carbon lay. Jen turned to Greg as they walked past a group of people huddled together.

'What did you think to the memorial service?'

'It was nice, and I noticed that everyone was supporting each other even if they didn't know each other.'

'Yes, there was a lady next to me who'd clearly come on her own. I ended up comforting her – she was beside herself. I don't think I realised before just how much the incident has affected this entire city. For someone to come alone to something like that memorial and openly express their grief … and there must have been dozens like her in that crowd today. I just wish I could have supported all of them.' As she spoke, Jen felt her resolve to solve the case become even stronger.

The cordons had been more or less removed, and the damaged building was now protected by chipboard which had been erected around the site in an attempt to stop any trespassing. The site entrance was guarded by a hired security firm.

'Hey, Geoff,' Greg greeted the security personnel, who was positioned at the entrance today.

'Detectives. How can I help you both this morning?'

'We were wondering if Karl Jenkins is here?' Greg asked as he looked through the gate at the shell of the nightclub.

'I don't think so. I haven't seen him around since yesterday, when he was here with some older bloke.'

'How did he seem?' Jen asked, wondering if this might give them some clue as to where Karl had disappeared to.

'Rude, arrogant, not the most friendly site owner I've met, I'll give you that. But I guess I have to give him some leeway, seeing as his business has just gone up in smoke.'

'Thank you, Geoff,' Jen said as she and Greg walked a little way off from the site entrance. 'I don't think we need to look round?'

'Not if Geoff says he isn't here. I'll wait till we're back in the office and see if I can get hold of the structural engineer guys, find out what the future prospects are for the site.'

'Fancy a trip to Hinkley?' Jen decided she just needed to voice what she'd been mulling over.

'Huh?'

'Well, Mr Jenkins is clearly not in Nottingham and not answering his phone. So I suggest we either head back to the office and wait to hear from the local Hinkley force, or we head over there and see if we can speak to him ourselves.'

'I guess it'll beat sitting around.'

'I'll check in with the DI, if you want to grab a pool car?' Jen said as they both headed back towards the office.

DI Chris Jackson

'Afternoon all. Welcome to our second incident command meeting,' Gil greeted the room, which was full of the same people who had been there the previous day, all looking equally withdrawn and exhausted. At least Chris would be able to hide in plain sight.

'Would you like to start us off with the fire service investigation, Graham?'

'We have greatly decreased our presence at the scene, leaving just the welfare unit and a small crew on site.'

'Is there any news on the fire investigation?'

'We received clearance from the structural engineers just prior to this meeting, so the investigation into the incident is being conducted as I sit here.'

'Can we be absolutely certain that this isn't a terrorist attack? I can't help thinking about the 2015 Bataclan incident in Paris, and, of course, the Manchester Arena bombing two years later.'

'From a firefighting point of view, there was no evidence that has suggested a suicide bombing attack.'

'There have been no early witness reports of anything that would point to such an event, and forensics seemed to have ruled it out, as we've already heard,' Lyndsey added.

'So where are you and Chris with your investigations?' the Superintendent asked.

'Chris and I have split the workloads between us. Chris and his team are focusing on the criminal investigation, and my guys are working on the venue side of things.'

'Chris?'

'I spoke to the venue manager yesterday, who, in my opinion, has a lot to answer for. We've also spoken to other potential witnesses, such as the band and duty manager. We received a raft of footage after the appeal, so with the help of Lyndsey's team, we're making our way through that.'

'Any cause for concern?'

'Not at this moment in time, sir. Though I do have some good news – we've identified the gatecrasher from the press conference and two of my team have gone out to visit him today.'

'Good. Where are we with identification and removal of the victims from the university?'

'My detective confirmed to me this morning that everyone who was at the gig has been identified and their next of kin informed,' Lyndsey answered.

'Okay, I guess that's something positive.' The Superintendent sighed.

'I can confirm that we've now discharged many of those who were in hospital, and we're working with the coroner regarding the dead being released back to their families,' Selina added.

'How are the hospital's coping, Selina?'

'We still have several critical patients, whose prognosis I am unable to comment on, but the tension seems to be lifting as we discharge more.'

'Thank you, Selina, for your hard work in coordinating this incident. If you could keep me informed on the remaining patients' prognosis?'

'Sir.'

'Kyle and the team from the major incident team have been stood down and returned to their base in Mansfield. Felicity, do you want to fill us all in with what the press are saying?'

'The press conference descended into chaos, thanks to our gatecrasher, but the output from the media seems to be pretty positive for the moment. Though I do have junior reporters from the nationals constantly on the phone after an update, no doubt so they can be the first to break any news of an arrest or new discovery.'

'I had a flick through briefly this morning, and I was glad to see they'd chosen *not* to follow up on two of our detectives and their rescue mission.'

'I suspect that they decided against it, sir. With other bigger stories happening and it not being election time, complaining about lack of resources isn't top of their priority list.'

'And the locals?'

'Our Mr Dale was mentioned and his outburst, but they don't seem to have followed up on his concerns. Their front pages were more focused on what had happened and our reaction. The media are a tricky bunch at the best of times. If we're open with them about how it's going and what we've got, they'll play fair with us. It's when we try to hide things, the sharks come out.'

'So you suggest we keep them informed?'

'Yes, sir. Maybe an odd press statement read out by one of the team once things get moving.'

'Okay. Thank you, Felicity. if you could work with the fire services' press department before you put anything further out, it may stop us duplicating the effort.'

'Of course, sir. They're already on my speed dial,' Felicity said, glancing over towards Graham.

'Unless anyone has anything else to add, I suggest we bring these daily meetings to an end and hand over to your teams on the ground.'

Finally, thought Chris. Now he could get on with some real policing rather than meeting after meeting.

'Graham, could I have a moment of your time after the meeting, please? I'd like to discuss with you how we move the investigation on,' Lyndsey cut in.

'Not a problem.'

'Thank you all for your time,' the Superintendent said, standing up and brushing himself down. 'Chris, do you want to follow me up to my office for a quick chat?'

'Meet you back in the office?' Chris turned and looked at Lyndsey, who was now standing up to talk to Graham. Lyndsey returned a nod and Chris fell into step with the Superintendent as he strode off up the corridor.

'Come in and take a seat Chris,' he said, when they'd reached his office and he'd unlocked the door.

'Sir.'

'Are you feeling any better?' Chris didn't quite know what to say and just stared at his boss for a moment. 'With what happened at Carbon and your hospital appointments, I just wanted to catch up with you about your health.'

'Everything is fine, sir. It was just the sudden rush of adrenaline and then fresh air …'

'Okay, Chris. You know my door is always open?'

'Thank you, sir.' Chris didn't really understand why he'd been invited into the boss's office to discuss his health. There was nothing to tell, was there? Or had someone else noticed something that he'd failed to hide from those around him and gone straight to the top? He felt okay, he was doing okay … wasn't he?

Or is that a lie?

Chapter Twelve

Jen Garner

Hinkley was just outside of Leicester, about an hour's drive down the motorway. As Jen was yet to pass her policing driving course, she was left watching the world go by.

'So tell me about yourself, Greg? How did you find yourself in the Special Ops unit?' Jen asked.

Greg laughed. 'What's with all the sudden interest in me?' he asked as he continued to concentrate on the road ahead.

'The team obviously knows all about me from the two cases I've been involved in. Hannah fills me in all about our DI … sometimes more than I want to know, to be honest.'

'Well, I came in when we were restructured and the Special Ops team was created.'

'Where were you before?'

'Oh, I was still in the Nottinghamshire area. I was just your plain old detective.'

'But why Special Ops?'

'I guess I just fancied a change. The kids had grown up and moved out.'

'Isn't that the point where you start to relax and spend more time with your wife?'

'Ha, she says I get in her way enough as it is!'

'So you spend your days being out of the way at work?'

'Something like that … But what about you? How come you've come back to policing?' Greg asked as he signalled to turn into a newly built estate.

'Truth be known, I wanted that buzz back … the excitement of the chase.'

'Why not go back to your old team?'

'Commitments and the ties that bind.'

'The kids and James then?'

'Yeah …' Jen sighed as she looked out of the window at the passing houses. If she was working this case as Lisa Carter with her old team in London, it would have been going in a very different direction. For a start, she would be running the show and they wouldn't be driving all over looking for Karl Jenkins. They would have known exactly where he was at any given time. Maybe she was losing her touch and changing into a completely different detective to the one she really was? She pushed the thought quickly aside. 'I don't think James was very keen on my return at first, but the longer I gave him to think about it, the more he came round to the idea.'

'I guess he wasn't expecting your first case off the starting blocks would involve you being woken up in the middle of the night and going MIA for the next twenty-four hours.'

Jen laughed. *Never a truer word ...*

Pulling up outside number 39 Crompton Avenue, Jen got out of the car and stretched. She ached and hadn't had the chance to exercise since before this had all started. Maybe she'd finally get the chance to go out for a run that night …

'Nice neighbourhood,' Greg commented as he looked around, taking in the scenery. 'Bit of money around here.'

Jen followed Greg as he headed up towards the house. There were no cars on the drive, but all the curtains appeared to be open.

'Doesn't look like he's here,' Jen mused as Greg rang the doorbell.

'We'll soon see.'

A weary looking man opened the door. 'Whatever you're selling, I'm not interested,' he snapped at them.

'Detectives Sanders and Garner,' Jen said, flashing her ID. 'We're here to speak to Mr Jenkins.'

'You'll have a problem with that one, I'm afraid,' the guy said vaguely as he studied their IDs.

'Do you know where we can find Mr Jenkins?'

'I haven't seen him since he went to work yesterday morning.'

'Can I just take your name?' Greg asked, pulling his notebook out.

'Samuel. Samuel Piper'

'Does he often disappear for days on end?' Jen asked, keen to find out where Karl could be.

'Not really, but given what has happened at Carbon, I thought it best to give him space.'

'Can I just ask your relationship with Mr Jenkins?' Greg asked, clearly remembering Jen's research that confirmed Karl lived alone.

'Yeah, I'm his partner.' Jen and Greg were taken back for a moment and Samuel laughed. 'Ahh, I see I'm still his dirty little secret. He isn't exactly open about our relationship.'

'How long have you been together, if you don't mind me asking?'

'Just over three years now. You'd have thought Karl would be comfortable with people knowing about me after all this time, wouldn't you?' Samuel paused for a moment. 'Why don't you both come in and I'll make us a cuppa. I'm guessing you have some questions.' Samuel stepped aside to let Jen and Greg into the house. 'If you go into the room on the right and make yourselves comfortable, I'll go and get us some drinks.'

Jen was sure that Greg was as equally shocked as she was by the revelation. No one at the Carbon offices had made any mention of Karl having a partner – even when they couldn't locate him earlier. She sat down on the leather sofa next to Greg and soon heard bone china teacups rattling as Samuel re-entered the living room.

'Detectives,' he said, placing the tray down on a side table. 'I'm guessing you're both happy with tea?'

'Please,' Jen responded as she moved towards the edge of the sofa, ready to accept the cup once it was poured.

'Has Karl said much about the explosion at Carbon?' Greg asked, immediately steering the conversation away from hot beverages.

'He was distraught when he came home that day. When his phone went off in the early hours, I just thought it was an issue at the club. It wasn't until I heard about it on the radio that I realised it was something more serious.'

'Karl didn't get in contact with you prior to that, to tell you what had happened?' Greg asked.

'No, I tried to phone him when I heard what had happened, but he kept rejecting my calls. I was so close to getting in the car and going to check everything was okay …'

'How come you didn't … if you don't mind me asking?' Greg asked.

'Like I said, he likes to keep our relationship quiet … I didn't want to make things more difficult for him. I've never met his work colleagues. There might have been questions if I'd just turned up.' Samuel fell silent and Jen was just about to fill the silence when he spoke again. 'I did question him about it when he got home. He just told me that he'd been too busy trying to sort everything out to get in touch. Then, when he didn't come home last night, I just assumed he'd slept at the office.'

‘Does he often sleep at the office?’ Jen questioned. The staff at Carbon had never said anything about that.

‘Sometimes. When we fall out, or when there’s a concert he wants to be at. Either that or he stays in one of those big posh hotels. It tends to depend on who he’s trying to impress.’

‘Can I just check, does Karl have any other phone numbers?’ Greg asked. ‘You mentioned earlier that he is, umm … keen to keep you a secret. It got me wondering whether he has a second phone?’

‘Ah, you seem to already know my partner too well, Officers. I have my own private hotline just in case I ring at the wrong time … as he puts it.’

‘Would you be able to give us that number, so we can cross check it and see if we can reach him there?’

‘You’re more than welcome to it, but I’ll tell you now, it’s turned off,’ Samuel said, reaching for his phone. A look of concern suddenly crossed his face. ‘Do you think something has happened to him? I mean, you said he wasn’t at the office …’ Samuel looked over toward to door, like he expected Karl to walk in at any moment.

‘I don’t want to cause any further distress, Samuel. We were just looking to talk to him about what happened at Carbon,’ Jen replied, trying to calm the increasingly nervous man.

‘Did Karl share with you who he thought might have been responsible for the explosions?’ Greg asked, obviously keen to move the conversation forward.

‘No, that was why he was so devastated about it. He was adamant it wasn’t terror-related and seemed to think it was to do with some odd punter they’d kicked out or something … but to go to those lengths.’

‘Do you know if there were any, shall we say, repeat offenders, or anyone who made threats to the venue or Karl’s staff?’

‘I’m afraid you’ll have to ask him about that. He’s never shared any concerns with me, but I’m guessing, as you are fast learning, he doesn’t tell me much.’

‘Do you think Karl could possibly be having an affair?’

Samuel nearly spat out his tea. ‘I very much doubt that. But who knows? Because I certainly don’t.’

‘I hope you don’t mind me asking, but do you have any concerns for yours or his safety?’ Jen asked.

‘What do you mean, Officer?’

'It's just my detective brain working: explosion at his place, him failing to come home last night …'

'Then no, he's probably just slept in a hotel. Biding his time, trying to salvage his empire.'

'Not to worry,' Greg said as he smiled at Samuel, trying to offer him some silent reassurance.

'Thank you for your time. You've been most helpful,' Jen said, finishing her cup of tea. 'If you do hear from Karl, would you ask him to contact me, please?' she said as she handed over her card. 'And, of course, you can get in touch yourself if you have any questions.'

'Thank you, Detective. You'll be the first to know as soon as I hear from him.'

Jen stood up and held out her hand.

Jen noticed Samuel standing and watching them as they climbed back into the car. Her mind was running at hundreds of miles per hour, and she knew that she and Greg had so much to discuss on the way back to the station. She felt like she was going to burst: this information about the secrets Karl had been keeping from everyone would most likely send the case in a new direction.

DI Chris Jackson

Chris had been back in his office for a while when his phone rang.

'DI Jackson.'

'Chris, it's Lyndsey. Graham has asked if you can make it over to London Road fire station.'

'Yeah of course. Give me five and I'll be on my way.

Once Chris arrived at the station, he showed his ID to the member of staff sitting at the reception. 'I'm here to meet Watch Manager Graham Styles.'

'Okay, sir. If you could just sign yourself in, I'll see if he's free.'

'Thank you,' Chris said as he completed the required information and moved over to look at the noticeboard which was full of information on fire safety, station open days and their annual carwash.

'Inspector Jackson.' Chris heard Graham's voice before he saw him walking down the stairs towards him. 'Thanks for coming over.'

'Not a problem. Lyndsey said you had something for us.'

'That's right. If you just want to follow me up to the meeting room. Have you driven over?'

'No, seeing as we're almost neighbours. Instead of being caught in traffic, I decided it would be quicker to walk here'

'I hear you there.' Graham chuckled.

'Are you guys finished up at Carbon now?'

'Yeah, we've done our bit. All up to the investigation team now.'

'Any closer to confirming the cause of the explosions?'

'Now, that's where it gets interesting ...' Chris followed Graham up the stairs and through some double doors. He could hear Lyndsey's slightly muffled voice coming from one of the rooms. 'Just to pre-warn you – if an alarm sounds, then there's nothing to worry about. It's probably my guys being sent out on a job.' Graham held open a door, revealing Lyndsey standing and talking to a couple of the station's firefighters.

'Ah, Chris, you made it.' She turned to him. 'Graham thinks he might have worked out which explosive they used on Thursday night.'

'As I said to Lyndsey, this isn't official till the fire investigation team confirm it, but …' Graham tailed off as he moved round the table that had been positioned in the centre of the room. 'Okay, so we're ruling out a suicide bomber – there's no forensic evidence, as we already explained.'

'Some of my team mentioned that a few of the witnesses reported a fruit-like smell,' Chris mentioned.

'Yes, I remember hearing something about that too and thought that it could be relevant,' Lyndsey agreed.

'They might have been close to our bomber at the time …'

Chris fell silent as he reflected on the fact that the people who had mentioned the smell were very lucky to still be alive.

'I present to you Acetone Peroxide crystals, also known as APEX,' Graham said with a flourish as he picked up a test tube which was lying on the table in front of them. It contained tiny white crystals.

'So you were right then. This did cause the explosion?'

'As much I like being right, in this case I sort of wish I wasn't. Yes, APEX was used.' Graham turned to look at Lyndsey.

'So we know what it is, but we're still not any closer to figuring out how somebody got it into the venue. Right, Chris?' Lyndsey asked and Chris nodded his response.

‘This can be made in your own homemade science lab and be left for a week or so at room temperature,’ Graham clarified.

‘God, that’s scary stuff.’ Chris shook his head in disbelief.

‘Our bomber wouldn’t have needed to create a lot of it to cause the amount of damage it did, and there’s also the fact that it can be set off by friction. If you speak to some of my colleagues, you’ll hear stories about many would-be bombers taking themselves out with this stuff …’ Graham explained.

‘APEX has been used most recently in some big terror attacks,’ Lyndsey added as she looked at Chris, waiting for him to agree.

‘If this stuff is set off by friction, how did our guy do it?’ Chris asked.

Graham’s expression turned grim. ‘With the evidence we’ve seen of the injuries, and going by what they’re saying on the ground, it appears as if your suspect filled bottles with APEX and simply threw them into the crowd. Then just sat back and let science do its job.’

Later on, Chris walked into his team’s office with a fresh cup of coffee in his hand. ‘I’m sure that Jen and Greg have filled you in on the latest information about Mr Jenkins,’ Chris said, putting down his coffee, then writing a name on the whiteboard and drawing a large red circle round it. ‘What’s everyone’s thoughts on this turn of events?’

‘The way his partner talks about their relationship is just weird. He described himself as, and I quote, “his dirty little secret”. Do we think Karl is homophobic?’ Greg asked. ‘Or perhaps just ashamed of his sexuality?’

‘I think that could be a possibility. Like I said in the car, keeping any big secret is hard enough, never mind having a constant reminder sitting at home,’ Jen responded. ‘But where does this lead us in the fire investigation?’

‘Lyndsey and I had an interesting meeting with Graham Styles, who was incident command on Thursday night. We’re coming round to thinking that the cause of the explosions was definitely APEX.’

‘APEX is activated via friction,’ Lyndsey added. ‘Graham thinks that our suspect most probably filled bottles with the stuff and threw them into the crowd.’

‘APEX doesn’t need a detonator; it will basically do the job for you,’ Jen said thoughtfully, clearly already familiar with the substance.

'Just think about how many club nights we've all been to between us where you drop a bottle on the floor by accident, or kick one out of the way during a concert,' Chris added.

'Dr Walsh wasn't the lead pathologist for Thursday night, boss,' Trudie cut in. 'But she pretty much confirmed that all wounds were from the waist down.'

'So it makes sense that whatever happened happened at floor height, and then shot upwards from there,' Jen concluded.

Chris ran his hands over his face and sat heavily down on a seat. 'Do we think someone is targeting Karl?'

'Not so long ago I had my money on it being Karl himself, but with it being a homemade explosive, I'm not so sure,' Julie said.

'But why blow up your own club, full of people?' Colin questioned. 'He could have easily done it at any other point, and there would have been less loss of life ... if it was for insurance reasons, or whatever.'

'I can't see this being a homophobic attack, or that somebody could be targeting Karl for that reason. No one at the Carbon offices seemed to have any inkling of their boss's sexuality, or even the fact that he's in a relationship for a start,' Jen said.

'But how sure are you on that, Jen?' Chris questioned.

'Isn't that obvious? No one mentioned it to us while we were at the offices. It's a juicy bit of gossip if nothing else!'

'Plus, if nobody has heard any different, Karl is still MIA.' Chris took a swig of his coffee, hoping that it would give him some clarity.

'I phoned around all the hotels in the area and no one has him checked in under his name anyway. Where the hell is he?'

'Well, mine and Julie's field trip turned out to be rather interesting,' Colin announced, clearly itching to share what they'd found.

'You found out something useful?' Jen asked.

'We most certainly did.' Colin sat down, putting his feet confidently up on the desk.

'Detective Goodwin, feet down. You're not at home.'

'Sorry, boss,' Colin said, hastily removing his feet.

'I'm still looking into that law firm in connection with Danielle Dale. So if you want to fill everyone in, Colin?' Julie spoke up.

'Law firm?' Chris asked, turning back to Julie.

'Let me look into it,' she said quickly. 'And then I can explain it all ... if it's relevant.'

'Okay. What have you got for us all then, Colin? The floor is yours.'

Colin stood up and moved to the front of the room. 'Well, other than where Dale Senior lives, which is something else in itself, Julie and I were greeted by the entire family. It was like we'd just walked into a business meeting.'

'Don't tell me he had his lawyer there as well?' Jen asked. 'Nothing shows guilt more than having your lawyer present when the police come to visit.'

'Oh, even better. Guess what the Dale sister does?'

'I think I already know the answer to this one.' Jen rolled her eyes.

'Nothing like keeping everything in family. Though, saying that, the family dynamic was very interesting.'

'How so?' Chris asked.

'I don't know if Julie will agree with me, because we didn't get a chance to talk about it on the way back, but Matt, Dale Junior, acts like a naughty child. We even had an apology from him for crashing your press conference, boss. It almost felt like Dale Senior was under the impression that his son had wasted our time, which seemed rather odd seeing as we're not exactly investigating them.'

'So Senior wasn't impressed that Matt had shone the spotlight onto the business?' Chris asked.

'I guess you could see it that way.'

'Correct me if I'm wrong though, boss.' Trudie spoke up from the back. 'We weren't investigating the Dales, were we?'

'No, which makes me wonder if we're missing something?' Chris replied thoughtfully.

'But I'm saving the best bit until last! Guess who used to be bar manager at Dale's?' Colin grinned round at a room of blank faces. 'Our very own Mr Karl Jenkins!'

'Wow … I wasn't expecting that,' Jen said to a now silent room.

'Oh yes, and Senior made some very derogatory comments about his sexuality too, much to his daughter's annoyance,' Colin added.

'It was all really strange. She was sitting there trying to object to his comments, almost like she was in a court room,' Julie said, popping her head up from behind the monitor.

'So where does Karl owning Carbon fit into all of this?' Chris asked, trying to steer the conversation back to the investigation.

'According to Senior, Karl came into some money, left Dale's and brought the land where Carbon previously was,' Colin informed the room.

'So there's no love lost between the two of them?' Chris asked.

'He said that Karl left on good terms,' Colin answered.

'I don't mean to throw another stone into all of this, but Danielle, the Dale sister, works for a big law firm in London. I just did a Google search on her. Anyone want to guess which firm she works for?' Julie asked the room.

'Go on, Julie,' Chris prompted.

'The exact same one I spent days chasing when we had Harry Greenidge in the cells downstairs … which means, guess who else they represent?'

'The Crawfords …' Jen responded at the same time as her head hit the table in defeat.

Jen Garner

'This isn't happening,' Jen moaned as she lifted her desk only to return it moments later with a thud.

'And on that bombshell,' Chris said as he looked over at his exhausted team, 'let's call it a night, go home and get rested so we can hit the ground running again tomorrow. Hopefully we'll have the surviving CCTV back and will be able to work through what we've got.'

'But sir, we need to discuss whether the Crawfords have anything to do with this,' Jen protested, standing up and looking over at Chris for his support.

'The rest of you gather your stuff together, and Detective Garner and I will discuss the Crawfords and feed back tomorrow,' Chris had clearly noticed the mood of the team change. 'Detective Garner, I'm going to grab a coffee. Can I get you anything? We'll discuss everything once this lot have cleared off.'

'Unless you've got anything stronger, a coffee will be fine,' Jen responded as her colleagues began to clear the office. 'Julie, will you leave me the name of the law firm so I can do some digging myself?'

'Of course, hun. I'll email you before I leave.' Julie continued typing away.

Jen thought she had finally seen the back of the Crawfords after the case last year involving a child they had rescued from a life of abuse. She often thought about Mikel and wondered where he was and if he was okay. He'd been taken swiftly into witness protection and luckily wasn't needed to give evidence during the trial, thanks to the huge amount of evidence stacked against the defendant and his network of child groomers. An involuntary shiver went down her spine as she thought about all the stuff that had been found in the house he shared with his wife, not to mention what they'd found when they discovered his warehouses …

Chris carried a tray of drinks back into the team's office, and she barely even acknowledged his arrival.

'Jen, before you say anything, I realise I'm just a street-level police officer and know nothing of what really goes on out there, but I really don't think the Crawfords are involved.'

Jen looked up at him. 'I think you're more than that, boss, and I think you more than proved that last year.' She selected a mug from the tray.

'I just don't see randomly turning up in Nottingham and blowing up a nightclub as something they would do.'

'I've read through all of Chloe's stuff enough times to know where they were dealing here in Nottingham, and Carbon and Dale's weren't on the lists. It's just hearing their name again and half expecting the next name to be mine.'

'You mean Lisa?'

'Yeah, the famous Lisa bloody Carter.'

'Well, we know she had nothing to do with it all, 'cos, like me, she was tucked up in bed when it all went down.'

Jen laughed weakly. 'She certainly was.'

'Look, I totally understand if you wanted to go running back to your guys in London, but let's see where this case takes us before we call in the big guns.'

'Have you spoken to Hannah?'

'No, not properly, but I'm pretty sure she's keeping an eye on you here.'

'You mean I'm keeping my eye on you?' She laughed again. 'I don't think the power has gone to Hannah's head like that just yet.'

'Oh damn, I almost forgot.' Chris sighed 'On a totally different subject, Hannah gave me a card for you. I was supposed to give it to you on your first day! It's in my office. I'll go and grab it now.'

'Not to worry, boss.'

Chris went to retrieve the white envelope. 'Sorry,' he said, as he arrived back in the office and handed it to Jen. 'I have no idea what's in it,' he told her. 'I was just told to give it to you on your first day.'

'Thanks, boss,' Jen said as she studied the envelope.

'Look, I've got some work I need to catch up on, so I'll be in my office. Get yourself home, Jen. There's nothing more that can be done here now.'

'Will do. Make sure you don't stay too late either, boss.'

Chris nodded and walked out of the office, leaving Jen to open the envelope and pull the card out, only to be greeted by a semi-naked, unattractive picture of Chris sprawled out on a bed. Jen knew immediately that there was no way Chris had known that Hannah had taken said picture, or that she had proceeded to get it stuck on the front of a good luck card. Jen sneaked another look at it, making sure she kept the front of the card opened flat on her desk, just in case someone walked in.

If you ever get in trouble with him, just think of this picture, Hannah had written. There was no way she'd be able to look at him in the eye now, she thought, as she stifled a giggle.

Jen quickly put the envelope back in her bag, before pulling out her phone from her back pocket to send Hannah a message to thank her for the card and to offer to send her a photo of James in return.

Chapter Thirteen

DI Chris Jackson

Sunday

'Sir.' Chris knocked loudly on the Superintendent's door. He had bypassed the Sup's secretary as he wasn't in the mood to get into an argument with the gatekeeper. He was fuming and had come straight to the top.

'Come in,' finally came the answer Chris had been waiting for, but the way he felt he was ready to kick down the door if he was turned away. 'Morning, Chris.'

'Sir, with all due respect, why wasn't I told about Flavor?'

'I'm not following, Chris?' Gil blew his checks out and exhaled. 'The way you barged in, I thought you had some news about Carbon.'

'No, sir. I heard on the radio on the way in that there were explosions at the gay night club Flavor last night. I wanted to know why I hadn't been informed.'

'Yes, I've just had Selina on the phone querying if they should be expecting any further admissions.'

'So … *why* wasn't I informed? At least an email! I mean I appreciate not being woken up in the middle of the night again, but to find out via BBC News—'

'The reports from control say that a Sergeant Gillroy was dealing with it.'

'Ah,' Chris responded, remembering well how things had gone down when he'd first met Sergeant Gillroy at a case in Long Eaton. Gillroy had been less than happy when Chris had informed him that *he* was going to be SIO and that the sergeant could stand down.

'Have you worked with him before?' Gil asked, seemingly picking up on Chris' reaction.

'I met him a couple of years ago in Long Eaton on the Chloe Seaward case.'

'To be honest here with you, Chris, I don't understand why neither of us were informed. This could be linked to what happened at Carbon, and the knock-on effect it's going to have on our hospitals, which are already overrun with Carbon survivors …' The Sup's expression said it all. Chris nodded, not wanting to give his opinion. 'In fact, I might ring my counterpart in Derbyshire and express my dissatisfaction, seeing as he's one of theirs.' Chris watched as Gil moved a couple of bits on his desk. 'I'm also going to chase up the reports on what happened, just in case we need to escalate it.'

'Shall I send a team over there now?' Chris asked.

'No, leave it for now. You've got enough on your plate with Carbon. Let me find out what's happened and I'll let you know if it needs investigating further.'

'Thank you, sir,' Chris said as he got up to leave the Sup's office, still angry – but at least he now knew where to direct it.

'Right, team,' Chris said marching into the office. 'Just so we're all on the same page, there was an incident at Flavor last night.'

'I'd heard something, boss,' Colin commented.

'It seems whatever happened caused mass panic and hospital admissions,' Lyndsey offered, having stayed quiet up until that point.

'Seems like I'm last to know as always.' Chris sighed. 'But do we think it's connected to Carbon? The Sup wants us to leave it for now while he looks into it himself, but I'm not so sure ...' Chris was met with a sea of blank faces.

'Remember after 7/7 boss, there were loads of false alarms because people were being overly cautious and generally panicking about anything?' Colin asked.

'Hmm,' Chris responded. He remembered that day well, and its aftermath, but didn't everybody? He was fully aware of how thin they were all being spread, so maybe it was best to leave the Flavor issue for the Superintendent to deal with … at least for now. 'Okay, well, let's talk through the CCTV footage. Tech guys did an amazing job with what they managed to rescue.' Chris reached for the print-outs that Lyndsey had provided and laid the massive map of Carbon out in the centre of the table. 'The explosives must have to have got into the venue somehow, and we need to work out where and how.' The team all left their desks and gathered around where Chris was standing. Chris was glad to see some of Lyndsey's team were also present so they could give their input.

'I'll start then,' Preston spoke up. 'I've been watching the CCTV of people entering and exiting the venue, prior to the explosion.'

'Great. Thanks, Preston.' Chris nodded his acknowledgement as his hand found its way to his next coffee fix. 'In the duty manager's statement, she says that they check every bag that people bring into the venue.'

'I can confirm that the security team did indeed check all bags. So, unless one of them was in on it, there's no way the explosives came into the venue via the entrance.'

'We can more or less put a cross against them coming in through there,' Chris clarified, reaching over and putting a red mark against the main entrance.

'But there is still a possibility that the explosives did come in inside someone's bag. Is a security guard going to question why someone has white crystals in their bag?' Lyndsey questioned.

'I think they would have at least taken them out and questioned if they were drugs?' Preston reasoned.

'I also think, from Graham's explanation about these things being set off by friction, carrying them in inside a bag would have been a bit risky,' Chris countered.

'I've been watching the CCTV cameras on the fire exits here and here.' Colin pointed on the map. 'At the moment of the explosion, like the other cameras, this one cuts out. I can confirm that there was nothing suspect. Pretty boring, really – no one exiting or entering.'

'If anyone was entering, then someone would've had to let them in.'

'Correct, boss.'

'I can confirm that the two cameras I have watched are also the same,' Trudie spoke up. 'Those ones are situated at the front of the stage,' she clarified.

'Has anyone seen anything of concern from the fire exit CCTV?' Chris asked.

'No, boss,' they all echoed back.

'We've cleared the front and staging area. Let's continue to the backstage area,' Chris said, moving the sheet of paper down. 'There was little to no damage to the backstage area from the blast as it was all contained in the main room. Who's been on the cameras here?'

'I think before we start looking at these,' Lyndsey cut in, 'if we can quickly run through what they used each room for?' Lyndsey reached across, pointing at each room as she spoke. 'We've the entrance here where all the equipment is brought into the venue.'

'Karl Jenkins confirmed in his statement that everything that comes into the venue equipment-wise is also handled by the roadies who work for Carbon, so nothing untoward came in that way,' Julie confirmed. 'I've watched the footage and it's all pretty boring, as the shutters are down after all the equipment is loaded into the venue. For most of the duration of the footage, it's just a view of a metal shutter until after the explosion when the panic starts and people begin trying to exit.'

'Anything from the other side of the shutters?' Chris asked.

'Other than yours and Detective Garner's rescue mission, there was nothing of interest,' Julie replied with a small smile.

'The entrance Jen and I entered … was there not a camera on that door?' Chris questioned.

'No, I think the camera I was watching of the other side of the shutter was supposed to be covering the courtyard. The door you and Jen entered is more out of the way, and we were told it's not accessed by all staff.'

'Looking at the map, the door Jen and I entered by leads into an open area. There's a locked room where I'm told the spirits are kept – a storeroom, basically – and stairs to the cellar below. Then there's also a corridor which leads to the backstage area,' Chris commented.

'When the panic ensued, a lot of people made it out of the shutter doors, which are triggered by hand in cases of emergency,' Julie explained.

'So why did Gabriel and Dean head out the way they did?'

'I tried to contact them both to check how they were doing after the memorial yesterday. From what I understand, they're both still in hospital,' Jen replied.

'Have they been looked at as suspects, boss?' Colin suddenly asked.

'In short, no,' Chris replied, wondering if he needed to get someone to look further into the boys – but with the injuries they'd both sustained, could they have lit the explosives and run?

'Off the backstage area, we also have a green room, several changing areas and toilets,' Lyndsey continued.

'Do we have lists of everyone who should have been backstage?'

'We do, Chris,' Colin spoke up. 'I also managed to get a list of the names of the people who were at the meet and greet. These people would've had their bags searched when they came into the venue and then would have been brought straight into the green room.'

'Could anyone have accessed the backstage area who shouldn't have been there?' Chris questioned.

‘I’d have thought they would’ve been stopped by security that were stationed at the doors here.’ Lyndsey pointed. ‘Which is the only way from the main room area to the backstage. Anyone else would’ve needed to come via the stage, which we know was only used by the road crew and the band.’

‘So we’re no closer to knowing where the explosives came in. We’ve checked all CCTV footage available. We know where all the dark zones are, which aren’t on camera – but they’re difficult places to get access to, as you’d need to go via security unless you were already in the backstage area.’ Chris was on the verge of hitting his head against the table when a nervous looking officer knocked and entered the room.

‘Excuse me, ma’am, sir, I think I’ve just found something at the venue that might be of interest.’

‘If it’s about to solve the case, I’m all ears,’ Chris said, looking towards the officer who had interrupted their meeting.

‘It might be best if you both come over to the site, sir.’

‘Okay, Officer ...?’

‘Golding, sir. Will Golding.’

‘Right team, I’m going to wrap up and head back to Carbon,’ Chris said, turning back to the table. ‘I know it feels like we aren’t getting anywhere, but let’s not give up just yet. Go grab yourselves a break.’

‘Boss,’ they all echoed and, for the first time in a while, Chris detected a hint of excitement in their voices.

‘I’m just going to grab my jacket from the office, Lyndsey. And then we can head over?’

‘Great. I just need to pop into the ladies. Meet you downstairs in five?’

‘Sounds good to me.’ Chris didn’t need anything from his office, other than more pills and a change of shoes that would hopefully be better for walking through rubble and left-over crime scene debris. Plus he could do with a couple of minutes alone to close his eyes and rub his temples in hope of staving off the impending headache.

Jen Garner

‘Here we are again,’ Jen said as she led the way up the drive towards Karl Jenkins’ home. She knew that Chris had told them all to take a break, but with there being no response to whether Karl had reappeared or not, Jen wanted to investigate further and was dragging Greg along for the ride.

'Well, there are two cars on the drive now, so it looks like Mr Jenkins might be back,' Greg said as he peered through the car windows. 'Yup, they certainly weren't here last time.'

Jen stood at the front door and knocked. From where they were standing, the house seemed eerily silent. Having visited the Jenkins' residence previously, something didn't feel right. Jen gave it a couple of seconds and knocked again.

'Okay, I'm coming,' came a voice from the other side of the door as a key turned and the door slowly opened.

'Oh, it's you again,' Karl Jenkins said as he opened the door, with his right arm noticeable in a plaster-cast.

'Good morning, Karl. We've been trying to get hold of you. I'm glad you're home this time. Can we come in?' Jen asked.

'No, not really. Can this not wait till I'm back in the office?'

'We visited yesterday after we couldn't find you at your office or at Carbon. We met your partner.'

'Partner?' Karl questioned.

'What was it he called himself?' Jen turned and asked Greg. 'Oh yeah, your dirty little secret.' Karl was silent for a moment too long.

'Samuel didn't mention anything.'

'Is he in now?'

'I'm afraid not. He's ... he's gone to the shops.'

'He was really concerned about you, actually. Like us, he couldn't get hold of you.'

'Not that it's any of your business anyway, but I spent yesterday in a meeting trying to salvage my business and last night sat in A&E.'

'What happened?'

'Look, Detectives, I don't have to answer any of your questions about my personal life, and I do *not* appreciate you turning up on my doorstep uninvited.'

'I'm sure I don't need to remind you, Mr Jenkins – just because it's your venue that's gone up in smoke doesn't mean you're not a suspect.'

'Well, I can assure you I had nothing to do with it. As I told you, and no doubt Samuel told you too, I was tucked up in bed when it happened.'

'That may be so, Mr Jenkins. But something on the scale of the explosions at Carbon takes a lot of planning, and just because you weren't there when it happened doesn't mean you didn't have something to do with it.'

'Well, maybe instead of standing here asking me about my personal life, you should be out looking for the person responsible?'

'We also need to make sure no one is targeting you personally. So I'll ask again: how did you break your wrist?'

'I got caught up in an incident and fell, okay? That's all. No major drama. A night at the hospital and I'm all back together again.'

'Were you at Flavor last night?'

'What if I was?' Karl stared at Jen, as if daring her to argue the point. 'I don't have to answer any more of your questions. Go catch whoever blew up my venue, and if I hear any more slander about my personal life you'll be hearing from my solicitor.'

'Mr Jenkins—' Jen started but Karl stepped back into the house and closed the front door in their faces.

'Well, that went well,' she muttered, turning towards Greg.

'I can't work him out at all.'

'I wish Samuel hadn't referred to himself as Karl's dirty little secret, because I can't get that bloody song out of my head!'

'Song?'

'By All American Rejects, I think?'

'Another one of your pop culture references I'm too old to know anything about.'

Jen laughed as they started to make their way back down the drive. 'I'll find it on my phone and play it for you on the way back,' she said as she hummed the tune.

'No, I'm good, thanks.'

Chapter Fourteen

DI Chris Jackson

They'd been met at the venue by Officer Golding, who had handed them both a hard hat before leading them through the now-familiar shell of Carbon. The balcony area that looked out onto the stage had been completely pulled down, and the main room was open to the elements. Now that it had been confirmed where the explosions had happened, and the fire investigation team were confident of the cause, it was their turn to find out how on earth the explosives got into the venue in the first place. As Chris made his way through the rubble, for the first time in ages he felt confident on his feet again; although he still made sure that he was careful where he stepped and thought ahead about the path he was going to take before they got to any challenging areas.

'I'm sure you're both aware that from the backstage, there's a corridor that leads to an open area, which is where you'd find access to the cellar, a back room and a room where all the spirits are kept,' Officer Golding explained as he led them backstage; an area which still looked in better shape than the rest of the club.

'We were talking about that just before you came in,' Lyndsey said.

'I noticed something in the back room earlier when I went in search of the fuse box to clarify a query from the fire investigation team. I don't know how much attention you guys have been paying to the windows in Carbon, but they're all painted shut, and some also have grills behind them.'

'Okay, go on …'

'When I was in the back room, I noticed that the window in there… well, all the paint has been chipped away around the opening.' Officer Golding spoke quickly, almost like the sooner he got the words out, the quicker he could get away. 'So I called one of my colleagues over and we managed to open the window without much force.'

'You've found a window in the club that opens?' Chris asked slowly.

'Yes, sir,' Officer Golding answered. 'If you follow me, I can show you.'

'Where does the window open to?' Chris followed Officer Golding into the area he'd previously been in only days before.

‘An alley, sir. It runs between the club and the university buildings that are situated behind Carbon.’

‘Could this be our mystery entrance for the explosives?’ Lyndsey questioned.

‘There is a slight problem though …’

Here it comes, Chris thought grimly.

‘The room has been accessed since the fire by various people, including myself. As for the alley, it’s no longer taped off either.’

‘So let me get this right … the public have been walking up and down this alley since the fire and the room has had continuous unmonitored access?’ Chris closed his eyes momentarily.

‘Yes, sir. I was advised to come and tell you before I got the crime scene tech in.’

Chris watched as Lyndsey looked around the room and inspected the window. ‘We might have found our entrance point.’

‘It’s just a shame that any forensic evidence is long gone,’ Chris said through gritted teeth, running his hands over his face.

‘Officer Golding, will you call the forensic teams in? Hopefully they can still find something.’

‘Yes, ma’am,’ he said, backing out of the room.

‘You don’t look too overjoyed,’ Chris commented to Lyndsey, whose face had turned to thunder.

‘Oh, I am. I just want to know how this was missed for two days since the explosion, and what the hell this room is being used for since the whole venue has been closed!’

Later on, Chris continued to stand at the front of Carbon as he listened to Lyndsey bark into her phone, ordering her team back to the site. The forensic team were a good half an hour away, stuck in traffic or something, no doubt.

‘I’m going to take a walk around the back,’ he told Lyndsey once she had finished shouting at whoever was on the other end of the phone.

‘I’ve called in for a couple of extra uniform, ma’am,’ Officer Golding said as he walked towards them, clipping his radio back onto his belt.

‘Thank you, Officer,’ Lyndsey responded before turning back to her phone.

‘Fancy taking a walk?’ Chris turned and asked him. ‘You can show me where this alleyway is.’

'Sir.'

'DI Shufflebotham, Officer Golding and I are going to find this alley that leads behind the club.'

'Okay, I'll get officers stationed on either side once they arrive.'

Chris and Officer Golding began their walk. 'How long you been in the police force?' Chris asked, trying to break the awkward silence as they headed down the side of the club.

'In Nottingham, just over a year, sir,' came the nervous reply.

'Please, it's Chris in private – or DI Jackson.'

'Okay. Thank you, sir, I mean Chris, I mean …'

Chris laughed. 'So, Will, tell me more about yourself.'

'Joined the police service just over six years ago, and I've recently transferred up from Cornwall. I was getting bored with investigating farm robberies and tourist theft. I needed some action.'

'Well, you certainly won't find any of those in central Nottingham.' Chris smiled.

'My game plan is to come and work with your team … you've got such a good reputation.'

Chris wasn't sure how best to respond to that one, so decided to keep walking and let the officer continue on.

'I'm currently on Sergeant Gillroy's team. I've told him I want to progress, but he doesn't seem very keen on letting anyone progress unless you're one of his favourites.'

'Have you spoken to your union rep?'

'No point, sir. He's one of the "favourites".'

'Ah ...' Chris wasn't really sure what the best advice to offer would be. He couldn't exactly tell Will that Sergeant Gillroy disliked him too.

They'd reached the courtyard at the back of the club, where he and Jen had previously launched their rescue mission.

'So whereabouts is this alley then?' Chris asked as he walked into the courtyard, which was now noticeably tidy of all the rubbish that had been there previously.

'From my understanding, it's further along the street, sorta behind the courtyard.'

Chris turned and headed back out of the yard and carried on walking, chatting to Will. Then, all of a sudden, his left knee decided not to bend as he walked, and he felt himself crumple towards the floor.

Chris heard his name being shouted from above, followed by the sound of police sirens and tyres skidding. As he sat on the floor, he tried to work out what the hell had just happened. One minute he'd been walking along happily, and then the next …

'Here, let me help you up,' Will offered as he put his hand on Chris' shoulder. 'You okay?' Will was clearly concerned. *Not surprising*, thought Chris. He'd probably never seen a grown man fall over like that before.

'Yeah, give me a moment. Not sure what happened there!' Chris attempted to laugh it off as he did a quick mental assessment of his body.

'You okay, PC Golding?' a voice that Chris knew all too well shouted.

'Yes, Sarg. Just helping DI Jackson.'

'What the hell are you doing on the floor?' Sergeant Gillroy bellowed. 'Falling over on the job, whatever next? Though you weren't looking too steady on your feet when I noticed you walking through Nottingham earlier.' As the words left Gillroy's mouth, Chris felt sick.

'I'm fine. Just tripped on something,' Chris said, finally managing to get up from the floor. 'Thank you, Will,' he muttered as he brushed himself down. No doubt, he'd have a graze or something, and he desperately needed to walk off the pain that now penetrated his ankle.

'Are you sure you're okay? Shall I get someone to come and check you over?' Will asked, frowning slightly.

'Don't be silly, PC Golding. Our detective inspector is as hard as nails.' Gillroy laughed.

'No, no, I'm good,' Chris reassured him. 'What's with the sirens?' *Time to try and move the conversation away from the fall.*

'I was told you wanted an officer stationed at each end of the alley. I've come so PC Golding can be stationed here and I can assist you. But, from what I've just seen, you're going to need more than just me to hold your hand.' Sergeant Gillroy laughed again.

'I'm fine. Thanks for your concern though,' Chris said through gritted teeth. 'Officer Golding will continue to work with me as we look at the alley. You're more than welcome to stand guard at this end until backup arrives.'

Sergeant Gillroy was clearly not best impressed with the idea as a thunderous look crossed over his face. 'I'm not here just to guard an alley,' came his reply.

‘Take it or leave it. Office Golding has made a breakthrough in this case, so will assist me for the time being.’

Chris noticed Will take several steps back, leaving him and Gillroy almost nose to nose. God, he hated this man, and he hated that he had just seen him fall on top of everything else.

‘It’s okay. I don’t mind standing guard,’ Will said quickly, clearly attempting to calm the situation. As Chris took a step back, he decided he’d be the bigger person and slipped into professional mode.

‘Officer Golding, if you’d like to follow me, please,’ Chris said as he turned to walk away. ‘Oh, and Sergeant Gillroy, if you could guard this side of the alley until I can arrange someone to take over from you.’

‘I don’t think so,’ came the response as Gillroy marched to the patrol car and spoke loudly into the radio.

‘After you, Officer,’ Chris said as he began to walk away from the patrol car.

‘The alley is just here, sir,’ Will directed him moments later, as they both stopped to look down a narrow passage that led behind the club on one side and the university building on the other.

‘Let’s go and see what we can find.’

Chapter Fifteen

DI Chris Jackson

'After you,' Chris said to Will as they both stood peering down the alley. 'I suspect that forensics won't be far behind.'

'Are you sure you don't want me to wait here and stop people from entering?'

'I think we'll be all right for now. If someone enters behind us, we can send them back, and the same if they enter from the other end.'

'Okay.' Will didn't seem as chatty and friendly since Chris's fall, almost like he was worried he might say something wrong … or could it all be because of Sergeant Gillroy's interference?

'Sir?' Will suddenly broke into his thoughts. 'I know you said you were fine, but you did just fall pretty heavily on your ankle.'

'It's fine, honest,' Chris said, giving his left ankle a shake to prove it was okay. Though there was still some pain there, he was sure he'd walk it off in no time.

As they made their way down the side of the club, all Chris could smell was the distinct stench of urine. Who in their right minds would want to take this shortcut with *that* smell guiding their journey, never mind the rubbish, cigarette ends, animal droppings and whatever else littered the path?

'I think Carbon must be somewhere about here,' Will said as the fencing gave way to brickwork.

'So which bit of Carbon is this? It feels pretty much like waste land back here.'

'I would say, at a guess, our window shouldn't be much further. It's only the two rooms that back onto this alley.'

They continued to walk a further ten metres and there, six feet off the ground, was the window. Chris could immediately see Will had been right; there were no metal bars or anything protecting the windows like all the others Chris had seen in the building.

'Like you said, it's a bit strange that this window isn't protected, given the public access route along here …' Chris mused.

'But would anyone take any notice of a window … unless they knew where it led to?'

'I didn't even know that the alley existed before you walked into the office earlier.' Chris snapped some photos on his phone and emailed them to himself. 'I'm not sure there's anything else we can really do here until forensics turn up.' As Chris finished his sentence and looked further up the alleyway, he saw what could have been easily mistaken as a scene out of *Monsters Inc.* as a group of five people in protective suits and goggles headed towards them. 'Ah, here they are now.'

'Right team, I have some good news and some bad news. So who wants to start?' Chris addressed everyone later on.

'Hadn't we better get your news out of the way first, boss?' Colin asked reluctantly.

'Okay, well … the good news, I guess, is that we've found how the explosives entered the club.'

'Brilliant!' came Colin's response.

'Not so brilliant when you find out that the entry point was missed by the original investigation team.'

'Ah … that would be why Lyndsey's lot rushed out suddenly.'

'It's looking like they came in through a window in a backroom near where Jen and I pulled Gabriel and Dean from.'

'How high up is this window, boss?' Colin questioned.

'A good six, seven feet – from the outside, anyway.'

'Does this put more into question what Gabriel and Dean were doing there then?'

Just then, Julie burst into the incident room with a tray of drinks in her hand. 'Sorry, sorry! There was a queue.' She immediately started passing the drinks around. 'I'm guessing I've missed the reason for the sudden exit of the other team?' she asked when she finally took her seat with her own drink in hand.

'Yeah, we think we've found how the explosives got into the venue.'

'Great!'

'Not so great when it turns out someone missed it first time round.'

'Ah.'

Chris repeated the findings to Julie, and then reached out and spread the map of the venue across the table again. 'Jen, this area here is where we found Gabriel and Dean.'

‘They were both there, near where the spirits are kept and the cellar. And now we’re saying the explosives entered in a similar area …’ Jen was visibly fidgeting in her chair.

‘Why did they not exit through the loading bay like everyone else?’ Chris questioned.

‘Didn’t you have to resuscitate one of them as well?’ Julie asked.

‘Yeah, until the paramedics got to him,’ Jen cut in.

‘I’m just not sure how they can be suspects, considering their injuries,’ Julie argued. ‘Are we saying whoever used APEX threw it into the crowd and ran? If it *was* them, why run into the carnage and not the other way?’

‘Putting Gabriel and Dean aside a second, there must've been someone else outside the club to pass the explosives through the window,’ Jen said.

‘Could they not have worked as a team with one of them entering the club later?’ Colin asked.

‘Come on, Colin! I pulled those lads out of that burning building. There is no way they were part of this. Chris?’ Jen turned to him, clearly wanting him to back her up.

‘We can’t completely rule them out, Jen, until we know their reasons for not leaving via the loading bay door.’

‘I’ll go and find out now, but it’s a waste of time, boss. There is no way they did this.’

‘Just hold your horses, Jen. I can tell you feel strongly about this,’ Chris said, trying to calm her down just a little. ‘Whoever is responsible for this either had someone working for them outside the club, or they set this up themselves to pull the bag into the venue on a piece of rope or something from the window.’

‘This cut-through is open to the public, right? Having the time to set the bag up and then get into Carbon past security on the entrance, and then more security to get behind the stage … How come no one using the alley in that time picked up this theoretical bag and investigated what was inside themselves?’ Julie asked.

‘When Officer Golding and I went to look at the alley earlier, it was so strewn with litter that a random bag propped up against a wall wouldn’t get a second glance with the amount of rubbish that has been dumped down there.’

‘I bet there isn’t much light down there either at night.’

'Correct, Colin. I wouldn't walk down there alone at any time, never mind at night.'

'Could the explosives not have been placed there before opening – sometime during the day, perhaps?' Trudie asked. 'Because I bet no one would've checked in there prior to opening.'

'That puts our Mr Jenkins back in the frame.' Jen suddenly perked up.

'Indeed, it does,' Chris replied, not totally unsurprised by Jen's new enthusiasm. 'I hear you went to visit him this morning?'

'Yeah,' Jen said, not giving anything away.

'Jen got threatened with being sued for slander,' Greg spoke up.

Not what I need right now on top of everything else going on with this case, Chris thought. 'Do I even want to know?' He sighed.

'Only if I mention him being at a certain nightclub again, and you know I'm not one to speak out of turn.' Jen raised her eyebrows. 'Our Mr Jenkins is home complete with a broken wrist.'

'He's made a reappearance, has he? What did he have to say for himself?'

'He claims he was in a business meeting all day yesterday, which was why no one could get hold of him.'

'The broken wrist?'

'He claims he fell, didn't tell us where or how, and, apparently, it's none of our business,' Greg summed up.

'Boss, we wondered if it would be worth getting hold of his medical records. That would probably tell us how he sustained the injury?' Jen asked.

'I'm not sure what that would gain us though.'

'We'd at least find out how and where he did it.'

'Why not just assume it was in the chaos at Flavor?' Colin asked.

'That's what I thought, but why would you be happy going to a gay club, but seemingly not want your colleagues to know that you're gay?' Jen said thoughtfully.

'What did he have to say about his partner?' Chris interrupted them.

'Something isn't right there, boss, he tried to deny his existence, and then, once he realised we had met him previously, he claimed he was out.'

'Greg?'

'I don't know, boss, it's like Jen said – if we're thinking that he's being targeted, then don't we need to rule out that the broken wrist wasn't caused by a mugging or something else?'

'I see your point.'

'I'm just concerned about Samuel's wellbeing, boss, based on Karl's reaction to us knowing he had a partner.'

'I'm not sure there is anything we can do, Jen. We don't have proof that anything untoward is happening between them.' Chris heard Jen's audible sigh and hoped she wasn't about to argue her point. 'Colin, I know you've probably looked at this list a thousand times, but I want to know everyone who was backstage from the moment the first security check was done prior to the gig to the point of the explosion. If you could also chase up any photos and videos we are yet to receive from the meet and greet. Who knows, there might be something in one of them we could use to help us identify our bomber?'

'Okay, boss.'

'Trudie, would you give Colin a hand?'

'Of course, boss.'

'Anyone got anything else they would like to throw into the ring?' He paused and was met with silence. 'Jen, Greg, I know how strongly you feel about this, but would you go and speak to Dean and Gabriel and see if you can find out how they ended up at the back of the club where we found them?'

'Boss!' Jen exclaimed.

'I know it's highly unlikely they're going to be suspects, but we're better crossing them off now than getting tripped up later for not speaking to them,' he said, doing his best to appease Jen. 'Julie, will you look into any further CCTV we're waiting for and chase it up? I think it also might be worth speaking to the university and finding out if they have any roof cameras or such that have a view of the alley. I know when Officer Golding and I went down there earlier I didn't spot anything, but you never know our luck.'

'Of course, Chris.'

Chris took his glasses off, rubbing his eyes. 'Everyone happy? Meet back here in, say, a couple of hours?'

As the room echoed his name, Chris scrunched his eyes up, just hoping that his vision would stop blurring and he could make it to his office without falling over again.

'The smell of this place never changes,' Jen said as they entered the hospital along with a whole raft of other people: all there to either visit an ill relative or for an appointment themselves, no doubt.

Jen had traced where Dean and Gabe were in the hospital and they'd agreed they could come and visit.

'Which ward did you say Dean was on?' Greg questioned as Jen instinctively turned towards the lifts.

'G22,' Jen replied as she marched over.

'You okay?' Greg questioned. 'You seem put out, like all this is a waste of time?'

'I can't help thinking it is, Greg. I feel like we should be back in the office looking into Mr Jenkins,' Jen said as she stepped into the lift and selected "G" floor.

'If nothing else, this job has taught me over the years that things aren't always as they seem.'

'Judging by their injuries and the state Chris and I found Gabriel in, there's no way they could have set those explosives off.'

'I agree with you, Jen, but why didn't they exit through the loading bay like everyone else?'

'I guess we're about to find out.' Jen exhaled heavily as the lift pinged for their floor, and they began the search for the correct ward.

'Detectives Garner and Sanders here to see a patient,' Jen spoke through the intercom on the wall.

'Good morning, Officers,' they were greeted as a nurse opened the door.

'Hi there. We're here to see Dean Wright, if you could direct us?' Greg asked, clearly poised to get his warrant card out at any moment if questioned.

'Dean Wright,' the nurse repeated. 'Ah yes, he's in one of our side rooms. He's had a very lucky escape that one.'

'How so?' Jen questioned.

'It's not every day a punctured lung turns into a heart problem.'

'I'm not sure I'm following?' Jen queried. 'They brought him in after the explosions at Carbon.'

'Yes, and he's been in that room ever since.'

They stopped outside room three. 'Is Dean's partner here with him today, do you know?' Jen asked.

'I'm not sure. I haven't been on for very long.'

'No worries. I'm sure we're about to find out anyway.'

As the nurse walked away, Jen turned and knocked on the door, waited a moment and then entered.

'Mr Wright?' she asked as the young man sat up in the bed.

'Yes, and you must be the detective who brought me back,' Dean said in a croaky voice.

'It was the least we could do after you dragged us into the building to help Gabriel.'

Dean smiled and nodded. 'That night was a bit crazy, if I'm honest with you. Who knew *I'd* end up being stuck in hospital when it was Gabe I asked you to help?'

'Is he not with you today?'

'He's just gone on the hunt for some decent coffee. He'll be back shortly.'

'Well, this is Detective Sanders,' Jen said, introducing Greg.

'Are you the guy I dragged in as well?' Dean asked.

'Oh no, you're thinking of our boss, DI Jackson.' Greg laughed. 'No heroics from me.'

'I thought he was more attractive …'

'Hey! I'm just getting old.' Greg laughed again as he stole a look at Jen; they'd make sure Chris knew about this revelation when they returned. As their laughter died down, the door to the room opened again and Gabriel appeared.

'Gabe! Super cop has come to visit us along with her partner,' Dean greeted him as he walked through the door, coffees in hand.

'Sorry! If I'd have known, I would've gotten an extra,' Gabe said as he shook Greg and Jen's hands whilst balancing the coffee cups. He walked around the side of Dean's bed and placed the drinks on the bedside cabinet. 'Good to see you again.'

'My colleague and I wondered if we could ask you both some questions about the other night?' Jen said. She noticed Gabe fidgeting as he sat at Dean's bedside.

'Fire away,' came Dean's response. He seemed far more at ease than Gabe.

'I don't know how much news you've been following since the other night, but we're starting to suspect that explosives were detonated during the gig.'

‘We thought that was probably the case. There were so many injured people, the amount of blood and …’ Gabe paused and looked out the window, clearly troubled by the memories.

‘It’s okay, take your time,’ Greg reassured him.

‘Can you talk us through the concert and what happened?’ Jen asked as she perched herself on one of the spare seats.

‘Well, it was just like a normal gig really. We got there midway through the support act. I wasn’t overly fussed about seeing them, so I’d say we arrived about nine-ish,’ Dean answered.

‘So just like any other concert you’ve been to?’

‘More or less. We made our way to the centre of the crowd, all ready for the McDermitts.’

‘Why more or less?’ Greg asked.

‘There seemed to be this weird atmosphere around the place. There’s usually like this … charge of electricity running through the crowd before a main act, but there didn’t seem to be one for the McDermitts. I don’t know whether the support band were shit and hadn’t hyped the crowd up enough, but everyone was just standing around talking really.’

‘In all the gigs I’ve gone to over the years, I’ve never experienced an atmosphere like it,’ Gabe added, bringing his attention back from the window.

‘Could it have been down to the age group the McDermitts draw in?’ Greg questioned.

‘Maybe, but then would there not have been a load of screaming, excitable girls?’ Dean responded as he sat up further in the bed, reaching for his coffee.

‘I remember this weird sort of smell …’ Gabe’s expression had clouded over. ‘I just put it down to someone’s perfume at the time but now I come to think about it, I just don’t know why anyone would want to go out smelling *that* strongly of citrus.’

‘When did you notice the smell?’ Greg questioned.

‘When Dean was dragging me to our usual spot in the crowd. Why … do you think it’s got something to do with what happened?’

‘I’m not sure, Gabe, but I’ll mention it to the fire investigation team back at the station.’ Greg looked meaningfully at Jen.

‘So the McDermitts came on.’ Jen tried to get the conversation moving in the right direction again. ‘Did you notice a change in the atmosphere?’

‘Oh yeah, they whipped the crowd up into a frenzy. Everyone was happy, singing and jumping around.’

‘When did you first notice that there was a problem?’ Jen asked.

‘You know how they say light travels faster than sound?’ Gabe began. ‘Well, not in this case, because there was this huge like … bang, followed by this really bright flash of light, and then there were more bangs and screaming, lots of screaming.’ Almost imperceptibly, he lifted his hands – almost as if he was about to cover his ears like he was hearing the screaming again.

‘Let me get this right, you heard a tremendous bang before you saw the flash of the explosion?’ Jen questioned, keen to understand if there was something that had happened prior to the explosion.

‘Yeah, and the look of horror on the band's faces as well. After the first bang, they all just kinda stopped playing at exactly the same time, then it just descended into chaos.’

‘Are you able to talk us through what went on around you both?’

‘I sort of instinctively grabbed hold of Dean’s hand, but there was so much screaming … I can still hear it now … especially when I’m in the flat alone … when I’m trying to sleep …’ As Gabe spoke, he took hold of Dean’s hand.

‘We just headed towards the fire exit at the front of the stage. The security team were all standing there as hundreds of people rushed past them,’ Dean continued, squeezing Gabe’s hand.

‘I know this is a silly question, but if you could think back to the moment after the second bang, when you said you grabbed Dean’s hand, Gabe, did you notice anything that was out of place or strange?’ Greg asked as he noted everything down.

‘No, not really, we just turned and ran. I feel guilty about it now because I should’ve gone to help some of the injured, but I just wanted to get out of there with Dean. No one else mattered in that moment. I just needed him to be safe.’

‘Okay, so you head to the fire exit, and then …?’

‘Yeah, there were hundreds of us going through this tiny door, all pushing and shoving, trying to get out at the same time, which is how they think I ended up with a punctured lung. Being pushed and shoved against body after body and getting nowhere as more people came in behind me, trying to get out of the same doors.’

‘Did you not notice at the time you had an injury, Dean?’ Jen asked.

'No, I was so concerned about getting Gabe and myself out of there. I just kept hold of his hand and pushed forward.'

'So you get through to the backstage area …?'

'At this point *I* was struggling to breathe,' Gabe continued as he instinctively put his left hand on his chest. 'And they were still trying to get the loading bay doors open. So I led Dean down this corridor, hoping there might be a way out that way. We came to this open area where you found us – I'm guessing it was some kind of storage place or something. I'd tripped over random stuff on the way out and must have cut my leg open at some point.'

'Gabe made me leave him, as he thought he was slowing me down and that I would be quicker on my own, so I promised I'd come back for him ...' Dean recalled as the tears started to fill his eyes. 'I didn't want to leave him … I was scared I'd never see him again, but I had no choice if we wanted to get out of there alive, so I just ran.'

'Which is when you came across me and Chris …'

'Yes, and then everything gets a little blurry,' Dean replied as Gabe reached for a tissue.

'Were you not in any pain or anything, Dean? You'd sustained a massive injury – that punctured lung?' Greg asked.

'I think I was just being carried on the adrenaline to get Gabe out … until I wasn't.' Dean fell silent.

'I think it should've been me that carried on,' Gabe joked. 'You were the seriously injured one.' There was a moment of tenderness that passed between them, and as Jen watched, she could see right in front of her what love really looked like.

'In the short time you were on your own, did you notice anything, Gabe?' Greg asked, shattering that moment.

'No, I was struggling to breathe and it was dark, and I must admit I was scared. Then you and that other detective arrived, and I felt relieved … well, until Dean went downhill.'

'I'm guessing you've been given a clean bill of health now, Gabe?'

'Yeah, they think I might be asthmatic … but compared to Dean, whose heart is basically not functioning properly, I think I'm the lucky one.' Now Gabe's eyes suddenly filled with tears.

'Come on, Gabe. They've already said I've probably had this underlying heart issue for some time. In a way, it's a good thing I've found out about it now,' Dean said as he squeezed Gabe's hand again.

'Bit of a stupid question, but do you have any idea why the incident happened?' Greg asked.

'None at all. The McDermitts are a great band, everyone loves them, and, as for Carbon, it's like the coolest music venue in Nottingham. The manager is meant to be a right cock but, hey, he has the right to be with all the amazing bands he gets in,' Dean responded.

'Thank you, lads,' Jen said as she began to stand up again. 'I think that will be all.'

'Oh, okay.' Gabe had recovered and now looked a bit confused. 'Are all the victims getting this special treatment?'

'No, only the ones we had to pull out of the building.' Jen laughed as she reached into her jacket pocket. 'Probably a good idea if you take my card – in case you have any further questions or you remember anything else. My contact details are on there.'

'Thank you,' Gabe said, reaching to take it.

'You two look after each other,' Greg told them both. 'You've been through a lot together. Don't let it tear you apart.'

'I appreciate it,' Gabe said, standing again and moving away from Dean's side. 'I can see you both out?'

'I think we're okay, thank you. Greg and I have been to this hospital enough to know our way out by now. But if we end up going in a circle, we'll be sure to come and ask you for help.'

Gabe and Dean both laughed as Greg and Jen made their way out of the room and ward G22.

'Tell me you think they did it?' Jen said triumphantly, turning to look at Greg as they waited for the lift.

'I hope my wife still looks at me the way those two looked at each other,' Greg responded with a slightly dreamy expression.

'I also think we need to look at Carbon's evacuation plans, because if Dean ended up with a punctured lung from trying to evacuate, there has to be something not right there.'

'Hmm, and I'll make sure Chris knows he's got another admirer.'

'I'd better warn Hannah too.' Jen laughed as they both stepped into the lift.

'Does anyone know if the boss is in?' Jen asked as she strolled back into the office later with Greg trailing behind her.

‘I’m not sure,’ Trudie answered, standing up to greet them. ‘Everything okay?’

‘Yeah …’ Jen replied, taking a seat back at her desk. ‘Just wanted to report back on our little visit to the hospital. There is no way Gabe or Dean set those explosives off – they just made the wrong decision when it came to exiting the club. They were trying to avoid the crush to get out of the loading bay.’

Jen pulled out her phone and noticed a message from James.

Had boss on the phone all morning. Something’s still wrong with the network. Need to get it sorted ahead of Monday, so I’ve asked Max if he’ll watch the kids for a bit. Assume that you’re busy. Jxx

Jen couldn’t remember the last time she had properly spoken to Max, her former boss from her service days. She’d been in this job for less than a week and it was already swallowing up her life! Maybe she’d be lucky and actually manage to get home at a decent time, and at least be able to see Max in passing.

‘Guys, I think I’ve just found something!’ Colin suddenly shouted, dragging Jen from her thoughts. ‘I’m looking at those meet and greet photos Chris asked me to source.’

‘Anything to drag me away from waiting to go and give Karl a piece of my mind,’ Jen muttered as she scooted across the office on her chair.

‘As much as I love looking at pretty girls and washed-up rock stars, I noticed something in this picture,’ Colin said as he loaded the photo on to the screen. ‘Tell me what you can see.’

‘Well, that’s the lead singer, Alistair, isn’t it?’ Jen questioned.

‘Yes …’

‘They’re not exactly in the green room either, where the meet and greets were supposed to be taking place,’ Greg offered. ‘It looks like the backstage area from here.’

‘Correct, but there’s something else. Look at the background of the photo.’ Colin increased the size of the photo while the other three stared. ‘What’s there that shouldn’t be?’

Jen squinted, trying to see what Colin was seeing. To her it just looked like a busy room with Alistair standing with his arm around some pretty girls.

‘Give up?’ Colin asked after a while.

‘Is it like one of those Magic Eye things? The more you stare at it the clearer the photo becomes?’ Trudie asked.

'Okay, okay. Call yourself detectives?' Colin moved the mouse to a figure in the background. 'He shouldn't be there.' Colin circled the cursor round the image of a young man who had been captured walking past as the photo was taken.

'Okay, you've lost me. Why shouldn't he be there?' Jen questioned.

'That gentleman there is our Matt Dale,' Colin told them triumphantly, finally letting them off the hook. 'The list of people who should've been backstage during the gig does not include him. In fact, he doesn't appear on any of the lists: the injured, those who were unharmed, those who were lucky enough to not even make the gig ...'

'So why is he there?' Jen questioned. 'And, more importantly, why isn't his name on any of the lists of attendees?'

'Your guess is as good as mine, but right now we've no suspects and no clue as to why Carbon went up in the first place, so he's our first anomaly.'

'Good spot, Colin. And, well, I hate to rain on your parade, but how many other people are going to be in those photos who shouldn't be? Just because you're familiar with Matt Dale—' Jen started.

'True, but why is he there when he's not on any of the lists? From the time the doors opened, the only way to get backstage was past the security team,' Colin argued.

'Either security weren't doing their job properly, or he managed to sneak past them,' Greg suggested.

'So do we need to start looking into Matt Dale as a suspect?' Colin questioned, clearly keen to get the gold star of the day.

Jen felt like she was starting to go stir crazy; all this procedure and you couldn't go dragging someone in because you disliked them – even if you were pretty sure they were guilty of something! Then there was the undercover work; in her old job, she'd have had someone in Karl's life monitoring what was going on behind closed doors by now. This felt like a longer game than she was used to playing ...

'Guys, I know we're in the middle of discussing Matt's appearance in these photos,' Jen interrupted. 'But I need to get out of here for a bit. Go for a run or something to clear my mind.'

'A run? Are you crazy?' Colin looked incredulous.

'Nope, but you're more than welcome to come with me if you want. That's if you think you can keep up.'

'I'll give it a miss. Thanks for the offer though.'

'Any time,' Jen said, giving him a knowing wink. 'Give me a call when the boss reappears and I'll be straight back. I just need some time away from this …'

'Have fun ...?' Colin stared after her in confusion as she headed out and away from the office.

Jen knew she wasn't dressed to go for a run, and she didn't have any spare running gear at work, so she decided to walk through Nottingham instead. She headed towards the Arboretum, found a seat next to the lake, and then pulled out her phone and studied it. She needed to get this stuff with Karl Jenkins out of her head. She was so focused on the idea that something was going on between him and his partner that she was starting to become obsessed. But there were so many people, women *and* men, out there who were suffering because of an abusive partner. *If I could just stop one of them.* Then there was the smallest possibility that the Crawfords could be involved as well …

She took a deep breath and pressed "Call" on one of the contacts on her phone.

'Hey, Jen. I'm just with the kids in the park. Everything okay?' Max almost immediately answered.

'Sorry, I totally forgot. I'll call back later.'

'No, it's fine. They're just on the swings, so we've got approximately ten minutes before they're bored again. What's up?'

'It's this case, Max. If I was still Lisa Carter …'

Chapter Sixteen

DI Chris Jackson

Chris was sitting in his office licking his wounds. His head hurt and his vision seemed to be playing up again, so much so he couldn't focus on the computer screen. With the fall earlier, he was beginning to doubt everything: his job, his ability, what everyone must be thinking – especially with Sergeant Gillroy's arrival to find him crumpled on the floor with a uniformed officer offering to help him up.

'Chris,' Superintendent Gray said as he knocked on his open office door.

'Sir?'

'Are you free?'

'Of course, sir,' Chris said, standing up and moving to the front of the desk. 'Is everything okay?' he asked cautiously, wondering why on earth the Sup had come down to his office.

'I was speaking to Sergeant Gillroy earlier ...'

This is it – the end of my policing career. The prick had gone running to his boss to tell him about Chris falling over earlier. The Sup knew Chris had been attending regular hospital visits since last year, and here he was coming to tell him he needed to step away from the case and go off sick as he clearly wasn't well enough to be in work, never mind investigating such a high-profile case. Chris braced himself.

'I asked him why he hadn't passed on the information to you and DI Shufflebotham about the incident at Flavor.'

'Sorry, sir?' Chris questioned, now confused more than anything.

'You've gone rather pale. Chris. Are you sure you're okay?'

'Yeah, yeah. Sorry. I think I just misheard you or something.'

'I came to tell you that I've had a word with Sergeant Gillroy about not sharing the information with the team about what happened at Flavor on Saturday night,' he repeated.

'Oh, right ... okay,' Chris replied, scrunching his eyes up and feeling his way around his desk back to his seat. 'Take a seat, sir.'

'I'm not stopping, thank you, Inspector. Sergeant Gillroy has promised to write up his notes and feed back to you and DI Shufflebotham.'

'Great. Thank you, sir.'

'Not a problem. Personally though, Chris, it might be worth you taking a trip to Flavor yourself and speaking to the staff instead of relying on someone else's notes. Plus they might have more of an idea now about what went on themselves.'

'I'll grab Julie now and we'll head over there.'

'Good plan. Everything okay otherwise?' The Sup paused for a second.

'Yeah, yeah, all is good.'

'Well, you know where I am.'

'Thank you, sir,' Chris said, standing up as the Superintendent made his way out. There were so many questions going round in Chris' head: Why had the Sup asked him if he was okay? Had Sergeant Gillroy told his boss about his fall when he asked about Flavor earlier? Chris found himself wishing that he and Sergeant Gillroy had gotten off to a better start when they'd first met. It seemed it would have saved Chris a lot of trouble …

'Right, team, tell me what you've got,' Chris said as he strode into the office later, head held high with a slightly forced smile on his face. 'Jen not back?' he asked, looking around.

'She's gone for a run, boss,' Trudie replied. 'She asked Colin if he wanted to go with her, but he chickened out.'

'I did *not* chicken out!'

'He wouldn't be able to keep up with her anyway,' came Greg's response.

'Okay, well, except for Jen's athletic ability and Colin's lack thereof, please tell me we've had a breakthrough with the case?'

'I did find something of interest, boss, I was searching through the pictures from the meet and greet and noticed someone in the background of one of them who shouldn't have been there.'

'Tell me more.' Chris sat himself down on one of the desks.

'Well, our Matt Dale, otherwise known as your good friend the press conference gatecrasher, appears in the background of this photo.' Colin brought the image up on the main screen.

'Okay?'

'He isn't on any of the lists, boss – not the ticket list, the hospital list. In fact, I doubt he's even on your Christmas card list.'

'So … let me get this straight. He was backstage and he wasn't on *any* list?'

'Yes, boss …'

'Well, he's the first person we've found who definitely shouldn't have been there … Okay, great, good spot. Have we been able to pick him up on any of the other CCTV footage from the venue?'

'Not as such, boss,' Trudie answered.

'There is also no way Gabe and Dean set the explosives off, boss,' Greg added. 'I think they just made the wrong decision when it came to finding an exit.'

'I bet Jen was happy about that.'

'Very much so, boss.'

That'll be why Jen's gone out for a run, Chris thought. *To clear her head before she becomes too focused on Karl.*

He carried on. 'Well, I've just had the Sup in my office, and he's suggested I go and speak to the management at Flavor about what happened the other night.'

'Wouldn't it just be easier to speak to Sergeant Gillroy?' Colin asked.

'Chance would be a fine thing,' came Chris' response. 'Fancy a walk, Greg, seeing as both of our partners have jumped ship? I'm guessing Julie is still out sourcing CCTV.'

'No problem, boss. Not much else I can do here at the minute.'

'Trudie, Colin, keep going with the photos and social media. I don't think Greg and I will be out for long, and hopefully we'll all be back in the office for a full feedback before we clock off for the day. Greg, meet you downstairs in five.'

'How's Jen getting on?' Chris asked as soon as they both broke free from the stagnant air of the Nottingham city police station.

'She seems to be doing okay. Think she might be struggling a bit with the slower pace of local policing.'

'Trust me, Greg, after a couple of days in their world you'd be begging to come back to a slower pace.' Chris laughed to himself, remembering everything being decided on a moment's notice last year when he'd found himself experiencing Jen's old place of work. 'Take Mr Jenkins, I don't doubt her instincts for a second. But I've learned over my many years that we can't just go crashing in there without proof of anything going on.'

‘I think that’s what she’s missing. She was at the top of her game when she decided to settle down. To now be back as a detective in local policing, it must be different to what she’s used to,’ Greg agreed. ‘I’ll keep an eye on her, boss,’ he reassured Chris as they continued to walk towards the club. ‘And how’s young Hannah, by the way?’

‘She’s good, thank you. Probably sitting in her office right now with her feet up doing her nails.’ Greg had a vague idea of what Hannah’s team did, but Chris had never told him, or anyone else for that matter, the full details. He had left it up to them to fill in the blanks.

‘You keep hold of that one, Chris. She’s had an amazing effect on you.’

‘What do you mean?’ Chris asked, slightly taken aback. He didn’t think he’d changed since meeting Hannah. *Had he?*

‘I don’t think you realise it, but I’ve definitely seen a change in you for the better.’

Chris was silent for a while as he remembered the change in him that was happening right now as his own immune system attacked itself, stripping his nerves of their protective layer. ‘I dread to think how I was before,’ he replied, hoping to deflect away from what was really going on in his mind.

‘It’s the little changes, boss. Nothing to worry about! You’re still as moody and arsey as ever.’ Greg laughed.

‘Good to know,’ Chris said as they walked up to the main entrance of Flavor and pressed the entry console at the side of the door.

‘Are they expecting us?’ Greg asked.

‘I’m not sure, but we’ll soon find out.’ As Chris spoke, a chirpy, young voice came across the speaker.

‘Flavor nightclub, can I help?’

‘Hi, Detectives Jackson and Sanders here. I was wondering if we could talk to someone about the incident last night?’

‘Erm … I’m not sure. If you could just wait a moment, I’ll speak to the manager,’ the voice said and then cut off.

Chris was beginning to think they’d been forgotten about when a striking six-foot blonde unlocked and opened the main door.

‘Katie Wainwright, venue manager,’ she said, offering her hand to the detectives. ‘I hope you don’t mind, but if you could show me some ID before we speak any further?’

‘Of course,’ Chris said as he got his warrant card out. ‘Detective Inspector Jackson, and this is my colleague, Detective Constable Sanders.’

‘Thank you, Officers. I’m sure you’ll understand we have to be incredibly wary of unexpected visitors claiming to be the police.’

‘We totally understand, Ms Wainwright.’

‘Please, it’s Katie,’ she said as she stepped aside and let the detectives into the nightclub. ‘My PA said you were here about last night.’

‘Yes, we just have a couple of questions, if that’s okay?’ Chris said carefully, very aware that Sergeant Gillroy had already been there previously, no doubt asking the same questions he was about to ask.

‘Please follow me. Can I get either of you a drink?’ Katie asked as she showed them both into one of the bar areas. ‘We’ve got a full range of whiskeys … if I can tempt you both?’

‘I’m afraid we can’t when we’re on duty, Ms Wainwright,’ Chris replied, although he suddenly found he was craving a whiskey.

‘If we start drinking this early, you’ll probably not get us out of here.’ Greg joined in, no doubt experiencing the same craving.

‘Have it your way,’ Katie said, casually pouring a large whiskey for herself. ‘So what can I do for you both? I’m guessing you're here to follow up from your colleague?’

‘Yes, we were hoping you’d be able to talk us through last night.’

‘Before we start, can I just say I have never, in all my time working here, met someone so rude and disrespectful to the LGBT community,’ Katie said with a look of pure disgust on her face.

‘I can only apologise for my colleague’s behaviour, Ms Wainwright. Can you confirm which of the officers you are referring to so I can get their behaviour reported to my bosses?’ Chris said, getting his notebook out.

‘Oh, there’s little point in that, I reckon … you’ll all stick together, like one big old boys’ club.’

‘I can assure you, Ms Wainwright, I’ll personally make sure we investigate his behaviour.’

‘Enough of the “Ms Wainwright”. Katie, please …’ she said, raising her hand before knocking back her whiskey.

‘Sorry, Katie ... if you don’t feel comfortable discussing this issue with myself or DC Sanders, I will happily send someone else over to meet you.’

'Like I said, there's little point in making a formal complaint. We often find ourselves in need of your assistance and I don't want to go upsetting the night shift.'

'It's up to you, but if I leave you with my card in case you change your mind?' Chris said, feeling into his back pocket. It felt strange offering his card this early on in the proceedings.

'Well, okay … but enough of that. I suppose we better chat about what happened last night.'

'Yes, I wondered if you could tell us any more about the incident? I suppose you must realise that we're interested because of what happened at Carbon …'

'Such a sad loss of so many young lives.' Katie bowed her head momentarily. 'We weren't exactly open on last night, if I'm honest with you. Obviously, it's normally our busiest night of the week but after the memorial, the staff and I decided that we'd open our doors, just in case people wanted somewhere to be … instead of, you know, sitting around at home worrying about the future?' Chris nodded for Katie to go on. 'We see ourselves as somewhere people can come together, no matter who they are, whatever their orientation or sexual preferences. Believe it or not, Detectives, some Saturday nights our clientele just want to come together and talk, find comfort in being around like-minded people, that sort of thing.'

'That's good to know.' Greg nodded.

'But last night we just seemed to just get busier, whether it was because we were the only place open in Nottingham, I'm not sure, but we dimmed the lights and put some music on. People just started dancing and enjoying themselves. It sort of felt like a release; just a really great atmosphere, despite everything.'

'So what went wrong?'

'We believe someone set off a smoke bomb and firecrackers at both the front of the dance area and at the back. This sent the attendees into a major panic, and they all attempted to leave the building at the same time,' Katie said, pouring herself another drink. 'I suppose they all thought it was another bomb, with what happened at Carbon …'

'Well … this is one of the reasons we wanted to come and speak to you, actually,' Chris said.

'Oh?'

'My team is currently investigating the explosions at Carbon and wondered if there were any connections between yourselves and the other music venue?'

'Not that I can think of. I do know that the owner, Karl Jenkins, often comes to Flavor.'

'Does he?' Chris questioned, trying to act surprised.

'Oh yes. He tries to blend in, but he sticks out like a sore thumb.'

'I take it he's a regular then?'

'If there isn't something more important going on at his place, that is.'

'Was he here last night?' Greg questioned.

'Yup! And he left with a pretty nasty injury, if I remember rightly. He was screaming and shouting like he was about to drop dead at any moment.'

'Did you speak to him?' Greg continued.

'He was trying to hide from anyone who would recognise him. I think the paramedics got the brunt of it.'

'Couldn't have been that bad then, if he waited for them to arrive?'

'Oh! Who knows with him? I mean, I feel sorry for the guy – it's awful what happened – but he's such a rude, weaselly little man.'

'I know you mentioned that there were two incidents at the back and the front of the dance area,' Chris said quickly, trying to steer the conversation in the right direction. 'I don't suppose you know of where Karl was situated when the incidents happened?'

'I'm afraid not, probably lurking somewhere like an oil slick. Why are you so interested in Mr Jenkins?' Katie looked confused.

'With the explosions at Carbon and your confirmation that Mr Jenkins was here last night, I'm starting to wonder if someone might be targeting him.'

'Why would anyone in their right mind waste their time targeting him?' Katie sniffed disparagingly. 'They've already destroyed his pride and joy by all accounts.'

'That is what we're trying to investigate.'

'Nothing against the man, but …' Katie tailed off meaningfully.

'Not to worry, Katie. We appreciate your time and honesty. I'm guessing all your CCTV went with the investigating officer?'

'Oh no, he said he'd come by and collect it at some point.'

'I'm more than happy to take it now if you have copies ready?'

'I'd just need to pop back into my office and collect the discs, Detectives,' Katie said, moving around the other side of the bar. 'Just be a moment,' she called as she disappeared, leaving both Chris and Greg sitting there looking at the range of drinks that were on offer, not daring to ask what the other was thinking.

'Okay, here you go. Five DVDs worth of footage from the other night. I have looked myself, but you can't really see who set the smoke bombs off,' she explained as she returned.

'Thank you,' Chris said, hopping down from the bar stool and feeling the uneven flooring underneath him. *Oh god, please don't let me trip again*, he thought as he carefully felt his way past the other stools.

'If you ever change your mind about making that complaint, I can assure you we will most certainly make sure it's investigated,' Greg said, clearly trying to convince Katie to name names. But Chris already had a good idea who it would have been.

'I'll think about it.' Katie regarded them knowingly.

'Thank you for your time, Katie,' Chris said as he held out his hand.

'It was my pleasure.' Katie shook it.

'You have my card if there's anything else you can think of.'

'Indeed, I do …' She winked.

Jen Garner

She hadn't been able to speak to Max for long, but what he had said had reassured her that, though her instincts had never been wrong in the past, street-level policing – as he called it – was very different to her old job. The things that Jen and the team had got away with would have had them strung up at a local level. Which, alas, included beating the crap out of Mr Jenkins till he admitted he'd blown up his own club too. Her conversation with Max had left her thinking about what would have happened if he'd never recruited her all those years ago. Would she still have been part of the force, perhaps at street level? Or was it being allowed to get away with so-called underhand tactics that had made her who she was now?

She had been sitting alone in the office for a while, wondering where everyone else was and what she had missed since her walk around the block and phone call. She probably should have rung James and checked in with him after the message he'd sent about being busy. Though when he was stressed with work, it was best just to leave him to it and be on hand to pick up the pieces afterwards. She was just about to grab her phone and ring one of the team when Greg and Chris returned.

'Enjoy your run?' Greg immediately asked as he sat down at his desk.

'As you can probably guess, it didn't happen. Not exactly dressed for the occasion,' she replied, looking down at her crumpled office wear. 'I went for a walk around the Arboretum, actually. Never been there before, if you can believe that. After all the years I've lived in Nottingham ...'

'It's more of a student hang out these days,' Greg commented as he logged his computer back into life.

'So … where's everyone else? Did I miss something?' Jen asked, concerned that her wander to the park had left the team one down.

'Well, Chris and I went up to Flavor to speak to them about the other night, and Julie was collecting CCTV from the universities that might give us something on our alley.'

'I know Colin found a photo with Matt Dale on it before I left.'

'Yes, he showed me that too. It sounds like you and I were pretty much on the same page that his presence might not be as significant as Colin thinks,' Chris replied.

At least I've been right about something today, Jen thought as Trudie and Colin entered the office.

'Do we know if Julie is back in?' Chris asked as Jen rocked back on her chair.

'Not sure, boss,' came the response from Trudie.

'I'm going to head back to the office and type a couple of things up. I also want to give Lyndsey a call and see whether she wants to join us before we all head home for the day.'

Jen checked her watch. Maybe with a bit of luck she really would get to see Max tonight, providing there were no major incidents along the way. As she began to plan it all in her head, she suddenly noticed how tired and drawn Chris was looking. She was in no doubt over how much stuff he had on his mind right now with the case, but she almost felt like she should go up to him and give him a hug or something. If he had been one of the girls, she'd have brought him chocolate, but he just looked so exhausted she found herself wondering whether any amount of chocolate would fix whatever was going on with him. Maybe she'd ring Hannah … but then she felt bad about ringing the girlfriend of her boss to ask if he was okay. Perhaps she should just keep out of it all and concentrate on the case, finding out who could have possibly wanted to, or even had the materials to, blow up Carbon.

Chapter Seventeen

DI Chris Jackson

'All sitting comfortably?' Chris asked the room of eagerly waiting detectives, who were either keen to go home or to get on with the case. He'd managed to get hold of Lyndsey, who had confirmed that shit was pretty much still hitting the fan. She was eighty per cent positive that they'd found the way the explosives had come into the venue but would be able to feed back better tomorrow. She also said she had a pretty good idea who had cocked up big time, but he'd have to wait for the office gossip to find that one out. Chris wondered if his fall earlier that day had made canteen gossip yet, and what Sergeant Gillroy's company would have been like if he'd had to join him along the alley instead of Officer Golding.

'I have some good news and some bad news,' Chris began as he looked around the room at his detectives, all hanging on to his every word. 'Lyndsey won't be able to feed back any news from Carbon until tomorrow at the earliest, so I've decided that we should probably all call it a day.'

Chris noticed his team immediately start to fidget around in their seats, clearly ready to get out of the office ASAP. 'I don't think there's much more work we can do, so head home and see your families. The bad news is I want everyone in for seven-thirty tomorrow morning, so make sure you get a good night's sleep. I need you all bright-eyed and bushy-tailed.' As Chris finished the sentence, the whole atmosphere in the office suddenly shifted to one of relief with thoughts of heading home.

DC Colin Goodwin

As soon as his wife picked up the phone, he could hear his daughter crying in the background. He felt the guilt wash over him.

'Hey, love.'

'Hey.'

'Lizzie, I am *really* sorry but I'm going to have to work late.'

'Okay?'

'I was hoping to get away at a decent time, but the boss wants me to look into something.' Colin hated lying to her, but what choice did he have?

'Do you know when you'll be back? Am I saving you some dinner?'

'It shouldn't be too late, love.'

'As you can hear, things here are a bit chaotic ... but I'll see you later, I guess.'

'I'm so sorry, Lizzie.'

'It's fine, just remember you owe me.'

'Love you. Tell Cassie Daddy misses her.'

'Will do. Stay safe,' Lizzie said as she hung up the phone.

He swore as he put down the phone. Why the hell *had* he lied to her? She'd be just as understanding if he told her the truth about what he was doing. It was just the fact Chris and the team didn't know, so he wanted to keep it to himself. There was no way Chris would have let him go out for a drink in Dale's to try to catch Matt in a lie. Colin put his phone back in his pocket and turned away from the police station, heading across the road towards the pub. He wasn't sure how busy it would be at this time in the evening, or whether Matt would even be there.

Dale's was situated close to Carbon and Flavor on Upper Parliament Street near to the shopping centre, the theatre and many other shops and pubs. The street was also one of the main roads through Nottingham with the one-way system flummoxing many a non-local driver.

As Colin got closer, he could hear the unmistakeable sound of one of the McDermitts' hits blaring out from inside the pub. *Maybe I should have brought some ear buds with me.* He couldn't believe that he used to enjoy going to places like this; the damage it must have done to his ears over the years! Colin stopped for a moment outside of the pub, moving from one foot to another, wondering whether this was really a good idea and what on earth he thought he was going to discover from Matt Dale, even if he lied and said he wasn't at the gig. It wasn't like Colin could arrest him on the spot. He knew backup from uniform wouldn't be far away if requested, but was this just a wild goose chase? Although he *had* told Lizzie he'd be home late so he might as well make the most of this. Pushing open the door, he was met with the smell of ale, and his mind suddenly informed him that he really could do with a drink ...

Like many clubs and bars, the place looked different in the dark. The dinginess was hidden by low lighting and crowds of students who weren't there to look at the décor; they were there for the cheap drinks and a good night out. Colin couldn't help wondering how busy this place would have been if there hasn't been an attack Carbon and Flavor wasn't also closed.

'What can I get you?' a young barman greeted him.

'Pint of Stella, please, mate,' Colin said, putting his hands into his jacket pocket in search of his wallet.

'Three pounds, please.'

'Is Mr Dale in?' Colin asked as he handed over the money.

'Junior or Senior?'

'Either.'

'Well, Senior isn't often here, so you might want to grab him while you can.'

Colin took his pint and moved to one of the tables at the side of the bar. He was used to looking for seating positions in undercover settings which gave him maximum observation. It wasn't the first time that he'd wished he'd been undercover in the bar the night Chris and Hannah met. He'd seen the CCTV footage … who hadn't? But to have experienced the action of that night, if only for his boss's comical dancing, would have been enough of a reward. Or maybe, in his wildest dreams, Hannah would have chosen him instead … and *that* would have been a whole different scenario to have to explain to his wife. Well, Hannah was incredibly fit, there was no denying that. He sighed. *Oh well.* He was on his own personal stake out now, alone at the bar with a pint of Stella, completely unsure what the hell he was doing there in the first place or what he thought he'd achieve alone.

As he sat and drank his pint, two older guys appeared behind the bar. He recognised them immediately as Matt Dale and his father. Colin couldn't help noticing how the bar staff seemed to be worshipping the ground the older of the pair walked on. Maybe the days at Dale's he remembered so fondly were also the days the bar was run by Senior, and it had gone downhill since he'd started to hand the business over to his son.

He was almost halfway through his pint and people watching when the music suddenly stopped, and an argument between the two men could be clearly heard.

'This place is turning into a dive.' Senior was making no effort to keep his voice down. 'I know I shouldn't have handed the business over to you. Your mother warned me this would happen.'

'Dad, be a bit quieter.'

'No, son, I won't. I'm fed up with telling you that your staff need to be told to buck up their bloody ideas. This place used to be filled by this time back in my day.'

'Dad—'

'You dare blame your competitors, or the smoking ban again! We had bigger problems in my day, son, and Dale's still came out on top.'

'Dad, please, you're making a scene.'

'No, son. Carbon might be closed for now and that homosexual place up the road … but their loss should be your gain.'

'So why was *he* here all day yesterday?'

Colin was sitting quietly taking in this whole argument between the two generations of Dales, while making sure he wasn't caught staring. He noticed that some people had also started to leave the bar. It seemed they didn't want or need front row seats – they'd come for a good night out, not a domestic. Moments later, the music was suddenly restored, but the argument continued. Except now Colin couldn't hear what they said. The bar staff appeared embarrassed as they desperately attempted to look busy to avoid being caught in the crossfire. The two Dales stopped arguing and moodily shook hands as Senior made his way out of the pub, leaving his son to clean up the carnage. *Second pint time*, Colin decided as he got up and made his way over to the bar.

'Same again, mate?' he was greeted by the same barman.

'What the hell was that all about?' Colin asked.

'Beats me. They always end up arguing like that,' came the response as the barman turned to pull the pint.

'What brings you here, Detective?' Colin heard a familiar voice. *Rumbled*. 'Sorry about all that. My father get bit anxious … he likes to make a scene.'

'Matt,' Colin said, holding out his hand. 'Fancied a pint after work. The DI is a bit of a slave driver.'

'Well, this one's on the house,' Matt said as he moved the pint closer to Colin.

'Thank you, but I'm afraid I can't.'

'Don't be silly! I won't tell if you don't.'

'I'm afraid it's the rules,' Colin said, reaching into his pocket, pulling out a fiver and offering it to the barman.

'Your loss,' Matt said, moving away from the counter.

‘Keep the change, mate,’ Colin called as he got up and went back to his stool. Being bought drinks by a possible suspect wouldn’t impress Chris, and would no doubt have him straight into disciplinary – *especially* as this visit hadn’t been sanctioned and Colin had just gone off on his own, Robin Hood style.

Jen Garner

‘Honey, I’m home!’ Jen shouted as she opened the front door. She’d already seen Max’s car parked on the drive, so wasn’t expecting much response from anyone. She could hear the shower running upstairs, which was a sure sign that James hadn’t been home long either. Looking at her watch, she realised how late it really was. Jen decided she better intervene and get the kids into bed; they had school tomorrow, and no doubt Max would be completely exhausted himself after at least four hours with the Garner children.

‘What do we have here?’ Jen asked, walking into the front room where the noise was clearly emanating from to find Max in a chair struggling to keep his eyes open while the kids played loudly on some computer game.

‘Mummy!’ Alex shouted, jumping up and running towards her.

‘Hey, little man.’ Melanie was less interested in her mum's arrival and continued playing. ‘Melanie?’ Jen asked to no response. ‘Good day out?’ Silence. ‘Melanie?’

‘She’s sulking,’ Max said, getting up from the chair.

‘Do I want to know?’

‘I’ll fill you in later,’ Max said with a knowing look.

‘Hate to break up the party, but you two need to be getting into bed.’ At that point, Alex clung to her extra tightly.

‘They’ve both read their books and Alex is ready to change his.’

‘Great. Thank you so much, Max,’ Jen said, detaching herself from Alex.

‘Not a problem. I need to be getting back anyway. Book club is at mine tonight.’

‘I’m so sorry. You should’ve said! I’d have come home earlier.’

‘Don’t worry, I know how busy you are. Plus I told Isabelle to let herself in if I wasn’t back.’

‘Isabelle?’ Jen questioned, unsure who he meant.

'Mansfield? Safe house?'

'Oh, that Isabelle. You two kept in touch?'

'Of course.'

It was just then that James appeared, smelling strongly of aftershave. He stood behind her and planted a kiss on her cheek. 'You look like you've had a rough day,' he casually mentioned.

'If only that was the half of it,' Jen said, involuntarily gritting her teeth. 'Thanks again for keeping an eye on the kids.' She moved towards Max.

'I like doing it.' He enveloped her in a hug.

'Thanks for the chat earlier as well,' Jen added quietly.

'Chat?' James questioned.

'Any time,' Max said, moving towards the living room door, shaking James' hand and ruffling Alex's hair. 'See you soon, Melanie.'

'Bye,' she replied curtly.

'I'll come out too, actually. I need to move my car.' Jen followed Max out onto the drive. 'What's happened with Melanie?' she asked, wondering if she had missed something important.

'Nothing to worry about,' Max replied as he headed towards his car.

'Okay.' Jen wasn't completely convinced as she moved in for another goodbye hug. Sometimes, when Max wasn't looking, Jen breathed him in, imagining it was her real dad hugging her. 'I trust your judgement.'

After Max had left, Jen walked back into the house and was met by James, cup of tea in hand. 'Go and get in the shower. I'll get the kids into bed and sort food.'

'At least I won't fall asleep in the shower,' Jen replied, remembering the last time she'd been ordered to get clean before dinner.

'With you, Mrs Garner, anything is possible.'

Later on, clean and refreshed, Jen kissed both the kids goodnight. James had somehow managed to get them both into bed before she'd got out of the shower. She decided not to broach whatever had happened earlier with Melanie and would judge her mood tomorrow when she woke up, if Alex didn't tell her what had happened first, of course.

'Better?' James greeted her at the bottom of the stairs.

'Yes, thank you,' Jen said, walking towards him as he held out his arms. 'Shall we just go to bed and sleep forever?' she asked as he held her.

‘Chance would be a fine thing, after the day I’ve had,’ came his response as Jen breathed him in.

‘Did you make a start on dinner, or shall we just get takeaway?’ Jen assumed that if James was as tired and worn out as she was, then perhaps the thought of cooking dinner was too much for him as well.

‘No, we’re good, dinner is in the oven. Nothing fancy – just one of those chicken things from Aldi.’

‘The ones we have to force Melanie to finish?’

‘That’d be the one,’ James said, pulling away and kissing her on the forehead. ‘Go and get a bottle of something from the garage.’

‘On a school night?’ Jen teased.

‘Make that two bottles then.’

After retrieving a bottle of wine, Jen returned to the kitchen to find James sitting at the table with his laptop on, muttering to himself.

‘Now, come on, Mr Garner! Leave work alone. It can wait until tomorrow. After all, you said you’d had a shit day so you’re better off leaving it anyway.’

‘Yeah …’ he responded, moving over quickly to check on the peas.

‘Am I okay to move your stuff?’ Jen asked as she cleared the table and then went to retrieve a corkscrew and some glasses. James returned to the table, dutifully shutting his laptop and moving it to the other side of the kitchen.

‘Want to talk about it?’ Jen probed.

‘Just everything going wrong, faulty equipment, broken networks … how we’re meant to continue to work from home, I’ll never know. It all just got on top of me today.’

James had worked for a big insurance company as their technical director for the past eight years. Fixing anything that was broken or faulty from machinery to people – usually more the former. Jen knew he’d dealt with the odd crying employee in his time. He was good like that: caring and compassionate for the people he worked with.

‘How come it’s gone wrong all of a sudden?’ she asked.

‘You know how everyone was issued with a new laptop? Well, they all came with new logins and programmes to use. It was one person after another at the end of last week telling me something didn’t work and they needed help.’

‘Fun? Still better than my week’s been then,’ Jen said as James moved back over towards the oven.

'Is that what you and Max were chatting about?'

'Yeah … I left work to go and cry to my old boss,' Jen admitted, because that was more or less what she had done, except there hadn't been any tears – yet.

'What's our favourite DI done now?' James always referred to Chris that way, since he'd been arrested by him well over a year ago.

'Chris has nothing to do with it.'

As Jen spoke, James started to get dinner out of the oven. 'Go on then, I'm listening.'

'Well … look, you know about my past?' Jen prompted, trying to think of the best way to phrase what she was trying to say.

'Yes, you were super cop.'

Jen laughed but then turned serious again. 'Well, I miss it …' James turned and glared at her. *If looks could kill*, she thought. 'Wait, just hear me out.'

'As long as you're not about to tell me you're going back and have enlisted again,' James said as he returned to dishing out dinner and bringing it over to the table where she was sitting.

'Oh no, not that.'

'What then!' James shouted. Jen could see he immediately regretted it when he obviously saw the hurt that spread across her face. 'I'm sorry. I'm just scared of losing you again. Things have been so great recently.'

'I know! That's why I rang and spoke to Max instead … I knew he'd understand.'

'What is there to understand?' James said, tuning off the hob and returning to the table where Jen was now sitting with her head in her hands. 'Help me to understand, Jen.'

'We've talked before about when I was in the service, and how, let's say, they chose the jobs for us.'

'Yeah, you were the middlemen … women.'

'Exactly. So, we went in there and got the job done, no questions asked.' Jen started to move her food around with her knife and fork. 'How do I put this? Street policing is very different, and that's what I'm struggling with.'

'So … you're saying you miss the action?'

'I'm missing not having to follow a bunch of procedures. Street policing is too slow …'

James burst out laughing. 'Too slow?' He continued to laugh. 'You've only dealt with an explosion at a music venue this week, no biggie.'

'I just need to kick some doors down again and use my instincts.'

'What did Max have to say?' James questioned as he popped a piece of chicken in his mouth and started chewing.

'Well … he said I was probably feeling this way because "Lisa Carter" was involved in the last two cases, so they thrust me back into the action and now …'

'You're just plain old Jen Garner?'

'Exactly. If it hadn't have been for Chloe's death, would I have even considered going back into the force? Would I still be pretending to be perfect?'

James looked at Jen as she spoke. 'You're still perfect to me.'

'Yeah, I'm just a messed up kinda perfect,' Jen said as she began chewing too.

'The kids think you're perfect as well.'

'That's because they know no different.'

'So what's the answer, Detective Garner?'

'To enjoy the highs when they come and learn to live with the procedures.'

'You know I'd never stop you doing anything, Jen,' James said after a while. 'But I just don't think I could cope if you enlisted again. You've only just gone into street policing and I'm already wondering what the fuck I've let myself in for.'

'I couldn't go back, James.' The lie seemed to slip so easily from Jen's lips. 'I have Melanie and Alex to think about.'

They sat in a comfortable silence and continued eating until Jen spoke again. 'I love you, James. You know that, don't you?'

'And I love you too, Mrs Garner.'

DI Chris Jackson

It was pitch dark outside by the time Chris got home, and he instinctively knew something wasn't right as soon as he stepped out of the lift onto his floor. For a start, his cat, Fluff, was on his doorstep awaiting his arrival. She'd usually greet him as soon as walked in purring and rubbing herself against his legs. Part of him was surprised to find that his front door was locked and, as he turned the key, a familiar fragrance hit his senses. He really didn't need this; he was tired, absolutely exhausted in fact. He wanted to sit back on his sofa, beer in one hand, some Netflix series on the television, and fall asleep in perfect bliss – but no such luck today, as *she* appeared from the bedroom door. As always, she looked beautiful.

'Who knew watching you on television could be such a turn on?' she purred as she stood in front of him in some frilly number she had no doubt bought specially for the occasion.

'Han …' He sighed

She paused and looked at him properly. 'Oh my god, Chris. What the fuck's happened? You look awful!' Dropping her defence mechanism, she rushed towards him. 'If I'd known, I'd have come to the station.'

'Hannah, I'm fine. Just tired, in need of a shower and sleep. That's all.'

'You go and get in the shower. I'll get dressed and get something in the oven ready for when you come out.'

'Thanks, Han. I'm sorry to spoil the surprise.'

'No, it's fine. I bet Fluff gave the game away anyway. She was meowing to get out as soon as I arrived. Anyone would think she hated me.'

'She clearly knew she wouldn't get any attention when I got in so went elsewhere.'

'Right! Shower, change, and then dinner will be ready,' Hannah ordered as she came over and kissed him. He partly expected his body to react the way it always did when she was close, especially looking like she did, but he was too knackered, and then there was everything else …

He jumped into the shower and let the warm water run over him. It felt good to get all the muck and dirt off. He honestly felt like he could sleep for weeks. In fact, he was so tired he'd only remembered to take his glasses off once he'd pulled into the underground car park. There was no denying that Hannah had clearly made an effort, and she'd looked stunning; it was just his head was in such a mess with work and his health and … well, he just needed a break from it all, although there was no chance of that happening anytime soon. Relieved to have showered alone without any interruptions from the two females in his apartment, he had a quick shave and pulled on a random pair of trousers and T-shirt he found lying around. Then he made his way to the living room. He stood and watched for a while as Hannah, who was now completely dressed with her hair pulled up into a bun on top of her head, attempted to clear away things that were piled up on his kitchen table. *What have I done to deserve somebody as amazing as her?* he wondered. And, although he had used the L word quite openly, there was something inside of him that was starting to believe that he really *did* love her. It wasn't just something he said in the heat of passion.

'Better?' Hannah asked as she turned and looked over at him.

'Much. Look, Hannah—'

'Shh.' She cut him off. 'It doesn't matter. Anyway, I think I've pulled together something suitable to eat from your kitchen cupboards, so take a seat, I'll grab you a beer and dinner will be served shortly.' Chris looked at her and smiled, plonking himself down on the seat that had been cleared for him, waiting to see what the hell she had managed to rustle up from the meagre contents of his kitchen cupboards.

'Beer,' Hannah said as she offered him a can of lager.

'What have you made?'

'Surprise! You're going to love it.'

'Let me come and help.'

'No. You, sir, are staying right there.'

Chris didn't want to argue with Hannah after she had made all this effort and then some. He thought he'd guessed what she'd sourced when he heard the microwave ping and the toaster pop up moments later.

'Beans on toast with cheese and a side order of chips,' Hannah said as she presented the meal. At that moment Chris thought he might burst into tears and tell Hannah everything, but something stopped him.

'You not having anything?' he asked instead.

'Hold your horses! I've already told you, you need to get a toaster that makes four slices at a time!' she said as she disappeared to return moments later with the same. 'Just like my mother always used to make it.' She sat down. 'Come on, dig in.'

'Han …' Chris began, but then he changed his mind again and simply picked up his knife and fork. He *was* hungry. 'So … how's work?' he asked instead.

'I think it should be me asking you that question.'

'Oh, you know … someone is blowing shit up in Nottingham and we're no closer to knowing who.'

'How's Detective Garner settling in?'

'Lighting fireworks and running away?'

'I'm sorry, but that's expected. Did you know the officers who went into the burning building on a rescue mission?'

'You're looking at one, and you can probably guess who the other was.'

'Ah … got you.' She looked thoughtful for a moment. 'Look, I know how territorial your team gets, but I can get on the phone and have my guys down here by morning.'

'God no, I can already sense that Jen is on a collision course with Sergeant Gillroy. I don't need Detective Brown down here stoking the fire as well.'

'Who's Sergeant Gillroy?'

'Oh, one of the officers from the investigation when she disappeared.'

'Ah, okay.'

It was nice having Hannah there after the day he'd had, and to have her acting normally was an added bonus. Meal finished, he helped wash up, fed the cat and then made his excuses.

'I'm so sorry. I know you've come all this way, but I really need to sleep.'

'Go for it. I'm not stopping you. I'll just grab my laptop from my bag and check a couple of things with London, and then I'll come and join you,' she said as she made her way into the living room to retrieve her bag and then set herself up at the table where they'd just had dinner.

'Night,' Chris said as he kissed her. 'And thank you – really.'

'Night.'

Chris didn't know what time it was when he felt the cat jump off the bed and Hannah join him. As she cuddled closer to him, he felt her breath on his back and then she kissed his neck.

'I love you, Christopher Jackson,' she whispered as her hand made it to the waist band of his boxers and rested there. Not wanting to let on that he was awake, he closed his eyes and drifted back into nothingness.

Chapter Eighteen

DI Chris Jackson

Monday

'Morning,' Chris greeted Lyndsey, who was already in the incident room setting up.

'Chris.'

Lyndsey turned to look at him as she spoke and he couldn't help but do a double take. 'I hate to say it, but you look shocking!'

'Thanks.' She laughed. 'I'm still trying to clean up after the major cock-up with the window in the storeroom.'

'Do you know who missed it?'

'Yup, they came to me and admitted it, so as far as I am concerned it's over and done with. Shame the Sup doesn't think the same, but as their boss I've taken the brunt of it all,' Lyndsey turned back to what she was laying out on the table as people started to filter into the room.

'Morning,' Jen sang as she entered. She looked so much more relaxed than when she'd left yesterday. Maybe the early-ish night had done her some good. He wondered if Hannah had been in touch with her after he'd arrived home yesterday to find her in his flat. They'd kissed on the doorstep as they both went their separate ways, not knowing when they'd be back in each other's arms once again. He couldn't help but think about the future and what lay ahead for his team, what with the boss falling apart and a highly trained undercover detective in their midst.

'I hear you fell over yesterday on the job?' Lyndsey commented, bringing Chris crashing down back to earth.

'Sorry?'

'I heard Sergeant Gillroy talking earlier in the canteen. He was saying you'd fallen over or something. Hope you're okay?'

'Yeah …' Chris tried to laugh it off, but his heart was racing faster. If it was now canteen gossip, how long before the Sup was back at his door again questioning whether he should be at work? 'I'm not sure what happened, but it was one of those things where you stand up and look round to check no one else saw. Except Gillroy chose that exact time to come blazing down the road in a patrol car.'

'You'd better get Julie to check there isn't footage out there of it.'

'I've still not lived down the nightclub incident from last year.'

'Nightclub incident?' Lyndsey looked curious.

'Long story. It was a drugs bust I got roped into, but my dancing skills apparently left a lot to be desired …'

'I might just have to find out more about that.' Lyndsey laughed.

'You're not missing anything.'

'Morning, boss,' Colin said as he practically rolled into the incident room.

'At least I don't look as rough as him,' Lyndsey said in a low voice.

'Morning, Detective Goodwin. What the hell happened to you last night?'

Colin looked slightly uncomfortable. 'You're not going to like this … but I went to Dale's for a couple of drinks.'

Oh God, not only were they gossiping about him in the canteen but now his officers were going off doing their own thing. He prayed that Jen hadn't gone and punched Karl Jenkins as well.

'What on earth made you suddenly decide to go for a drink there?' Chris heard Lyndsey ask him.

'Well, erm …' Colin stuttered.

'Take a seat, Colin, and you can fill us all in shortly,' Lyndsey replied, clearly mimicking Chris' leadership style. Colin quickly walked over and took a seat at the table next to Trudie, where he began talking to her in hushed tones.

'Okay. Everyone present and correct?' Chris couldn't help but feel he was starting to lose control. He wasn't only losing his health, his balance, but now an outsider had come in and seemed to be taking over.

'Chris, the floor is yours,' Lyndsey said, smiling at him and pulling Chris back into the reality of what he was supposed to be doing: his job, and he was bloody good at it.

He cleared his throat. 'We've got lots to get through this morning, so who wants to start?'

'I think I might be best to start,' Lyndsey cut in. 'Let's go back to the beginning of this whole case: the explosion at Carbon.' Lyndsey placed the large map of the nightclub back into the centre of the table. 'I'm sure the layout has been burned into all of our retinas, so I won't make you all stare at it for too long.' Lyndsey shifted her position. 'I'm sure you're also all aware now that this backroom here,' she pointed, 'had a window that wasn't secure like the rest. It's looking very likely that the explosives came into the club via this room. The CSI guys found trace amounts of one of the chemicals used to make APEX around the window ledge.'

'How confident are they that said chemical wasn't used for something else in the room previously?' Trudie questioned.

Lyndsey shook her head. 'I can't see why this chemical would be used for any other reason in that room.'

'If we're saying that this is where the chemicals came in, who had access to this area?' Chris questioned.

'All members of staff had access to it, but had no reason to enter the room prior to or during the gig.'

'So other than staff members, who does that leave?' Chris responded, knowing exactly who would answer.

'Greg and I went to visit Dean and Gabriel at the hospital yesterday and their stories check out. Having already been caught in the crush for the fire exits, which is where Dean managed to pick up a collapsed lung, they took the corridor, hoping it would lead to a different exit,' Jen explained.

'Gabriel is quite possibly asthmatic, so with all the panic to get out going on around them, it made sense for them to try and find an easier way out,' Greg added.

'There's no way that either of them had anything to do with the explosives, Chris.' Jen sounded like she was gearing up for a fight.

'I trust both of your judgements on them,' Chris responded, hoping to knock Jen slightly off from her high horse.

'Though they were a tad disappointed that you hadn't come to interview them, boss. If you ever get bored of young Hannah …' Greg said as the room broke out into laughter and Chris felt his face turn a shade of red he wasn't quite expecting.

'I'll bear that in mind. Thank you, Greg,' Chris said, finding himself laughing too, despite everything.

'So Colin ... time for that explanation,' Lyndsey prompted, bringing the room back to the task at hand.

'Well, let's start at the beginning… I'd been looking through all the photos from the backstage area from the meet and greets, and I noticed that in one of the photos we can see Matt Dale in the background. After talking it through with the team yesterday and re-checking lists, we agreed he was an easy spot because I know who he is. So I went back to searching for any other people who shouldn't have been there from the lists provided to us.'

'And your late-night drinking session?' Lyndsey prompted again.

'I know this sounds stupid, but we all clocked off last night and I fancied a pint. I thought if I went to Dale's, maybe I could get Matt talking and ask him about the gig. He'd make a mistake and say he wasn't there or something and then we'd have him.'

'Oh god,' Chris heard himself say out loud.

'Nothing bad happened, boss. In fact, I didn't even get to talk to Matt, only a barman … well Matt *did* offer to buy me a drink, but I declined,' he said quickly. 'So don't panic there. But what I did overhear was him arguing with his dad.'

'Dale Senior?'

'Correct. About, well … basically how badly the pub was doing and that he shouldn't have given the business to him, all that sort of stuff. Dale Senior went on to talk about Carbon and Flavor, in a particularly homophobic way may I add, and how his son should be sweeping up the business while the two venues were closed.'

'Flavor's closed?' someone questioned.

'Well, this is it, because it isn't. I checked on the way home … I mean I walked past. I didn't go in – honest!'

'It's okay, Colin. I believe you,' Chris reassured him. 'I don't think it would be your scene.'

'There was also a strange comment Matt made about someone being in meetings with his father all day on Saturday, but I didn't catch what else was said because the music came on again after that. I also didn't get to speak to anyone about the gig, so it was a wasted couple of hours, but it got me away from the missus a bit longer.'

'Team?' Chris paused, looking around.

'Good try on trying to get a result, Colin,' Greg congratulated him.

'What father and son were arguing over matched up with the business accounts,' Julie added.

'I wonder if it's worth looking into the Dale family dynamics some more?' Lyndsey spoke up.

'Colin, you've just won that award,' Chris announced. 'Everything about the Dales: their family, history, favourite chocolate, supermarket, that sort of thing. Just try to avoid going for a drink there again anytime soon.'

'Okay, boss.'

'I guess that just leaves mine and Greg's visit to Flavor yesterday then. Do you want to lead, Greg?'

'Can do, boss. So Chris and I went over to Flavor to speak to them about the incident on Saturday night. We spoke to the manager, Katie Wainwright, who, and this will interest Jen—' Jen suddenly looked up, all alert '—confirms that Karl Jenkins was in the club at the time of their false alarm.'

'She wasn't particularly complimentary about him either, if I remember rightly.'

'Do they know who or what caused the incident?' Lyndsey asked.

'Katie seems to think there were two separate incidents: one at the front of the dancefloor and one at the back of the room, which caused maximum panic as people believed they were trapped between explosions.'

'Katie also confirmed that Karl Jenkins was injured in the panic and was transported to hospital,' Chris added.

'So we now know where he got the broken wrist then?' Jen asked.

'I would say so. Wouldn't you, Chris?' Greg asked

'I think we can pretty much bet on it.'

'Another fan of Mr Jenkins. Maybe you two could start a club. What do you say, Jen?' Colin jibed but was met with a stone-cold stare.

'I know none of you guys are that stupid, but Katie also made a complaint against one of our officers. So please, if you need to head into Flavor, make sure you're respectful,' Chris said, glaring round to the room to make sure everyone understood him.

'I think the biggest question then is whether someone is targeting Mr Jenkins because of his sexuality?' Lyndsey voiced what they were all thinking.

'I'm not sure how we're going to be able to find that one out, if he himself doesn't even admit to being in a relationship with a man.'

'I find it hard to admit being married sometimes,' Colin joked and received another death stare from Jen.

'Jen will agree with me when I say that it's more than that, Colin,' Greg spoke up, trying to calm the situation.

'Guys, we're getting away from the purpose of this investigation: who blew up Carbon and why, not who hates Karl the most!' Lyndsey reminded them.

Was Chris really imagining it, or was Lyndsey seemingly trying to take control of *his* team, when hers couldn't even process a crime scene without missing a huge piece of evidence? He was being petty, he knew he was, but after how everything had been over the past couple of days … God, he hated that he was starting to become paranoid and jealous of a colleague who were probably just trying to help.

'If I move the subject away from Karl again then,' Julie offered. He had totally forgotten that Julie had gone on the hunt for additional CCTV of the alleyway. 'I'm afraid we're drawing a blank. No CCTV of the alleyway, no CCTV from the neighbouring buildings. There's some of the road in both directions towards the alley though ...'

Here it comes, Chris thought to himself, *she's going to announce to the entire room that she watched the CCTV of me falling over.* But the Julie he knew wouldn't do that, would she? She had been his partner for ages and was the one who had nagged him in the beginning to get to the doctors – although look how well that one worked out.

'There are numerous hours of footage of the road. You can't see anything but cars. A lot of this is due to the direction the camera was pointing.'

'No footage of mine and Chris's rescue attempt?' Jen asked.

'Afraid not.'

'So a waste of time,' Colin commented.

'I wouldn't say a complete waste of time, but I'm not expecting the camera to suddenly change direction anytime soon …' Julie tailed off.

'Trudie, anything interesting pinged on social media?'

'Not really. Lot of condemnation for whoever set the firecrackers and smoke bombs off at Flavor, but other than that, nothing.'

'I know that this is my favourite subject and all, but nothing on Karl Jenkins?' Jen prodded.

'Nope. Sorry, hun.'

'So … where are we in this huge mess of an investigation, team?' Chris found himself asking.

'We know the explosives came in via said window in the club, but still no idea who brought them in,' Lyndsey offered.

'I still say Matt Dale looks good for that, boss,' Colin countered.

'He seems to be the only potential suspect we've got right now,' Lyndsey agreed.

‘We know Karl started his career off at Dale’s from Julie and Colin’s meeting. Will you see if you can find out where the money came from to buy the Carbon site, Julie? And Jen, I know that we’re all sick of looking at CCTV, but will you just run your expert eye over the backstage footage and see if Colin has missed anyone?’

‘Of course, boss. Anything else you’d like me to look at?’

‘I think that’ll keep you quiet for a while. Colin, the ingredients needed to make APEX can’t just be bought in the local supermarket in those quantities. Will you contact local mail delivery companies and see if anyone has delivered anything they found suspicious or large quantities of anything out of the ordinary? Might also be worth contacting the bomb squad and maybe Hannah’s team to see if they have any thoughts on how this stuff gets to its intended recipient.’

‘I’d started looking into it, boss, so shouldn’t be too difficult to pick up.’

‘Great. Trudie, as we now know Karl worked at Dale’s, will you reach out to your contacts in the trade and see if anyone remembers anything about his time there?’

‘Are we heading down the route that someone could be targeting Karl?’ Lyndsey asked for clarification.

‘As much as I think we all despise the man, at the end of the day he is a victim of two attacks now.’

‘Where do you want me, boss?’ Greg asked.

‘You and I, Greg, are going to see the man himself.’ Chris didn’t dare look over to where Jen was sitting; the fact that he wasn’t sending her out to see Karl again could go one of two ways. ‘Lyndsey?’ Chris finally turned to ask if she was happy.

‘Looks like you’re all sorted, I’ll get my team to continue on with what they’re doing and will speak to the press officer about putting an update out.’

‘Thank you. Meet back here say about one-ish for a working lunch?’

‘Are they ever any different, boss?’ Colin asked.

‘Guess it depends on who’s working and who’s having lunch!’

'Thought I was in for a right telling off from the boss,' Colin declared once he was sure Chris and Greg has left the office.

'You impressed him, you know?' Julie smiled at him as she stretched.

'I'm not sure about that. I'm half expecting a disciplinary meeting when he gets back.' Colin laughed slightly nervously.

'Oh, he'll have you for the unauthorised field trip – but you used your initiative, and he likes that.'

'Well, as long as Lizzie doesn't find out I lied to her as well then I'm home safe.'

'You lied to *her*?'

'Yeah, didn't really have much choice. I really wanted to go into Dale's and catch Matt in a lie if he's the one behind all of this. But I think he'd be too clever for that.'

'Well, Chris seems happy enough for us to be looking at Dale's for now,' Julie responded. 'I just can't get out of my head how Matt reacted when we went over to speak to them. It really seemed like his dad was pulling the strings. It was like he was a shy kid, hardly speaking to us!'

'So why has his dad given him the business then, if he acts like a five-year-old?' Colin questioned.

'But didn't you say you heard Senior tell him that he shouldn't have given him the business? Who else would it have gone to?' Julie asked, her attention returning to the computer in front of her. 'Danielle, I assume?'

'Our high-powered lawyer representing some of the country's worst criminals,' Jen butted in now.

'Yeah, so what would she want with a pub? Isn't he better having her onside for legal representation?'

The room fell into a comfortable silence as the team got on with their assigned tasks.

Colin turned to his computer and wondered how the hell he'd go about shipping the ingredients he needed to make explosives to one address. Then it came to him: cleaning companies! There must be millions out there where you could buy what you needed in bulk with no questions asked. Lizzie would know more about this than he would because she was always getting her hair dyed. But the kits she brought didn't come with enough peroxide to blow anything up … although hairdressers must get their peroxide from somewhere, as he doubted it all came in a little box with a pretty model on the front. So that was where he'd start searching around online, looking at where he could buy mass quantities of peroxide, and, if he was still struggling, he'd phone up Lizzie's hairdressers.

'I'm not having much luck tracing where Karl got all his money to buy Carbon.' Julie interrupted the sound of people tapping away on their keyboards.

'A lottery win?' Trudie shouted across the office.

'I'm sure if you win enough to buy a piece of land you end up on a register somewhere, and there's always paperwork. You can't claim more than a hundred pounds from a retailer, and if it's more than fifty thousand, I think you have to claim that in person.'

'How much would a piece of land have been five years ago, and how much would it have cost to build a venue like Carbon there?'

'Wouldn't his insurance company know?' Jen offered, clearly keen to distract herself from the same photos for five minutes.

'But the cost to rebuild now would be very different to five years ago, because look at what Carbon is these days.'

'Maybe we need to look at his family, parents, grandparents … Samuel's family?'

'God, if only it could be as simple as a quick Google search.' Julie sighed, seemingly not getting anywhere. 'Anyone having any more success than I am?'

'I've got some of my pub contacts in touch. Once I mentioned Karl and Dale's, quite a few of them said they would get back to me,' Trudie answered.

'Something must've kicked off if people remember him and are willing to talk,' Julie said thoughtfully.

'I'm pretty sure if there was nothing to tell, they would've told me off the bat.'

'Colin – found anything?'

'Well, I now know where to buy twenty-five litres of peroxide from.'

'You can buy that amount over the internet?' Julie asked, shocked.

'Indeed, and I bet if I keep searching I'll find the rest of the ingredients,' Colin answered, feeling he'd achieved something without even having to ring Lizzie's hairdresser. Although he almost felt scared at how easy it was to buy bomb-making materials innocently over the internet. 'I've not got very far on the other job Chris gave me though: finding out all about the Dales.'

‘I can help with that if you want, Colin?’ Jen offered.

‘You ready to give in?’ Colin teased. ‘What’s that, Jen, I was right and there are no other unlisted people in the photos?’

Jen stuck her tongue out at Colin in response. ‘I didn’t say I was ready to give up, more like I don’t mind doing something different for a bit.’

‘When you’re ready to admit defeat, Jen, you know where I’ll be!’

Chapter Nineteen

DI Chris Jackson

'You okay, boss?' Greg asked as they began the now familiar walk across Nottingham towards Carbon's office.

'I think so,' Chris lied. His head was a mess. He now couldn't help but think Lyndsey had been sent in to commandeer his team and combine it with hers. The way she seemed to take over in the meeting … and her team wasn't even there. Maybe she should be concentrating on them more after the massive cock-up. Because what else could they have missed? Now he was being petty again. *You need to act professional and give her the fight of her life if she thinks she's going to push you out of a job*, he thought, gritting his teeth.

'Only think so?'

'Just tired, you know how it is. We seem to be getting nowhere with the case and the Sup is on my back …' Greg seemed to nod in agreement. 'Jen didn't seem too disappointed that she isn't off on this field trip, did she?' Chris asked, deciding to steer the conversation away from him and his life. If Greg knew half of the things that were going on with him at the moment, he'd switch into the fatherly figure mode; right now, he just needed him as a colleague and not someone else worrying about his health.

'Our Mr Jenkins seems to have really riled her up.'

'I noticed. I know she's been out of policing for a while,' Chris said, choosing his words carefully, 'and to come from high octane policing with Hannah to Nottingham's mean streets …'

'A slower pace of policing.'

'I'll say it again, Greg. I'd take Nottingham any day after working with them last year.'

Greg laughed as they continued to walk towards Carbon's offices. With every step Chris took he was conscious that he might trip and fall at any minute, and if Greg had already heard along the grapevine that he'd fallen the other day … Chris' mind was running at a hundred miles an hour and he'd started trying to second guess everything his body would do before it did. It was getting exhausting. He knew of toddlers that could walk without falling over. Why couldn't a grown man do the same?

'What's the plan, boss?' Greg asked, making him jump.

‘I think we just need to go in there and check he’s okay. Tell him we’re concerned about his safety after what happened at Carbon and at Flavor.’

‘It seems to be this secret partner, Samuel, that gets him on edge. I think that’s where he clashed mostly with Jen.’

‘Good point. Maybe we can just allude to it …’

Greg opened the door to the offices and Chris followed him in.

‘Detectives Jackson and Sanders. We’re here to see Mr Jenkins.’ Chris made their introductions to the receptionist.

‘Do you have an appointment?’ she asked.

‘Just tell him we’re here in a professional capacity.’

‘Okay, if you want to take a seat. I’ll call through to his office,’ the receptionist told them as they made their way over to the same old plastic chairs.

‘What’s the problem now?’ Karl Jenkins asked as he stormed out of the lift a little while after the receptionist had phoned through.

‘Mr Jenkins,’ Chris said, holding out his hand. ‘Is there somewhere we could talk in private?’

‘As I’m sure you’re aware, I’m very busy dealing with getting my business back off the ground, so unless you've caught the person responsible …’

‘My colleague and I wanted to come and talk to you about our concerns for your safety. To us, it’s increasingly looking like you could be the one being targeted.’

‘The only person giving me grief at the moment is that detective of yours. What’s her name again? Ah yes, Detective Garner.’

Chris noticed that Greg couldn’t help from smirking.

‘I’m sure you can understand our concerns, given what’s happened to Carbon and how you’ve since picked up a broken wrist.’ Chris tried to steer the conversation away from Jen.

‘As you can see, Detectives, my wrist is perfectly fine,’ Karl responded as he ran his hand over his plaster cast. ‘Now, if you excuse me, I’ve got work to do.’

‘Mr Jenkins, we would like to position an officer outside your house and have a clothed officer here for your safety.’

‘There’ll be no need for that.’

‘We’re only concerned for your well-being, and with this second incident …’ Greg joined in.

'Like I said, the only person targeting me right now is your detective, so if you could kindly get her off my back.'

'Still, Mr Jenkins… I would feel more reassured if there was one of my officers outside your house at least,' Chris said soothingly as he stole a look around the main reception where they were starting to draw an audience.

'Fine.' Karl seemed to be admitting defeat. 'You clearly know where I live, so position a car there if you must. But I'll not have one of your officers here. I have clients to think about.'

'Thank you.'

'But I don't want anything to do with them, and I don't want them too near the house.'

'You have my word, Mr Jenkins.'

Without another word, Karl turned and headed back towards the lift, leaving both Chris and Greg standing there watching him go.

'I think Jen has really got under his skin, boss,' Greg said, turning to Chris once he was sure they were no longer in earshot of anyone.

'I noticed that too, and it makes me wonder whether Jen can sense something more about him than we can.'

Greg nodded at the receptionist as they both headed out of the building and then turned back towards their offices.

'Greg, do me a favour, as I need to stay objective on this; when it's decided who's stationed outside the house, will you have a quiet word with them about our concerns for Mr Jenkins' partner?'

'Of course, boss. I was thinking the same, to be honest.'

'Let's keep it between us for now, eh?'

'So, team, how're we doing?' Chris asked as he walked into the office a little bit later on.

'Probably the same as when you left, boss … although Colin does now have an impressive online shopping trolley of items,' Julie said, standing up to greet him.

'I hope you've got something for me in that list, Colin?'

'Depends if you're planning on dying your hair boss, or starting a cleaning business.'

'I don't think my cleaners are too impressed with my current efforts, so maybe not a career change I should be considering.'

‘I’m just about to make a round of drinks. Chris, can I get you a coffee?’ Julie asked, spinning round to get the orders from the rest of the office.

‘Greg not come back with you, boss?’ Jen asked. Chris was unsure whether she was enquiring after her partner or just wanting to get the lowdown on Mr Jenkins.

‘He’s just popped in to speak to uniform. I’m guessing he should be back with us shortly.’ Chris knew there was no way he could lie. He couldn’t really say he was in the little boys’ room or something in case he reappeared in the office, declaring he had sorted stuff. Plus he wasn’t a very good liar, he knew that for sure; just good at pretending – or so he hoped. ‘If Julie is getting coffees, I guess I’d better gather all my stuff for our working lunch meeting in ten. Hopefully Greg will be back by then.’

Chris really didn’t know how much longer he could keep going like this. He was shattered, and what exactly had he done that day? It wasn’t like he and Hannah had got up to anything tiring the night before. He slept, she slept, they woke up together and went their separate ways. If they’d been up all night doing adult things, then he’d expect to feel as crap as he did. The more he researched, the more he learnt that fatigue was the most common symptom of his probable diagnosis and, oh God, was he feeling it. He had even gone as far as searching online for something he could take for it, but unless he was willing to buy prescription meds over the internet, there was no other option but to wait till he saw his neuro again … but how long would that be? How long did test results take to come in? Surely they could have seen instantly on his brain scans that something wasn’t right? He’d just have to sit in his office chair for the next ten minutes and close his eyes, hoping he could at least get five minutes, if that, of “quiet” time.

In what felt like an instant, it was time for Chris to get back to his team for their working lunch. When he arrived back in the office, they were all sitting down and chatting away to each other – he hoped about work, although there was nothing wrong with having a five-minute catch up about what had been on telly the previous night, of course. Having now decided it was the right time for him to put his glasses on, Chris found a chair, sat down and polished them with his shirt sleeves whilst waiting for the quiet to descend, signalling that his team were ready to roll. He had decided to not tell Lyndsey about the meeting; it wasn’t that important and she didn’t need to be involved. They were in charge of the criminal investigation whilst she and her team were supposed to be concentrating on the venue side of things anyway.

'Boss, spoke to uniform and they're arranging for a car to be parked outside Mr Jenkins' house every night from 6 p.m. till whenever Mr Jenkins goes to work the next morning.'

'Great. Thank you, Greg.'

'What happens if he decides to spend the night in a hotel, boss?' Jen questioned, clearly already seeing potential flaws in their plan.

'I don't think there's anything we can do, Jen. He didn't particularly want us there at all when Greg and I spoke to him.'

Jen sighed and returned to flicking through the hundreds of photos she had yet to view.

'Do we think we should ask him to inform us when he isn't going home?' Greg questioned, making Jen's head pop back up from her monitor.

'I suppose we could attempt to, but he definitely didn't want anyone at his workplace. Also, if you remember, he didn't seem that convinced about the idea that someone could be targeting him personally. Unless it was one of our own ...' Chris said, looking pointedly towards Jen.

'I'll give him a ring, boss. You never know, he might have warmed to me,' Greg replied as Jen almost spat her drink out laughing.

'I don't think he likes anyone, Greg, so good luck on that one,' Jen remarked as she mopped up the split tea.

'Colin. The Dales – what's their favourite ice cream?'

'Sorry, boss?'

'Thought you were about to give us an in-depth profile of the family.'

'Ah no. Sorry, boss. Been too busy doing a bit of internet shopping ... and I got strangely distracted by Danielle's Instagram page.'

'Been looking at pretty women again, have we, Colin?' Trudie asked from the back of the room.

'Worryingly, yes. Although this one is supposed to be a lawyer in training.'

'She's of the Instagram generation, I suppose,' Julie commented.

'You know those people who are born blonde and pretty who refuse to be stereotyped as a "dumb blonde" so go on to have high-powered careers just to prove they aren't stupid? Family aside, I'm wondering if that's her,' Colin mused.

'Maybe.'

‘Think the film *Legally Blonde*,’ Trudie joined in.

‘Isn’t that about getting a dog rights, or is that the second one?’

‘Wait, I’ll look that one up,’ Trudie responded as she pulled up IMDB to check.

‘While those two are busy with their pop culture searching, anyone got anything of interest from this morning's work?’ Chris asked. For some reason, he felt almost tempted to swing back on his chair, but decided not to risk it – for obvious reasons.

‘Colin knows where to buy twenty-five litres of peroxide from,’ Trudie spoke up as she scooted her chair to be closer to where Chris was sitting.

‘Thinking of starting a hairdressing business, Colin?’

‘Might be a viable career choice. It wouldn’t cost me as much to get Lizzie’s hair done then.’

‘Oh, domestic bliss,’ Chris responded in a dreamy-like voice to chuckles from his team. ‘Other than saving you money, Detective?’

‘To be honest, boss, I found it quite worrying how easy it is to buy materials you could use to make a bomb.’

‘You wait till you hit the sites telling you exactly how to make one,’ Jen said darkly, also moving closer to join the team.

‘So Colin … your next step?’ Chris asked, hoping that Colin could think on his feet.

‘Other than my hairdressing business?’

The joke wasn’t funny any more, but Chris knew that maybe he was being a bit too hard on the team when they were so used to taking his direction. With the way he was feeling, the fall and Lyndsey seemingly trying to push her way in, he needed to prepare them all for the worst.

‘I suppose I follow up on my call to the website, asking if they’ve had any orders recently that have been delivered in the local area?’

‘Gold star, Colin,’ Maybe his team were better prepared than he gave them credit for.

‘I can tell you now, Chris, I have no idea where Karl got the money for Carbon from,’ Julie cut in. ‘No lottery win, no signs of inheritances from either his parents or Samuel’s.’

‘So he rocked up at an estate agent with, what? Possibly a quarter of million? To buy a rundown venue that later goes on to become a prime location.’

‘Yes, I’ve looked, and I can’t find any mortgage on the property. Karl is the only person listed on Companies House as a director.’

‘There was no way he was being that well paid while working for the Dales either. Bar managers don’t earn that much, do they?’ Colin questioned as he pulled out his phone, no doubt to search for bar manager salaries.

‘It just doesn’t make sense to me where this money came from and why he left Dale’s in the first place.’ Julie looked like someone who had spent hours searching for something that she wasn’t going to find.

‘I might have something,’ Trudie responded triumphantly.

‘Anything that would move this case forward would be great around about now,’ Chris responded, noticing the tired faces of his team.

‘According to the people I’ve spoken to, once upon a time Karl and Matt used to be best mates, and, if one person is to be believed, they both ran Dale’s together quite happily.’

‘Well, that *is* an interesting turn of events.’

‘Yep, they were best of pals, were both known on the clubbing scene … then it just stopped.’

‘Stopped. What do you mean?’

‘Karl and Matt were no longer seen together, either in the pub or out on the town.’

‘Woah, from BFFs to nothing?’ Colin spoke up.

‘And no one knows why. Carbon was opened approximately six months after Karl left Dale’s. One day Karl was there, and the next he wasn’t.’

‘Something has to have gone off between the pair of them,’ Chris mused as he tapped his pen on his teeth.

‘If I may throw something into the ring, boss?’ Colin piped up as the silence dragged on.

‘Be my guest.’

‘What if something happened that made Matt flip and decide to blow up Carbon? Call it revenge, jealousy, a lost love, I don’t know …?’

‘I must admit, boss, I’m struggling to find anyone else in these pictures that shouldn’t be there,’ Jen cut in, seemingly backing up Colin’s theory.

‘Karl wasn’t at the McDermitts’ gig, so he wouldn’t have let Matt into the club for starters,’ Trudie joined in.

'You're telling me that Matt got into the club, retrieved the explosives from the backroom window, walked to the back of the crowd and threw them in?'

'I guess so, boss, and whether Flavor was Matt's second attempt or some copy-cat idiot trying to be clever ...?'

Chris stood up and walked over to the board at the front of the room. 'I guess this fits in with the theory that someone is targeting Karl, but why? If he and Matt used to be best of friends?'

'As I mentioned when we were at the house, Matt came across as a little child being told off by Daddy, but the guy we all saw during the press conference was very different,' Julie reminded them.

'I think I agree with you, Julie. It fits with how he was at the bar the other night.' Colin nodded.

'Okay, team,' Chris said, trying to calm the new excitement down. 'But why do it in the first place? We've got the potential suspect. Now let's find the evidence.'

Chapter Twenty

Jen Garner

'Right team, get to it,' was the last thing Chris had said to them before he disappeared, probably to his office or wherever he went these days. There was no way this was the DI Chris Jackson she'd worked with last year, or the one who'd hunted her down. Something was clearly going on, but what and was she really in a position to bring anything up? Yes, she was outgoing, driven and confident, but she also didn't want to step on anyone else's toes so soon into her new job. Who usually took the reins when Chris vanished for no reason? … Julie?

'Julie, is Chris, okay?' Jen asked hesitantly, making sure no one else was in hearing range first.

'What do you mean?'

'He just seems … distant and noncommittal. He literally told us to find evidence and then wandered off!'

'I think he's got a lot on his mind at the moment, and no doubt the Superintendent is breathing down his neck.'

'Guess I hadn't thought of that. He just seems different … it's not quite how I imagined working with him would be, you know … after last year?'

'We both know how much he put into that case, and he will again with this one. We just don't get to see what's going on behind the scenes sometimes …'

Jen acknowledged Julie with a "hmmm" and Julie made to move away.

'I've just heard back from Chem-Cell, and they had an order for a large amount of peroxide earlier this month. They're looking through their records as we speak,' Colin announced, breaking the comfortable silence that seemed to have descended in the office.

'Great news, Colin,' Jen answered, hoping this might be a lead they could follow up on. 'Did they give you a time-scale?'

'She says that she remembers the order coming in because she queried with her bosses if they were allowed to send such a large amount out.'

'Wow … okay, well, if she's got the payment details too, that'll be even better.'

'Already on that one.'

'My sources really do seem to confirm that something big kicked off between the Dales and Karl,' Trudie spoke up.

'I'm wondering if we need to take a trip to the pub for a lunchtime drink?' Greg suggested.

'I'm game if you are.' Jen decided that going out for a quick pint, or in her case wine, might make things clearer. 'Do we need to let Chris know first and check that it's okay with him?' Jen added, unsure what protocol was.

'I'll cover for you,' Julie offered. 'I'm sure he'll be fine with it if it means we get this case solved sooner.'

'Trudie, you coming too?'

'Nah. I'm going to keep digging and see what pops up. Thanks though, Greg.'

'Anyone else?' Greg asked, making sure he'd included everyone in the "escape to the pub".

'Bring me back some crackling,' Colin piped up, just as Greg followed Jen out of the office.

Jen and Greg made their way into an almost deserted Dale's where the barman was standing playing on his phone while another member of staff cleaned tables.

'Bit busy in here,' Greg joked as the barman finally looked away from his phone and acknowledged them.

'Yeah, always like this at the beginning of the week. I don't know why we stay open, if I'm honest with you. What can I get you guys?'

'Half a pint of mild, please. Jen?'

'Just a Coke please.'

'With ice and lemon?'

'Please.'

'Thought you said you were having a wine?' Greg raised his eyebrows.

'Yeah, well ... probably not the best idea on a school day.'

They watched as the barman slipped his phone back into his pocket and went about pouring their drinks.

'Been working here long?' Greg asked as the barman placed his pint in front of him and went back for Jen's.

'Just while I'm at uni. It's easy money.'

‘Especially when it’s this quiet, I guess! But, generally speaking, what’s it like working at the famous Dale’s pub?’

‘It’s okay. Depends on which side you catch the owner, and if his dad’s been in!’ The barman answered

‘The famous Dale Senior?’ Jen asked.

‘You mean infamous?’ came his reply.

‘Weren’t the McDermitts playing here when they were discovered?’ Greg joined in.

‘So the story goes … bit before my time though.’

‘It’s scary to think what those guys must’ve witnessed standing on that stage at Carbon.’

‘I know, and the amount of death and destruction that followed. I don’t think I’ll be watching gigs there again any time soon,’ the barman responded, becoming animated.

‘Bet you're glad you didn’t go?’ Jen asked, trying her best to get something out of this visit.

‘Yeah, before everything kicked off I’d have loved to. I couldn’t get a ticket so came to work instead.’

‘Many in that night?’

‘Prior to the gig, but once that started we were dead. Even Matt Dale gave up and went home early.’ The barman laughed. ‘Left the tidying up to the minions.’ Jen glanced over at Greg and a knowing look passed between them. This was a piece of information they definitely needed to report back.

Greg picked up his pint and followed Jen to a seat near the window, where they could watch the bar and the outside world going by.

‘Interesting place,’ Jen commented as she looked around. ‘Don’t think I’ve been here before. Doesn’t look like I’m missing much either.’

Greg laughed. ‘I’m surprised Colin doesn’t remember Karl working here. He must have been here in his partying days.’

‘Ah, but I bet he doesn’t remember much of it. You know the young – down as many cheap drinks as they can then head off to the nearest club?’

‘Well, looks like their options are going to be pretty slim for a while.’

Jen decided it would be the right time to check and see if she had any messages from the family or any important calls she’d missed.

‘Can you imagine your two coming here for a night out?’ Greg asked, distracting her from her scrolling.

'God, I don't even want to think about it.' Jen laughed. 'Melanie already has the attitude for it, and I get blamed as James tells me she only takes after her mother!'

'I can see where he's coming from.' Greg laughed as Jen gave him a playful nudge.

'Good afternoon, Detectives. To what do I owe this pleasure?' Matt said as he seemed to appear out of nowhere.

'Matt,' Greg said as he stood up to shake his hand.

'I heard you two talking shop with my barman, so I thought I'd better come and introduce myself.'

'We've come in for a sneaky pint. You know, get away from the office for a bit?'

'Anyone would think you guys were spying on me. Your other detective was in here the other day. What was his name? I forget now.'

'Oh, we're just keeping an eye on things, making sure the pub is safe,' Jen replied quickly, glad that they had the excuse of Matt's press conference stunt.

'It's a shame that it's taken something like what happened up the road to bring you guys out into the open,' Matt replied.

'We're always watching, don't you worry,' she responded as Matt laughed and turned away to head back towards the bar, where his barman was now cleaning up and most *definitely* not playing on his phone.

'Not sure how we're going to get much info now that Matt has appeared,' Jen said, taking a mouthful of her drink.

'At least we can report back what we've found out.'

'Wait … that's the office,' Jen said picking her phone up off the table and reading a message that had just come in. 'We need to head back. Colin's got something.'

DI Chris Jackson

'Nice of you both to re-join us,' Chris greeted Jen and Greg as they strolled casually back into the office.

'What's cracking? The message sounded urgent,' Jen said, clearly keen to know what was happening.

'The internet company came back with a delivery address and credit card details,' Colin answered, sitting up straighter in his chair.

'And …?'

'This is where it gets interesting.' Chris raised his eyebrows.

'Greg and I better get back to our desks then,' Jen replied as she crossed the office. 'We have news too, so yours better be groundbreaking.'

'I'm quaking in my pants,' Colin joked.

'Okay, children …' Chris addressed his bickering team. He turned to Colin.

'The internet company came back and said that they'd delivered the peroxide to an industrial unit in Lenton.' Colin stopped for dramatic affect. 'The card was in the name of K Jenkins.'

'*Shit.*' Jen momentarily closed her eyes. 'I want to say I didn't see that one coming.'

'So Jen … beat that!' Colin teased.

'Our news isn't *as* groundbreaking, but the barman at Dale's just told us Matt left early when the McDermitts played Carbon. Which I guess isn't as earth shattering now as it would've been ten minutes ago.'

'Team, we're at a cross roads. According to Samuel, Karl was in bed with him at the time of the explosion,' Chris summarised. 'We've a photo of Matt backstage where he shouldn't have been, and Greg and Jen have just confirmed that he left Dale's early that night.'

'Do we know who owns the industrial unit?' Jen asked.

'Just chasing that up now with the landlord,' Trudie replied, looking up from her computer.

'Didn't the duty manager from that night confirm to us, Jen, that Karl wasn't at the venue on the evening of the McDermitts' gig?' Greg cut in.

'She did, which puts a dampener on my argument that Samuel could be lying to protect his partner.'

'But the internet company confirmed that the credit card was registered to K Jenkins, so that's got to mean something,' Colin argued.

'Okay, settle down,' Chris interrupted. 'There's something else we haven't found out yet. We still don't know why Karl left Dale's all those years ago, and where the money came from to buy the venue.'

'Let's get him in here then, show him the evidence from the internet company and demand answers,' Jen spoke up, still just as keen to have it out with Karl.

'But what if Karl and Matt are working together? We get one of them in here and the other one goes on a rampage with whatever explosives they've got left?' Julie was the voice of reason, as always.

‘Julie’s right,’ Chris said as everyone got animated, throwing their opinions into the ring. ‘Anything, Trudie?’

‘Well, personally, I’d have liked to have been the one to pull the rabbit out of the hat, but guess who the lock-up is also being paid for by?’

‘K Jenkins.’ This time they all responded in unison.

‘I think we need to get our Mr Jenkins in here for a chat,’ Chris said once the noise had died down.

‘What are we waiting for then?’ Jen stood up.

‘Can I suggest that someone goes and sees Matt at the same time? Like Julie said, if they’re working together and the other one finds out …’ Colin interrupted Jen’s obvious growing excitement

‘Okay, this is how we’re going to roll. Greg and I will invite Karl for a chat and will conduct the interview. Jen, you take Colin and visit Dale’s, have a chat with Matt about Carbon and about Karl’s time there.’

‘Are we okay mentioning the photo, boss?’

‘Don’t see why not, but use your best judgement, because there might be a reasonable explanation as to why he was there.’

‘Even though he wasn’t on any of those lists …’ Colin muttered.

‘Trudie, Julie. If one of you could watch the interview in the recording suite and the other keep on with the research and take any appropriate actions necessary?’

‘Okay, Chris,’ they both echoed.

‘Everyone happy?’ Chris regretted asking because he knew Jen would want to be at the forefront of the action with Mr Jenkins. But he needed to keep her contained for now …

Chapter Twenty-One

Jen Garner

'Take a seat, Detectives,' Matt said as he led both Colin and Jen into his office.

'Thank you for agreeing to see us at such short notice.' Jen pulled out a chair. Matt's office was pretty much how she imagined: calendar of topless women – check, notice boards full of A4 sheets – check, CCTV cameras flickering in the corner – check, coffee-stained desk – check, comfy office chair – check. His office couldn't be more stereotypical if it tried.

'It's my pleasure. I'm sorry I didn't get a chance to talk much when you and the other detective were in here earlier.'

'We just needed to get away from the boss for a while. He's a bit of an—'

'Arse,' Colin jumped in.

'I understand, Detectives. You're both welcome in here anytime. Now what can I help you with?'

'We were hoping that you might be able to give us some information on Karl Jenkins?' Jen watched as Matt's face suddenly looked really confused.

'What sort of information are you looking for?'

'When we spoke to you on Saturday your father mentioned that Karl used to work here as a bar manager and, to be honest, we're wondering why he left.' Colin cut to the chase.

'I think that's obvious: he moved on to bigger and better things.'

'We were just a little bit surprised at the massive jump from being a bar manager to owning something as big as Carbon?'

'Well, it's not like there's anything left to own now, is there really?'

'If you want to look at it that way.' Colin raised his eyebrows.

'What was he like to work with?' Jen jumped in.

'Who, Karl?'

'Yes, we understand you two used to get on really well.'

'We did in work, you know the odd bit of banter, but Karl came into some money and decided that the grass was greener on the other side.'

'And was it?'

'Clearly not now.'

'Are you two still friends then?'

'No, not really. He doesn't come in here any more since he left.'

'That's strange, if you two were such good mates.'

'Exactly: *were*. Anyway, my dad didn't like him much and, as he was running the business at the time, he always had the last word,' Matt said, reaching for an empty glass on his desk. 'Can I get either of you a drink?' he offered as he rose from his chair.

'I'm good, thank you. Colin?' Jen asked as she exchanged glances with her partner at this possibly staged interruption to the questioning.

'If you excuse me both, I'm just going to pop down to the bar. I won't be two seconds.' Matt left the office, and Jen and Colin sat there looking at each other in a confused sort of way. They both knew better than to discuss the case while a potential suspect was out of the room.

'How're things with Lizzie?' Jen asked, desperately trying to grab something to talk about other than the case.

'She's good, thank you. Cassie is being a nightmare at the moment, but you know yourself what small children are like.' As Colin spoke, Jen continued to exchange looks with him. She nodded, motioning for him to keep it going until Matt returned. She realised they couldn't leave him on his own, just in case he found out about what was happening with Karl.

'Ah yes, when does she start school?'

'Next September. Lizzie says it can't come soon enough.'

'Then I guess it'll be time to start thinking about another one to add to the family. You know, a little brother or sister?'

'Lizzie isn't keen, but I'm working on her,' Colin said, lifting his shoulders into a shrug at the same time.

'Ah, but it would be lovely for Cassie to have someone to play with.' Jen was now using all the lines that had previously been used with her when she'd had Melanie. Luckily, just at that point, she was cut off.

'Sorry about that, Detectives. I just needed to refresh my glass,' Matt said, returning to the office with a pint in hand. 'Where were we?'

'We were just asking about Karl Jenkins and his time working here,' Colin reminded him.

'Ah yes, there isn't really much I can tell you about that, I'm afraid.'

'Karl didn't offer you a job at Carbon then?'

'He tried, but I wasn't interested. I was about to inherit this place.'

'How are you finding stepping into your father's shoes?'

'It's been good. I just need to get him to let go of the strings now and let me get on with running the business.'

'If I remember rightly, your mother seemed to think that would be sooner rather than later?' Colin prompted.

'Yes, my father isn't getting any younger, and he needs to start enjoying life and not worrying about this place.'

'Can I just ask you, Matt, about what happened at Carbon on Thursday night?'

'Of course. Such an awful incident, and for something similar to happen at Flavor as well. Anyone would think someone was targeting Karl,' Matt said with a chuckle, leaving both Jen and Colin even more confused about what was so funny.

'Did you attend the gig, Matt? I don't remember seeing you on any of the ticket holder lists we were given,' Jen probed.

'Yes, I popped in to say hello to the band and congratulate them on their success.'

'That'll be why you weren't on the ticket holder list then?'

'I know some of the door security. They also work here on gig nights, so they let me sneak in.'

'Were you not injured by the explosives?'

'Oh no, I'd left by then.'

'Ah okay,' Jen replied, trying to decide which way to take the line of questioning next.

'Have there been any rumblings in the trade about who might have blown it up?' Colin asked.

'Not that I am aware of … but it's obvious, isn't it?'

'Humour us.'

'Karl Jenkins, of course. One great big insurance job.'

'What, and kill and maim people in the process?'

'The only person Karl cares about is Karl and his back pocket.'

Matt certainly isn't lying on that point, Jen thought grimly.

'But why go on and cause trouble at Flavor?'

'To cover his own arse? I heard from one of the bar guys he sustained an injury in the process of that one.'

'Broken wrist so we heard.' Colin nodded, glancing over towards Jen.

'Has Dale's lost many bookings since the events at Carbon?' Jen decided to ask, knowing full well what had been said at the press conference and at Senior's house.

‘No. In fact we’ve been gaining them, if I’m honest with you. Everyone is looking for somewhere to play now Carbon is a pile of dust and Dale’s is stepping back into the limelight,’ Matt said with poorly concealed excitement in his voice. ‘Like my father said, I overstepped the mark at the press conference and I would still very much like to apologise to your DI for that.’

‘We’ll pass on your apologies.’ Jen made to stand up, ‘Well, I think that’s everything, Mr Dale. You’ve been very helpful.’

‘No, no, it’s the least I can do, given the chaos I’ve already caused,’ Matt said as he stood up to shake Colin and Jen’s hands. ‘If there’s anything else I can help you with, or you’d like to speak to my father about Karl’s employment, please feel free to contact me.’

‘Thank you. We shall bear that in mind,’ Jen said as she turned to follow Colin from the room, expecting Matt to follow – but he didn’t, leaving them to wander around looking for an exit.

‘Hope you remember the way out of here?’ Colin turned to ask.

‘I think we need to head for the stairs ...’

‘I’m sure if we get lost we can call for backup,’ Colin laughed.

‘Yeah, and never be able to live it down, you mean?’

DI Chris Jackson

‘Mr Jenkins, if you could please take a seat. I’ll just get the recording equipment set up,’ Greg instructed as Chris placed the cups of coffee on the table.

‘I think this is over the top and totally unnecessary,’ Karl barked at them.

‘Mr Jenkins, this is for both your and our protection,’ Chris soothed.

‘But I haven’t done anything wrong! When will you get that into your thick skulls?’

‘Then you’ll be up and out of here in no time.’

‘I only agreed to come in to get you off my back and away from the front of my house.’

‘All set up,’ Greg interrupted, taking his seat next to Chris.

‘In the room is myself, DI Chris Jackson, my colleague, DC Greg Sanders, and Karl Jenkins, who has declined legal representation at this time,’ Chris spoke into the tape.

‘I don’t need legal representation,’ Karl muttered.

‘Karl Jenkins, you are under arrest on the suspicion of the murder of twenty-two people on Thursday seventh June—’ Greg began

‘This is stupid,’ came Karl’s response while Greg continued the speech.

‘Before we begin, Mr Jenkins, can you just confirm that this is your signature, please?’ Chris asked, producing a sheet Karl had signed only moments earlier.

‘Of course it is. You saw me signing it, you idiots.’

‘Brilliant. Can you confirm where you were on the night of seventh June?’

‘I was at home.’

‘Can anyone confirm your whereabouts?’

‘Yes.’

‘Would you please confirm who this person is?’ Chris could already sense that this would not be an easy interview.

‘No.’

Chris decided he’d let that one go, as both he and Greg already knew who it would be.

‘As you will know, Carbon, your live music entertainment venue, was subject to an attack which left twenty-two people dead and others injured—’

‘Yes, can we just get to the point?’ Karl interrupted.

‘Karl, do you know how to make an explosive device?’ Greg asked.

They’d decided that he’d ask the big questions so Chris could watch out for how Karl reacted, but right now he wasn’t giving Chris anything. They wanted Karl to think that Greg was stupid.

‘No,’ came the answer they were expecting.

‘Have you ever, let’s say, looked it up?’

‘No. What would I want to know that for?’

‘Do you own any other properties, Karl? Any garages, lockups, hairdressers maybe?’

‘As you know full well, I own Carbon and I started renting the office space after Carbon became too small to house my expanding staff.’ Karl couldn’t resist a subtle boast, even here.

‘So no investments in any other businesses?’

‘No! Why are you asking these stupid questions that you clearly already know the answers to?’

‘We’re trying to build a picture of your property portfolio,’ Chris responded, hoping that seemed a good enough reason for Greg’s questions.

‘In that case, I also own a house part mortgaged in Hinkley, which you’ve been to already.’

‘Do you know any hairdressers?’ Greg asked.

‘Only my barber? What sort of questions are these? I thought I was here to talk about my business, which you’ve already pointed out was attacked.’

‘Karl, do you use the internet company Chem-Cell for anything?’

‘Not that I know of … never heard of them.’

Greg reached into the folder that Karl had been looking at suspiciously on and off since the interview started. ‘Mr Jenkins, we have an order here made from your credit card for six two-litre bottles of peroxide.’

‘What? I’ve never ordered anything like….’ Then it seemed to click. ‘Hang on, you think I ordered peroxide to make explosives or something … to blow up my own club!’

‘Your name is on the invoice and receipt, Mr Jenkins, and a credit card in your name was used to pay for it.’

‘Then you need to speak to the bank because someone has cloned my card.’

‘See, this was a newly opened credit card account, Karl, with the U Credit Company?’

‘This isn’t me! Someone is pretending to be me,’ Karl tried to argue.

‘While we were investigating where this peroxide was delivered to, we also discovered the unit you own, Mr Jenkins.’

‘What?’

‘The unit, which you have rented for six months,’ Greg said, sliding the second piece of paper over.

‘This isn’t me either.’

‘But the signatures match, Mr Jenkins.’

‘Yes, but like the peroxide, it’s nothing to do with me. Someone else is using my identity.’

‘You see, Karl, us detectives like to be very thorough when we investigate these sorts of things, so we spoke to the letting agent at the unit and he described you exactly: your mannerisms, your arrogance and rudeness down to a tee,’ Chris told him.

'But it wasn't me!'

'Who was it then?' Chris shouted.

'I have no idea, but I'm being framed.' Karl stopped to take a breath. 'Hang on, but you know I wasn't at the venue when the explosions happened.'

'You weren't there, no, but you could've easily been working with someone.'

'I'm not … I mean I'm being set up! I keep telling you this.'

'We haven't released this information for obvious reasons, Mr Jenkins, but we now know how the explosives got into the club, so you could've easily left them for someone else to pick up and throw into the crowd to cause maximum impact.'

'What the hell!?'

'And what happened at Flavor, Karl?' Greg asked. 'Did you try to blow somewhere else up and get caught in the crossfire?'

'Why the hell would I?'

'Well, this is it, Mr Jenkins. Though we are yet to work out why you decided to blow your own business up, we strongly suspect that you tried to throw us off the scent by targeting Flavor, hoping it would be classed as a homophobic attack.'

'Someone is clearly targeting *me*.'

'You see, there's a problem with that scenario, Mr Jenkins. Myself and my officers have been trying to offer you protection ever since this first happened and you've been completely uncooperative. Now we are showing you the evidence that makes you a possible suspect you are screaming and shouting that you're being targeted. Which one is it?' Chris was getting really fed up now and just wanted this man out of his sight.

'I've been trying to protect myself from you guys and look what's happened.'

'If you'd been cooperative in the first place, I think we'd be more inclined to believe that there was no way it could be you.'

Karl didn't have a response for that one. 'Look, I was at home in bed with my partner at the time Carbon was attacked. He'll provide me with an alibi.'

'Is this the mystery person you mentioned at the beginning of the interview?'

'Yes, and before you say it, I'm not the master mind. It's not that somebody else is attacking these places for me either.'

'Okay, Mr Jenkins, I think it's best we take a break,' Greg said, gathering up the papers. 'An officer will escort you back to the cells.'

'There's no way I'm going in one of those things.'

'I strongly suggest you source some legal representation, Mr Jenkins, because this isn't going away.'

Karl just looked at them in totally bemusement.

'Interview terminated at 3 p.m.,' Chris said, reaching over to stop the recording.

'So … what are your thoughts?' Chris said as he walked back to the office with Greg.

'I don't know, boss. *Could* someone be using his identity?'

'The landlord at the unit seemed pretty positive it was him when he handed over the keys.'

'Maybe it's time to have a look inside this unit and meet said landlord?'

'Yeah, I was just thinking that. And maybe we should take the bomb squad along with us … just in case.'

Chapter Twenty-Two

Jen Garner

'Team, I'm going to keep this quick. Greg is on the phone to the bomb squad as we speak.'

'Has he confessed?' Jen immediately asked.

'No, he's denying everything. I've contacted the landlord at the unit and he's going to let us in for a look round.'

'Can he do that?' Jen questioned.

'He said he can, so right now I'm not going to argue with him if it gets us in without having to go to court for a warrant,' Chris replied. 'How did it go with Matt?'

'Hmm, it was interesting. He claims that the security team let him into the venue so Colin is just on the phone trying to get confirmation from Clarissa, who was the duty manager that night, and a list of door staff so we can start ringing around.'

'Great. Let me know how you get on. I'll be on my phone if you need me.'

'Will do.'

Chris turned and left the room and his remaining team members to their tasks, which now mainly revolved around trying to prove Matt's whereabouts.

'Julie.' Jen scooted over to her colleague's desk

'Hmm?'

'You saw Chris just then, didn't you?'

'Yeah … why, hun? What's up?'

'Is it just me or does he look better than he has done all week? The spark seems to be back!'

'Not that I noticed. Maybe it's just that the case is at last moving in the right direction and is starting to pick up some steam?' Julie suggested.

'We're into the closing act, you mean?'

'Hopefully all the main players are in place, and no one misses their cue.'

They'd been outside the unit on the Lenton industrial estate for the past thirty minutes, waiting for not only the bomb squad but also for the landlord. If anyone had been watching, they would have had the press on their backs. The secret wasn't out yet.

'Ah, here we go,' Chris muttered as he noticed the bomb squad's truck arrive, followed by a beaten-up Merc, which was obviously the landlord.

'Detective Jackson.' Chris held his hand out to the military man who marched over from the van.

'Can we get this over with?' A short man followed, shouting at the top of his lungs.

'Mr Southyard,' Greg said as he moved over towards the landlord to try and calm his rage.

'What have you got for us, Detective?' The army officer seemed to be doing his best to ignore what was going on with the landlord.

'Suspected bomb making factory.'

'It's not every day we see one of those in an industrial unit.'

'Well, we've got a suspected ready-made one right here for you,' Chris replied. 'Mr Southyard, if you could pass me the keys, please?'

'If you can let my guys enter the facility first, we can assess the situation before endangering any more lives.'

'Not a problem, Officer,' Chris said, standing back and letting the team do their work.

'I never imagined when I hired the unit to the guy I'd end up letting the bomb squad in six months later,' Mr Southyard muttered as they watched from a distance.

'I don't think any of us planned on standing around here when we all got up this morning,' Greg quipped as a machine that looked like something from *Star Wars* was manoeuvred out of the back of the van and straight into the unit.

'The number of times I've watched this happen in my career, Greg, and it never gets less surreal when R2D2 comes rolling out the back of their van.'

'It really is like something from a sci-fi film,' Mr Southyard observed. 'The machines are taking over the world.'

'Inspector Jackson,' the army officer shouted from his command position.

‘That’s me.’ Chris was pleased to excuse himself from the impending discussion about sci-fi movies. He moved over to where the officer was positioned with his bank of computer screens. ‘What have you got for me?’

‘Inspector, what we have here is nothing short of an evil scientist’s lab.’

‘One capable of making APEX?’

‘Oh, I’m certain of that … but what’s left here now are the waste products from the looks of things.’ The officer looked grave. ‘Follow me, Inspector and I can show you,’ he said as he marched towards the building. The first thing Chris noticed was the sickly-sweet smell and then the discarded containers of assorted chemicals, Bunsen burners and various other chemistry equipment.

‘I don’t think my school was ever this well-equipped,’ Chris murmured as he peered into the unit.

‘I’m afraid we’re seeing these set-ups more and more, Inspector,’ the officer explained, leading Chris further into the unit.

‘Is it safe to enter?’ Chris asked cautiously.

‘As far as we can tell. The explosives look to no longer be on the premises.’

‘The more scary question is where the hell are they then?’

‘That, Inspector, is your job to work out.’

‘I guess that’s our next step,’ Chris said, holding out his hand.

‘I’ll get my guys to remove anything potentially dangerous and return the site to yourselves.’

‘Thanks.’ Chris retrieved his phone and took a couple of snaps of the inside of the unit, and then returned to find Greg and Mr Southyard.

‘Everything okay, boss?’ Greg asked as he noticed Chris walking back towards them.

‘Well, depends how you look at it. Luckily for us, there isn’t anything dangerous in there at the moment.’

‘Can I see how much damage the idiot has done to my unit?’ Mr Southyard asked, starting to head over.

‘That might not be the best idea. We don’t want you contaminating evidence,’ Chris said, quickly standing in front of him.

‘But some maniac has been making explosive devices on my property!’

‘The property is now in the possession of the Nottingham Special Ops unit, Mr Southyard. You have nothing to worry about.’

‘Great.’ He sighed. ‘I won’t be making back lost income anytime soon.’

‘You informed my officer, Mr Southyard, that the current occupant rented the property six months in advance?’ Greg interrupted.

‘Yes, but that isn’t the point.’ Mr Southyard started marching across the courtyard towards his car. ‘Call my office when I can have the keys back.’

‘I’ll go after him, boss,’ Greg said, obviously noticing the worried look on Chris’ face.

‘Ask him to look at the photo of Karl again and see if we can get a positive ID.’

‘Will do.’

Chris looked around at the other buildings that surrounded the unit – a car showroom, a recycling plant – all places that would no doubt have gone up as well if their bomber had made a mistake. *The fire service would have been battling to control the blaze for weeks*, he thought grimly.

‘Mr Jenkins.’ Chris walked into the interview room with Julie following behind later on that day. Greg had been left to arrange an unmarked car to be stationed close to the unit in case someone unexpectedly turned up. He’d also managed to calm the landlord down and told him he needed to keep what was going on in the unit quiet until they had caught the mystery renter – just in case he managed to tip someone off and they had another incident on their hands.

‘Inspector, have you come to tell me this is all a mistake and I can go home now?’ The Karl Jenkins sitting there in the interview room seemed a very different man. He appeared to have lost his fake confidence and bravado. Chris couldn’t help but notice how his previously perfectly ironed clothes were now creased and untucked, and his hair was all over the place, making Chris grateful he’d put gel in his own that morning.

‘I’m afraid not, Mr Jenkins,’ Chris said, almost missing the seat as he sat down. ‘Interview with Mr Karl Jenkins resuming at 6 p.m. on Monday eleventh of June. In the room is …’ Chris continued to run through the procedures.

'Mr Jenkins, I take it you've decided not to seek legal advice?' Julie asked, once he'd finished.

'I keep telling you people. I've done nothing wrong.'

'Okay, Mr Jenkins. We've just got back from Lenton and the unit you claim to have not rented, and I wanted you to look at some photos.' As Chris spoke, Julie produced the photos from the same brown folder and laid them on the table in front of Karl. The man looked at them and then at the detectives, and then back again.

'Is this what I think it is?' he asked.

'Depends on what you think it is,' Chris responded.

'This is where the explosives were made to blow up my club, isn't it?' Karl slid down his chair.

'You tell us, Mr Jenkins?'

'How many times do I need to tell you that it's got nothing to do with me!' Karl straightened up again.

'Then you need to give us something, because right now you're our number one suspect.'

'But I keep telling you! I was at home with my partner at the time of the explosions, so I couldn't have set them off.'

'Then who are you working with?' Chris probed. 'Because it seems a little strange to me that on Thursday night, instead of staying to watch the band as you normally do, you left early.'

'I wasn't in the mood for partying. I just handed over to my duty manager and went home instead.' Karl looked down at his hands. 'Surely there isn't anything wrong with that?'

'But according to your staff, it's totally unlike you.'

'Then there's the incident at Flavor …' Julie continued, taking over from Chris' questioning.

'Which I was very much injured during. You know, my broken wrist?' Karl said, raising his arm to remind the detectives it was still broken. 'Plus, if I remember rightly, there were two loud bangs. How could I have let them both off?'

Though this would not help the case, Karl had at least now confessed he'd been at Flavor at the time of the false alarm and also backed up what the manager had said.

'So why go to so much trouble to hide?'

'Oh, come on, Inspector. People talk. I was in a gay club, next thing you know they'll be splashing my personal life all over the papers ...'

Karl was right in some respects that he'd have been sold down the river, being the boss of a big music entertainment venue who clearly worked so hard on his macho image and persona.

'Tell us about your time working at Dale's,' Julie said in her calm, relaxed voice; the voice she used when trying to convince people she was on their side.

'Ha!' Karl spat. 'A barrel of laughs, that was. Did you know that before all of this, before Carbon, I was going to be the one to take over and run that place? Not that spineless son of his.'

'You and Matt had some form of falling out? Because, from what we've been hearing, you two were best of friends. So what happened?' Julie continued to probe carefully.

'That was in the past.'

'Doesn't Matt frequently come into Carbon though?'

'Not on my watch.'

'He was there the night of the explosions.'

'Lucky for him. Hope he sustained life-changing injuries.'

'Mr Jenkins!' Now Julie was putting on her schoolteacher voice.

'As far as I'm concerned, Matt is welcome to the shit hole. Him and the rest of his family can go to hell.'

'What happened, Karl? What happened at Dale's to make you hate them so much?'

'Get this, Dale Senior found out about my sexuality, and that was it. I was out of the door and the pub was his son's again.' Karl sighed. 'Look, I need a break. Can someone get me a coffee or something?'

'Interview terminated at eighteen-thirty.' Chris turned off the tape. 'I'll arrange to get something sorted for you,' Chris said, leaving Karl sitting in the interview room. He could feel that they were getting closer to the truth, but Karl had decided that enough was enough. It was definitely time for a breather.

'Anyone got anything useful?' Chris asked as he walked into the team's office. 'Karl is denying everything as expected, so I could really do with something positive right now.'

'Well, Matt confirmed he left Dale's to go to Carbon to watch the McDermitts and was let in by the door staff, even though he had no ticket.' Colin set the ball rolling.

‘If I remember rightly, Matt doesn’t appear on any of the CCTV entering the club,’ Julie offered.

‘I can back you up on that one too,’ Trudie spoke up from her desk.

‘The only footage we have of him is in the single photo Colin found.’ Chris sighed as he sat down heavily on the table.

‘I’ve just got off the phone with the last of the door stewards. None of them recall letting Matt into the club.’ Jen put the desk phone down with a flourish. ‘I also spoke to the duty manager, and she said the same. She doesn’t recall seeing Matt in the venue at all.’

‘We’ve got Karl in the cells denying everything, still claiming he’s being framed. Matt getting into Carbon somehow, and even through to backstage, but no one else seeing him do it,’ Chris summed up. ‘Do we know anything more about Karl and Matt’s relationship? Could Matt be working with Karl?’

‘Don’t get me wrong here, boss, but Matt has a motive! The pub is losing business fast, and there is his old work friend and competitor raking it in,’ Colin spoke up. He seemed more confident than Chris had ever seen him before.

‘Okay, so you think Matt needs looking into more?’

‘I think he needs questioning properly at the station.’

‘So now we have two suspects: Karl Jenkins and Matt Dale. Colin, your money is on Matt and I can understand your reasoning … but to go to all those lengths, apply for credit cards, the unit in Lenton?’

‘I know the bomb squad removed everything dangerous from the unit and we’ve got a car sitting outside, but could we get a CSI in there to look for fingerprints?’ Greg now put in his two pence.

‘I must admit I’ve been thinking the same, but if whoever is behind this is watching the unit—’

‘Then they already know they’re in trouble because we were there earlier,’ Greg cut in.

‘Okay, hear me out. Colin and I both saw where the Dales live, and there is no way that a single pub in Nottingham has brought that amount of cash in. What if, and this is a big what if, Senior bought Carbon for Karl as some kind of pay off?’ Julie suggested.

‘Karl did say in the interview that Dale’s was going to be his originally,’ Greg mused, backing up Julie’s thoughts.

‘But why? This is what I don’t understand! If this is about some family argument, isn’t there a better way to sort it out than blowing each other up?’

‘Senior was also not very complimentary over Karl’s sexuality, and if I remember from watching the interview, didn’t Karl state he left because Senior found out?’

‘But why buy him Carbon then?’

‘This also puts Matt back in the picture. If he’s found out that Daddy brought Carbon for Karl, not only is he blowing up Carbon because of the loss of business, he’s cutting a revenue stream from his father’s income.’

‘Okay, so let’s go to the court and get warrants to search Matt’s home, plus the Dales’ and Karl’s homes and offices, to see what we can dig up.’ Chris decided that there was only one way to sort this out and they definitely had enough evidence to get warrants now.

‘I can head straight to the courts first thing, boss,’ Greg offered.

‘And I’ll get on to uniform for some backup and get the raids coordinated.’ Trudie picked up her phone.

Chris jumped off the table with some renewed energy and headed to the whiteboard where he started to write.

It was at that moment that he dropped the pen and everything started to spin, but this was worse than normal; he couldn’t just blink it away. *No, no, this isn’t happening*. He felt his body crumple to the ground. He closed his eyes as he heard seats scraping and people shouting his name. He needed to be on the floor because he knew the floor was solid, but it seemed to be spinning even down there. As he’d keeled over, he’d crossed his legs like a naughty school child, and now he rested his head in his hands, squeezing his eyes closed. ‘I just need everything to stop spinning,’ he said to no one in particular until he sensed someone kneel next to him.

‘Chris, you okay?’ they asked.

‘Can someone get him some water?’ another voice shouted.

He felt a reassuring hand on his shoulder and slowly looked up, afraid to open his eyes.

‘I just need everything to stop spinning,’ he said again.

‘Do we need to get an ambulance?’ someone else shouted. *God no, the last thing I need is to be shipped off to A&E. I’ll never live it down.*

‘Chris?’

He did a quick check over of his body. It didn’t feel like it was spinning any more so, keeping his head down, he opened his eyes and looked at the floor. That wasn't moving either, so things were looking better. He gradually lifted his head, looked at the wall in front of him and then up at Julie, who was knelt down by his side.

'Chris, are you okay?' she asked again.

'I don't know … I think so,' he said slowly.

'Let me help you up, boss.' Greg's voice came next as someone grabbed him under his arms and lifted him slowly. He kept his eyes focused forward; it scared him to look around just in case it brought the sensation back. He was helped on to a chair and a glass of water was thrust into his hands.

'I'll call an ambulance,' Chris heard Colin saying.

'No, no, I'm fine. I just went a bit dizzy,' Chris heard himself saying. He had used this excuse a thousand times before and they'd bought it, but he'd never hit the floor like this before.

'Are you sure, Chris?' Julie asked again. Chris noticed the tone in her voice had changed. She was worried about him.

'No, no. I'm good, honestly,' Chris said as he tried to stand up and then wobbled dangerously again. *Shit*. He lowered himself back onto the seat. 'Jen, if you could take over writing on the board for me, that would be great.' He needed to switch back into boss mode. He needed his team to concentrate on their suspects and not what they'd just witnessed from him.

'Chris?'

He felt his team were questioning him. They were starting to doubt him. They were losing faith in him.

'I'm *FINE*,' he shouted from his seated position. 'Jen – to the board, please.'

Chapter Twenty-Three

DI Chris Jackson

Was this the beginning of the final scene in the film of his policing career? His team hadn't been the same since he'd crumpled into a heap on the floor. He'd felt them watching every move he made, almost second guessing him for the rest of the day. Then there were the comments he'd brushed aside from Gillroy about watching him fall at the crime scene. His boss knew he was regularly visiting the hospital since that brain scan that had kicked it all off last year, when the white masses appeared that changed everything. He'd done a good job of holding onto everything, hadn't he? He'd continued on when the world spun, he continued on when everything went blurry. Whatever was going on in his head hadn't affected him in such a dramatic way until today. Would he arrive at work tomorrow and be met by the Sup and HR telling him he was too much of a liability, and he needed to consider early retirement due to ill health, or at least to take time off until things got back to normal for him? He almost laughed, despite everything. When was the last time that he'd felt normal? Then there was the voicemail icon that was currently flashing at the top of his mobile phone screen. He knew exactly who it was but was too scared to listen. He didn't know what he'd do with his life if he couldn't work, because working was everything to him. From the day he signed up to join the police force, he'd loved every minute of it. God, it had been stressful, but he'd thrived until now.

He knew it was getting late – who knew what time he left the office? – and here he was in his living room overlooking the football ground. What would he do without the force, that buzz of excitement when he got close to cracking a case? He moved into the kitchen to grab a beer as the cat weaved in and out between his legs.

'I wouldn't get too close. I might end up falling on you.' He laughed bitterly at the ball of fluff that was always so happy to see him, no matter what had happened or how long he left her with next door. Maybe this was how it was going to all end: him and the cat.

As he pulled out a bottle of beer, his eyes fell on the photo stuck on his fridge of him and Hannah: the most amazing girl in the world, who he loved – and it hurt to admit how much he really did. He'd been planning on taking her to meet his parents, he'd already met hers. God, he was almost ready to ask her to marry him, if he was honest with himself. But he couldn't do that to her. He couldn't ask anyone to spend the rest of their life with him when he was falling apart. He wouldn't let anyone so full of energy, so brilliant, so beautiful be trapped looking after someone who was about to become as useful as a chocolate teapot. He needed to end it with her before he got any worse; yes, he'd go down to London first thing. No doubt she'd just walk away like she did last year, not bothered about it because who was he to her anyway? It would only be his heart that would shatter because he had made the mistake of falling in love. At least he could blame their respective careers because that's how *he'd* been dumped time and time again. He wouldn't need to tell her the truth, just that it wasn't working and blame their jobs, but everywhere he looked in his flat were reminders of her. He needed to be proactive; he needed to get her out of his head and eradicated from the flat.

He found a bin bag and started piling her stuff into it. This was the end; he was going to make a clean break from her. He stripped his bed, and Fluff jumped off and went and curled up under the radiator like she was trying to tell him something; trying to tell him that it was okay, she didn't really hate Hannah, that she was happy to sleep under the radiator whilst she was here, but Chris didn't believe in signs, so he continued ridding his flat of all of Hannah's stuff. *A clean break.* That's all he needed.

After this, he'd listen to the message his neurologist had left and find out what bad news he'd need to take into the office with him tomorrow in an attempt to salvage his career.

Chapter Twenty-Four

Hannah Littlefair
Tuesday

'Hannah Littlefair,' Hannah said, putting on her best phone voice. She didn't need distractions. She had enough reports to write as it was.

'Sorry, ma'am. There's a gentleman downstairs requesting to see you.'

'Can you find out what it's about and whether one of the other detectives can deal with him?'

'I'm sorry, but he's requesting to speak to you. He says he's a detective.' Hannah heard whispered voices down the phone as reception tried to establish who was looking for her. 'Sorry, ma'am. He's just shown me his warrant card. Detective Inspector Christopher Jackson?'

What the hell was Chris doing in London? Didn't he have enough going on in Nottingham?

'I'll send one of my detectives to meet him,' Hannah said as she picked up her phone, checking she hadn't missed any calls.

'Thank you.'

Hannah got up from her desk, brushing her clothes down as she did. Maybe a break away from report writing would help, but she couldn't let herself get carried away with him, plus she wasn't exactly dressed for a rendezvous in the staff changing rooms.

'Sam, our favourite detective inspector is downstairs. Will you meet him and bring him up?' she said, putting her head out of her office door.

'Chris?' she questioned. 'Of course I will … but what on earth is he doing here?' She didn't wait for an answer, just got up and did what Hannah had asked.

'Are you going out?' one of the other detectives asked as Hannah headed back to her office.

'Not planning to. Is there anything you needed to speak to me about?'

'Yes, boss. I need a word about the Kristoff case.'

'Give me an hour and I'll be with you.'

'Thanks, boss. It won't take long.'

There goes me getting up to too much with Chris any time soon …

She had just managed to apply a quick spray of perfume and some lip gloss when she heard Chris and Sam entering the main office.

'Chris!' Hannah said as she moved towards him and kissed him. 'I wasn't expecting to see you again this soon,' she purred at him. But something was wrong. She could sense he wasn't his normal, relaxed, friendly self. He seemed tense and very … well, police officer like.

'Hannah, can we go somewhere and talk?' he asked immediately.

'Yeah, my office is free.'

'Okay, great,' Chris replied curtly.

'Is everything all right?' Hannah asked as she turned and led the way back to her office, but her question was met with silence as he followed her in.

'Hannah,' Chris began, as soon as they entered. He didn't even bother to sit down.

'How come you've driven all the way down here?' Hannah said, sitting back behind her desk.

'I needed to talk to you.'

'Well, I'm all ears, and then you can take me out for dinner after work,' she said cheekily, hoping it might spark something between them.

'Hannah, there's no easy way to say this but … I think we need to call things a day. Things are moving too fast and, with our different lifestyles, it's just not going to work out.'

'What on earth are you talking about? It is working, isn't it?'

'I'm sorry, Hannah … I think we both need to move on.'

'What about everything that we've been through together?'

'I really am so sorry. I've made up my mind.'

'Chris, you're not making any sense.' Hannah stood up and moved towards him as she felt her heart beginning to break.

'I can't do this any more.'

'Chris!' She looked into his eyes, searching for the reason he was doing this. 'What the hell!'

'I'm so sorry, Hannah,' he apologised again as he tried to walk past her.

'You are *not* ending things without giving me a proper explanation!' She was angry now, the feelings of hurt and rejection already disappearing. Something wasn't right. Why had he come all the way to London to dump her? 'Come on, Chris. I'm waiting,' she said in a low and dangerous voice.

'Look, Hannah, it's over, okay? But now you need to let me pass so I can get back to Nottingham and the case.'

'You aren't going anywhere till you give me a proper explanation,' she said, more loudly now. She didn't care if she made a scene.

'The rest of the office are starting to look over.'

'I don't care what they all bloody think.'

There was a knock on the door and Sam peeked in. 'Is everything okay?' she asked meekly.

'Bloody fine and dandy,' Hannah shouted. 'Now you can go and report back to the rest of the team that their boss has just been dumped by her boyfriend.'

'Oh … I'm sorry!' Sam squeaked, looking stricken as she closed the door and backed away.

'Well, that's the entire office informed,' Hannah said as she tried to suppress the tears that were about to fall. There was no way he was going to see her cry.

'I'm ill, okay?' Chris said as he exhaled, looking like all the air had left his body. 'That's why I'm calling it a day. I've been seeing a neurologist for the past year.'

'The emergency brain scans last year?' she questioned.

'He thinks I've got a chronic illness. By this time next year, I could be in a wheelchair, unable to function without constant care.'

'Hang on?' Hannah said, raising her hand to try to stop him mid speech. 'The loss of balance and that thing you do with your eyes … the unopened letters from the hospital ...'

But it seemed now that Chris had started talking about it, he couldn't stop.

'Goodbye job, that God only knows how I'm managing to cling onto. I won't have you feeling obliged to care for your useless boyfriend, when you've got so much more to give to the world … I love you too much for that …'

Hannah took another step back. The Chris she loved was no longer standing in front of her; he had morphed into someone she didn't even know, but things were starting to add up. Why the hell had she just brushed all these things aside and chosen to ignore them?

'Goodbye, Hannah,' Chris said as he turned and made his way out of her office.

'Chris, please wait,' she shouted after him as he strode through the main office whilst everyone looked up from their computers. As Hannah hurried after him, she noticed Sam standing up and motioning in the direction Chris had just headed off in with a look of concern etched on her face. Hannah nodded towards her, hoping to give her the cue that it was okay and that she could go after Chris. Returning to her office, she closed all the blinds, locked the door, sat on the floor and sobbed. What had she done? Why hadn't she said something before when she'd first noticed him struggling?

DI Chris Jackson

'Boss, I know you said you didn't want to be disturbed …'

'What's the problem, Jen?'

'I'm sorry, but I've only just had a chance to look at my phone … and I saw a message from Hannah.'

'Hmmm.'

'She wanted me to let her know when you got back to Nottingham. So I thought I'd better check you were okay.'

'I am fine and dandy, thank you, Detective.'

'Boss.' His door was flung open a second time, startling both him and Jen.

'What part of "I don't want to be disturbed" is everyone having a problem with?' Chris shouted.

'Sorry, boss, but we've just received a call from the Nottingham Arena. They've come across a suspect package …'

'Okay, let's go.' Chris suddenly clicked back into operation mood. He was done with brooding; this was more important than his doomed love life. 'Julie, I want those warrants chasing up. Greg should be back from court by now. I want the bomb squad over to the Arena without causing mass panic till we know what we're dealing with.'

'Boss,' Julie said, backing out of Chris' office.

'Come on, Detective Garner. We've got an arena to secure.'

Jen Garner

Not wanting to make a scene with dozens of police cars pulling up outside, they walked quickly across Nottingham to where the Arena stood, towering over its neighbours.

'Detectives Jackson and Garner,' Chris said, holding his warrant card up as they arrived in the venue's foyer.

'Thank you for coming over so quickly,' the security guard said.

'We've alerted the bomb squad. They're mobilising as we speak. We've also sent an alert out to the other emergency services to be on standby just in case things worsen.'

'Thank you, Detective. What do you need from me and my team?'

'I take it you've cleared the area where the suspect package has been found?' Chris asked.

'As best we can. We have Esquire playing here tonight, so you can imagine things down there are a bit chaotic.'

'Are you happy to direct me and my colleague towards this package and we'll take a look?'

'You sure that's a good idea? I mean, before the bomb squad gets here?' The security guy appeared confused.

'Detective Garner here is well up on her explosive devices, so I'm sure we'll be fine.'

Jen turned and looked at Chris like he was crazy. *Well up on her explosive devices*? What did he actually think she'd done before she joined Chris' team?

'If you're sure.' The security officer turned and started to speak into his radio.

'Chris, are you insane?' Jen turned and hissed. 'I'd very much like to be going home to my family after this.'

'It'll be fine, Jen. Remember the explosions at Carbon didn't go off until someone had thrown the bottles into the crowd? Our suspect might well be expecting these to be set off by the vibration coming from the concert above tonight, plus, unless someone says otherwise, this might just to be a false alarm and people panicking over nothing.'

'Detectives, my keys are still in the lift control panel. The lift will take you straight down to where you need to be.'

'Thank you.'

'Inspector Jackson?' Jen questioned again. Was he so unhinged that now they were getting into a lift in a building where a bomb could go off any second?

'Don't worry, Detective. This is the lift the emergency services use.'

'Isn't there another way down?'

'Only through the loading bay or via the arena staging area. I'm afraid this is the quickest route.' The security guard answered with his foot in the lift door to stop it closing.

'Detective Garner, are you joining me?' Chris asked as he marched over towards the lift. 'Or shall I just report back later?'

This was mad! What the hell had happened in London that morning to make Hannah so worried? And then there'd been the incident the day before …

As Jen got in, the door closed and they were trapped in the lift, descending to what could possibly be a ticking bomb.

'With all due respect, Chris, what the hell is going on?' Jen asked him as soon as she knew no one else could hear them.

'Nothing, Detective. We're going down to see what our suspect has left us this time.'

'You know that people like this tend to escalate?'

'I'm here with the famous Lisa Carter, who pretty much bounces back from anything. I'm sure I'm going to be just fine.'

'Chris, because you're my boss and I respect you, I'm going to pretend I didn't hear you say what you just said. You don't have a clue what I've been through these past two years.'

'But you've still come back like nothing's happened.' As Chris said his last word, there was an almighty boom and the lift began the shake violently, forcing them to grab hold of whatever they could to keep themselves standing up. Then there was a second boom but quieter this time before everything stopped and fell silent. Jen wasn't sure if it was her heart she could hear or some other random noise the lift was making.

'Chris, you okay?' she asked as she looked over toward where he was heaped on the floor. 'Chris, are you injured?' she asked again as he swore and pulled himself into a standing position before turning and starting to punch the lift doors.

'Fuck, Fuck, there goes my career, my pension, my life,' he shouted as he kept smashing his fist into the interior of the lift.

'Chris, please?' Jen said, moving over towards him, but he wasn't listening. 'Detective Inspector Jackson!' she shouted at him as she tried to grab for his wrist. He stopped and sunk down towards the floor with his eyes squeezed shut. Jen couldn't believe what she had just witnessed as Chris sat on the floor with his right hand dripping with blood.

'Chris?' she asked again, unsure whether he was going to start ranting and raving again. Jen took her jacket off and started ripping at the arm. She hadn't liked the bloody thing when James had bought it for her anyway. She knelt in front of Chris, who had gone from raving mad man to silent child in the space of seconds. 'You going to let me look at that hand?' she asked softly. 'Let's get something on it to stem the bleeding.' Jen reached forward for Chris' arm, but it wasn't going anywhere. Jen stood up again and felt for her mobile phone, 'Damn it, no signal,' she said, moving towards the control panel and pressing the emergency call button to no avail. 'Chris, I need you to check your phone and see if you've got any signal,' she said firmly to the almost catatonic detective in front of her.

'I've really fucked up this time, haven't I?' Chris moaned.

'No,' Jen lied.

'What the fuck is wrong with me?' Chris gasped out.

'I don't know what you mean, boss.'

Chris barked out a small laugh.

'We all make mistakes, boss. It's just how we bounce back from them that matters.' Chris fell silent again and Jen let him as she too decided she might as well sit down and await rescue.

'We had him, Jen. We can be pretty certain Matt's got something to do with this now.'

'And we've still got him. Greg is getting the warrants as we speak.'

'While you and I are sat trapped in a lift.'

'Chris, what's *really* going on?' Jen asked, fearing his response. 'The others have noticed it too. You seem distant, not the same Inspector Jackson whose team I really wanted to be part of if I couldn't return to London.'

Chris swallowed. 'I'm ill, Jen.'

'What do you mean ill?'

'I've been seeing a neurologist for the past year. In fact, he phoned me yesterday and left a message. He wants me to go in and speak to him about my test results. I'm going to be no use to anyone soon.'

'Chris, don't be stupid. You've got your entire team and Hannah who need you.'

'We broke up.'

'What? Why? You two are made for each other! Two people who desperately need someone to go home to and decompress with when the job's done.'

'I went down to London this morning and ended things with her, and my performance over the last couple of days has probably sunk my career too.'

‘Chris, you’re not talking sense.’

‘It’s over, Jen, and there is nothing I can do about it. The runaway train of my life has finally come off its rails.’

‘Chris?’ she asked him again, trying to make sense of his rambling.

‘Like I said, I’m ill. I’m falling apart … nerve by nerve, cell by cell.’

‘So this is your answer to that then, is it?’

‘What, getting in a lift to inspect a potential bomb with a fellow detective?’

‘Besides that. We can’t change that bit. But, you and Hannah, you went through so much together last year trying to save Mikel, and I’ve seen myself how she’s changed for the better because of you.’

‘None of that matters any more. It’s over.’

‘You don’t think she’d support you with whatever you’re going through, is that it? So you’ve found an excuse to dump her.’

‘It’s going to be too much to ask of anyone, Jen.’

‘If you love someone, then nothing else matters. You support each other no matter what.’

‘That’s the problem. I do love her.’

‘Then why the hell are you splitting up with her?’ There was a silence between the two of them as they sat suspended in time in a lift shaft going nowhere. Jen tried her phone again but nothing. Then they heard a shout from above.

‘Is everyone okay down there?’

‘All good, one hand injury, but other than that Detective Jackson and I are fine.’

‘The fire service has just gone to get some equipment to hoist you back up again.’

‘I’m guessing the bomb exploded?’ Jen shouted back.

‘We’re not sure. The bomb squad has gone round there now to check on the situation.’

‘We heard two explosions, so I think we can be pretty sure it’s gone off,’ Chris shouted, seemingly picking himself up.

‘Yeah, us too, though we wondered if it was some kind of earthquake as the floor shook violently here.’

‘But possibly not setting the explosives off like at Carbon?’ Jen mused.

‘Just be five more minutes and they’ll have you outta there.’

'Thank you,' Jen shouted back. 'So, Inspector Jackson, what are you going to do now?' Jen turned and looked at him.

'Hand my resignation in before they sack me?'

'Get a hold of yourself, Chris. I understand you're in a dark place right now, but you need to pull yourself the fuck together and finish this. What if you'd fallen apart like this when you were with Mikel?'

'That was different.'

'You're telling me you're not on a one-man mission to get yourself killed?'

'I'm sorry.'

'Tell that to James and the kids when I don't come home later.'

Chris was silent again.

'Okay, the fire service are going to start pulling you up now,' came the voice again.

'Chris, it's make or break time, and even if you're giving up, I'm *certainly* not giving up on you or this case.'

'Jen, look—'

'No. You look, Chris.' Jen could feel the lift moving upwards to safety. 'When we get out of this lift, you are going to stay here and sort whatever has just gone down. I'm going to rally the team and go and get our Mr Dale.'

At last Chris stood up and pulled his tie off to wrap around his bloody hand. 'He thinks I've got Multiple Sclerosis. We know that it's all downhill from there.'

'MS?' Jen turned and looked at Chris as the doors to the lift were wrenched open.

'Detectives! Everything okay?' a firefighter asked them as he held out his hand to help them both from the lift.

'Yes, thank you. DI Jackson is going to take things from here. I've got a suspect to arrest,' Jen responded as she stole one last look at Chris, trying to digest what he'd just revealed.

Chapter Twenty-Five

DI Chris Jackson

Chris watched Jen run out of the Arena on her way back to the office, and as she ran, he could see his policing career following. He wanted so much to hear Hannah's voice right now. He had been fighting this battle alone for so long, and when the lift had shaken violently and he had waited to plunge to his death, he had realised how much he loved her. He'd been so wrong to rush up to London that morning to end it all. Having told Jen moments earlier about his pending diagnosis, a weight had momentarily lifted from his shoulders, and he had felt better than he had done in a very long time. Though before he could celebrate any breakthroughs with his health battles, he had a job to do.

'What the hell happened?' he asked one of the firefighters.

'We think it might have been some form of minor earthquake, boss,' came the response.

'Great timing. Is everything still secure under the stage?' He turned to ask one of the army officers he knew to be part of the bomb squad.

'As far as we're aware. I've sent two of my team to check out the situation. They have chosen to go the sensible way round,' the officer mocked.

'Yeah, yeah I know,' was all Chris could muster in response. He didn't need to justify his reasoning to the bomb squad because maybe, just maybe, he had been on a suicide mission and had almost taken the best officer he had on his team right down with him. 'Let me know when you hear back from the team.'

'Will do, Detective.'

Chris decided he'd better find the security officer who they'd first spoken to when they arrived.

'Detective Jackson, I didn't expect to see you alive again.' The security guard in question greeted him.

'You know what they say about bad pennies…'

'What do you need from me?'

'First your name.'

'Callum.'

'Okay, Callum. Have you managed to get everyone evacuated from the building?'

Callum laughed incredulously. 'You must be joking,'

'This is no joke, Callum. I think it would be safer if we got everyone the hell out of here. You must've seen the damage that the explosions at Carbon caused last week. Well, I suspect it could be a lot worse here.'

Callum just looked at him with a confused expression on his face.

'I know I should've initiated this when we arrived earlier but …' Chris shrugged.

'Not a problem, Detective,' Callum responded, suddenly understanding what Chris was trying to say to him. 'I will contact the duty manager and begin the full evacuation procedure.'

'Good man,' Chris said. 'Thank you.'

Callum spoke into his radio and then raced off, not looking back for a second or questioning why there'd been a delay.

Well, I might as well end my policing career in style, Chris thought darkly.

Jen Garner

Jen raced across town and back into the office. *This is Lisa Carter's moment*. As she ran through reception, swiping her card on the way, she couldn't stop thinking about what Chris had said about his diagnosis. She didn't know much about MS but she'd make a point of looking it up as soon as this was over. She near enough flew into the office to be greeted by the team.

'Oh my god, Jen. Is everything okay? We feared the worst when the ground shook.' Trudie looked terrified.

'We're all good. The Arena is still standing.' Jen stole a look over at Julie. Did she know about Chris and what was going on with him? 'Where are we with these warrants?' she asked. There was no time to worry about her boss at the moment. She needed to click herself back into operation mode.

'Greg is on the way back from the courts now with all the warrants we requested for Karl's home and offices, Matt's home and Dale's pub.'

'Great. Thanks, Trudie.' Jen's two personalities started fighting with each other; she knew she needed to do this but at the same time was so scared of stepping on anyone's toes. She was still new here, even if she *was* the fearless Lisa Carter. Who usually took over when Chris was away? Julie? She paused and stuttered for a moment before the old Jen suddenly came rushing out to play again.

'Colin, I need you to go and speak to Karl. It's unlikely he's involved with whatever's at the Arena because he's been here overnight and they'd have found it earlier if it had been left before. I need you to talk to him and see if he confirms our suspicions about the money and anything that will confirm Matt's involvement in this. Trudie, the officers that are currently sitting outside Karl's house – I need them to start knocking on doors and getting access to the place, either via the partner or by force. I want to make sure we're not missing anything.'

Both Colin and Trudie jumped up and straight into action, not questioning where Chris was or why she was now giving the orders. Was she the only one who didn't know about Chris' health issues, or had the last couple of days made them all realise that something really was up with their captain?

'What do you want me to do?' Julie asked, and as Jen looked over to her, Julie smiled at her ever so slightly and nodded. Maybe Jen *did* have the team behind her and she was wrong to ever doubt that she wouldn't have?

'Can you organise tactical support and possibly the bomb squad to meet us at Matt's house? We could, for all we know, be walking into a trap, plus we don't exactly know where he is right now.'

Jen looked at her watch. Would it be wrong to put in a call to James and make sure he got everyone out of the office just in case the Arena was *really* about to go up. She knew she couldn't think like that; she couldn't risk the whole area of Nottingham going into panic mode about something that she hoped to God wouldn't happen. She thought back to Flavor and what had happened there. It might do more harm than good.

'I'm going to organise us some backup,' she said resolutely, turning to leave the incident room again. 'Report back here in ten,' she shouted as she headed for the stairs to run down to where she knew she could find the shift's sergeant. Though she was yet to meet the famous Sergeant Gillroy, she had a city to protect and a man who had gone a bit too far with his chemistry set to be involved in a pissing match.

'What did I miss?' Greg said as he came flying into the office with envelopes in hand.

'You know, we've all just been sitting around doing nothing really,' Jen replied from the desk opposite.

'Where's everyone else?'

'Well, Chris is at the Arena – they've found a suspect package under the stage. Colin is with Karl Jenkins trying to get information out of him, and Trudie and Julie are rushing around organising stuff so we can get the show on the road.' As Jen spoke, Trudie and Julie appeared back in the office.

'All set and ready to roll. The team outside Karl's are trying to gain entry as we speak,' Trudie advised.

'And the tactical units are ready and awaiting further instructions.'

'Great.' Jen stole a look at Greg before continuing. Just because the others had fallen in line, it didn't guarantee Greg would do the same. He was the father figure of the group, and maybe he knew about Chris; they'd been working together a lot recently. 'There are four of us that know this case and we've four warrants to serve. In my opinion, Matt's house is the biggest risk.'

'Well, I'll take Karl's then, seeing as I've just been on the phone to the team outside his house,' Trudie said, relieving some of the tension Jen felt about taking over.

'Thank you, Trudie. I'd like to take Matt's house. All being well, he'll be there and we can bring him in safely.'

'So that leaves Karl's office and Dale's to us, Julie,' Greg concluded.

'I've been into Karl's offices before – so if you don't mind, Greg, I'll take there and you can have the pub.'

'We're all sorted then. Uniform are standing by for further instruction.'

'What about Chris?' Greg finally asked.

'I think he's got enough on his plate at the Arena,' Jen lied. 'Let's find Matt and get this case closed.'

'And Colin?'

'He should be interviewing Mr Jenkins as we speak …'

DC Colin Goodwin

'Good morning, Mr Jenkins. I trust that you slept well?' Colin said as he walked into the interview room where Karl was already sitting and waiting in exactly the same clothes as yesterday, although they now looked even worse.

'Please tell me you're taking the piss,' Karl said as he attempted to stretch in his chair. 'Where is that DI Jackson anyway? As I'm still stuck in here when I'm one hundred per cent innocent.'

'Mr Jenkins,' Colin said as he took a seat opposite and started to fiddle with the buttons. 'Interview resumed on Tuesday twelfth June. Present are Detective Constable Goodwin and Karl Jenkins.'

Karl rolled his eyes as Colin spoke to the tape, clearly fed up of this already.

'Mr Jenkins, I have come to ask you for some help.'

'Ah, so that's why they've sent you, is it? Butter me up with the youthful good looks.'

'Mr Jenkins ...'

'Karl,' he said in a sarcastic tone, like he was fed up of reminding people.

'Karl, you may be relieved to hear that overnight someone planted a suspicious package at another music venue.'

Karl laughed. 'So that means I'm off the hook and I can get back on with my life?'

'No, Karl. We're hoping that you're going to help us identify the person who actually did this.'

'How am I supposed to know? You thought it was me who blew up Carbon. It could be the Pope for all I know.'

'Karl, something that has been baffling us detectives is how on earth you managed to pay for the land and property that is now Carbon?'

'Was,' Karl corrected him in a monotone voice. 'I was lucky. I just came into some money, and what with being kicked out of Dale's, I thought what the hell? I'll go it alone.'

'See, Karl, there is and has been no mortgage on the property, there are no loans in your name, and no inheritance we can find for either yourself or your partner. So where did the money come from?'

'I don't see how this is relevant. I had some money, I bought a shell of a building and made it big.'

'See, if you borrowed this money from, let's say, a loan shark, and have missed a payment or something, they could be suspects. It could be them who are framing you. Maybe there are other suspects we're not aware of yet.'

‘I can tell you now that the person who gave me the money won’t have blown the club up. They benefit too much from their little investment.’

‘Karl, we could really do with knowing who this person is to help with our enquiries.’

‘Okay, okay, but I’m telling you now that he wouldn’t have done it. Dale Senior bought me the club as a leaving present … to make up for Dale’s going to his son and not me …’

Chapter Twenty-Six

DI Chris Jackson

The same robot they'd met a day or so before was closing in on the package to assess its danger. Knowing how things were shaping up, Chris half expected it to be a bottle of coke or something and this to have been another big cock-up. He was now standing outside the Arena at the entrance he and Jen were told to enter originally. If only he had listened and had waited for the bomb squad …

'Inspector Jackson.' It was the same army officer as well as the same robot. 'It's the substances to mix APEX, all right?'

'Great. So … what now?'

'I'm going to send one of my guys in and get the stuff separated and removed to a secure location for disposal.'

'Can I confirm that the Arena is no longer at threat?'

'I can't say for certain, but it would be best to get my guys to do a complete search before we let anyone else back into the building.'

'Okay, I'll let the venue management know that the gig won't be happening tonight and that they might as well send their staff home.'

'Good idea, Inspector. And I advise you walk around the building this time.'

Oh brilliant, Chris thought. *He already knows about the lift incident.*

'You've got my mobile number. I'll head back round to the other side of the Arena and inform management.'

Chris started to walk and the same feeling of being unsteady on his feet sneaked in as well as his eyesight blurring. *Please God, let me just get through today and then you can have my badge and I'll stop*, he told himself. Everything around him seemed to be carrying on as normal: the traffic was heavy, the buses still stopped to let passengers on and off, couples still walked by hand in hand, blissfully unaware of what was going on in the building next to them. He thought briefly about the thousands of disappointed fans who wouldn't get to see their favourite band tonight, because some idiot had decided to try and blow another venue up ... although he supposed it was better than the alternative. And with Karl being locked in the cells, it was looking increasingly unlikely that it could have been him. Under the stage would have been busy with people loading in equipment yesterday for the gig; so if something had been there before, it would have surely been found earlier. In Chris' mind, Matt was looking more and more guilty … but why the hell turn on the Arena?

Jen Garner

'This is the police! Open up!' Jen hammered on the door. She had been surprised that the commander had let her knock in the first place. Usually, they would burst in there without a second thought. Though right now Matt was seen as a dangerous man, and if entering the house safely was the best option then Jen would knock and shout for as long as it took until someone opened the door. Greg had reported back to her that Matt wasn't at the pub and that they were starting the search.

'Excuse me, what the hell is going on here?' a voice shouted from behind them.

'If you could move away from the area, sir,' Jen heard the commander say as she continued to knock.

'Matt, this is your last chance to end this peacefully. If you don't open the door in the next twenty seconds, I won't be able to hold the tactical command team back any longer.'

As Jen started to count out loud, she employed the exact same tone she used for Melanie and Alex when they'd done something naughty. Although, she realised that if it didn't work for a ten- and seven- year-old, there was no chance it would be working now.

'You won't be going anywhere! This is my son's house and you have no right to be threatening him.' It was at that point that Jen stopped and turned her attention to the scene unfolding at the bottom of the drive. She had a decision to make: Matt could be inside destroying evidence while she was standing outside his house being distracted by the person who appeared to be his father.

'Ma'am, if you could step aside, please,' one of tactical command told her as they made the decision for her, clearly not wanting to wait for what could come. After several barges at the door, the wood cracked and they gained entry. Jen stood there as men with guns and tasers rushed into the house, not bothering to even wipe their feet as the welcome mat instructed.

She listened out for various "cleared" commands as she made her way towards the angry man and the uniformed officer who'd been assigned to dealing with him.

'Detective Garner,' Jen said, holding out her hand to him.

'Matthew Dale Senior,' he replied, ignoring her hand. 'What the hell is going on?'

'Do you know the whereabouts of your son, Mr Dale?'

'No, I was looking for him myself.'

'Suspect is not in the house. I repeat, the house is clear,' Jen heard in her ear piece.

'Do you have any idea at all where he could be?'

'No, and if I did, it wouldn't be any of your business anyway.'

'We need to speak to Matt as a matter of urgency, Mr Dale.'

'Well, in that case, you'll need to contact our solicitor.'

'Ma'am, I think you need to see this,' somebody shouted from the house. Jen excused herself from Mr Dale and headed towards the property with him hot on her tail.

'I trust you have a search warrant,' he was barking after her.

The officer on the door acknowledged her and then put his arm across the entrance to stop Mr Dale following. 'I'm sorry, sir, this is an active crime scene.'

Jen entered Matt's home to find a production line of plastic screw top bottles and small plastic bags with a few clear-looking crystals left on the living room table.

Shit…

DC Colin Goodwin

'So did Matt know that his father had paid you off?'

'He didn't pay me off, it was … I don't know what it was. An investment?'

'Then why call it Carbon and not Dale's, or, I don't know, some other family name?'

'He gave me the money and told me to buy the venue and send him a percentage of the income every month. Senior isn't stupid. He knew that bands were looking for somewhere to play that held a smaller capacity than the Arena and much more than your local pub. He also knew that I was *very* good at my job, even if he hated my guts.'

'So you went away and made it a success. Happy days.'

'Indeed they were.' Karl chuckled, in spite of his situation.

'Okay, so tell me about working with Matt. Did he know his father had given you all this money?'

'Hell no, that was one of the conditions. The money is deposited into a bank account every month, but I have to make sure it doesn't look like it's come from me or the club.'

'And this is all above board?'

'Yeah, my accountant deals with it.'

'What if Matt found out about it?'

'I don't know. I guess he'd be pissed.'

'Pissed enough to try and blow up his dad's money-making project?'

'Matt got everything he ever wanted when his dad agreed to give him that pub.'

'So why did you leave then?'

'Because I was given Carbon.'

'Pull the other one, Karl. There is more to this than you're making out.' Colin swung back on the chair. 'There's something you're not telling me.'

'No, that's everything.'

'What were the other conditions of you having Carbon? You said the money was one condition. Where does your partner fit into all of this?'

At that point there was a knock on the door, and Colin stood up and moved towards it. He opened it to a uniformed police officer who handed him a piece of paper.

'For the tape, Officer Haywood has just entered the room and handed over a note for me to read,' Colin said as he read the note.

No sign of Junior, all locations secure, we really need you to pull something out of the bag. Jen.

'He has nothing to do with this,' Karl continued as Officer Haywood left and Colin sat back down. 'Samuel is my partner and that's the end of it.'

'But you keep him, and your sexuality, hidden?'

'Wouldn't you?'

'I'm not sure what you mean. Society is more willing to accept people of all sexualities these days. I remember one of my mates came out when we were younger, and he got a bit of trouble then, but hardly anyone would be bothered at all now. We've progressed, thank God, and there's no need to be ashamed any more.'

Karl didn't seem to have any response to that one and just sat staring into space, until he finally spoke. 'But I bet your mate never got hurt so badly the only option was to keep it quiet.' Now it was Colin who didn't have an answer.

'What do you mean? What happened between you and Matt, Karl? Best mates one minute and bitter enemies the next.'

'That's life for you, I guess.' Karl wasn't making this easy.

'Let's sum up: you and Matt used to be best of friends, then one day you left Dale's and went on to have a successful business in Carbon. Little did anyone else know you were bought the club as, like you describe it, a leaving present, and each month you send Dale Senior a percentage of the profit. You and Matt are no longer friends though, and no one knows why.'

'That's correct.'

'Tell me why you called Matt spineless in an earlier interview?'

'Sorry?' Karl looked confused now.

'When you spoke to Chris, you stated: "Did you know that before all of this, before Carbon, I was going to be the one to take over and run that place. Not that spineless son of his." I suppose I can also tell you I heard Senior inform his son recently that the business should've gone to someone else and not him.'

'He's just a jerk.'

'Anything else you want to call him?'

'You know what? I'm fed up of this bullshit. Do you really want to know what happened? Well, let me tell you … Dale Senior caught me and his precious son in … let's say a compromising position, and he hit the roof. I was kicked out of Matt's house and told to never come back there or Dale's ever again.'

'So … Senior found out you were in a relationship?' Colin asked, in almost disbelief.

'Yes, and you know what, his son didn't even stand up to him? He just scurried off back to Daddy's side. I was stupid and thought he was going to follow me off into the sunset. I told Senior that this wasn't going to end well and I wouldn't just be disappearing into thin air, that I was in love with his son and his son loved me too ...'

'So he bought you Carbon to keep you quiet …?'

'I think he knew I wouldn't just give up on his son, and no son of his was going to be a "poof" as he would put it. So he decided to buy my silence instead. I sometimes wish I'd stood up to him … I wish I hadn't given up on Matt so easily ...'

Chapter Twenty-Seven

Jen Garner

'Okay, tell me someone has found Matt?' Jen was met with resounding silence. 'Where the hell is he? His house alone is enough evidence to convict him of the attack on Carbon, and he hasn't been back to the unit, according to the team who are keeping watch there. We've cleared Karl's house and office, and Dale's. So where *is* he?'

'Sorry,' Colin said, rushing into the room. 'This whole thing is ten times worse than we originally thought.'

'Meaning?' Jen asked.

'The short version: Matt and Karl were in a relationship, Senior caught them and told Karl to leave and never come back. Karl played the knight in shining armour and Senior paid him off with Carbon.'

'*Shit*! If Matt is on rampage and has finally flipped, we need to get a car and armed response over to Senior's now to make sure they're all safe and okay,' Trudie said.

'Well, I can reassure you all that Senior is in no danger whatsoever,' Jen said, breaking the panic that had suddenly started to spread throughout the room.

'How can you be so sure?' Trudie questioned.

'Well … mainly because he is currently safely in one of the rooms downstairs, seeing as he appeared at Matt's house just as we were about to go crashing in.'

'Yeah, and his daughter is here as well.' Julie turned to the team as she put down the phone.

'So they must know what's kicking off then, if Senior's already called the heavyweights in,' Trudie commented.

'If he isn't at home with Daddy, Karl is in the cells, where else could he have gone?' Jen questioned, though she'd been thinking exactly the same thing as Trudie since the appearance of both Senior and Danielle downstairs.

'Samuel?' Greg picked up his desk phone to inform the team who were still situated outside the house.

'Look, I'm going to speak to Dale Senior. Hopefully he'll be able to answer the questions we're still in the dark about,' Jen said, already knowing that it was none other than Lisa Carter who was about to go into that interview room and demand answers.

DI Chris Jackson

Chris couldn't believe that this was how his police career would end, walking from one side of the Arena to the other and then back again. All because he selfishly decided to get in that lift. Yes, he had a radio that he could have spoken to the bomb squad through, and the same with the management, but maybe the walk would help clear things in his head. The Arena wasn't about to explode; the bomb squad had made sure of that, and Jen had made it pretty clear when she left him that he should sort stuff here whilst she went to find out what was happening with Matt. What use would he be back in the office anyway? Maybe once this was all cleared and handed back to the Arena management, he'd sneak back in. His hand still ached where he'd smashed it into the doors of the lift over and over in frustration with this stupid illness and the situation he was in. No doubt the blood from his knuckles would've stemmed and clotted by now. He just wasn't ready to find out what other damage he had done.

As he arrived, he noticed that the military had now moved on, no doubt checking the rest of the Arena for anything suspect. Their vehicles were all still parked there and it was quiet. Maybe using the radio *would* have been a better idea. Seeing as there was no one around, he decided to look at his phone. Perhaps one of the team had sent him a message to keep him up to date with what was going on? Not likely, but it was worth checking just in case. Five text messages and three missed calls. *Gee, I'm popular.*

Chris, I need you to call me. I'm worried about you. Hannah.

Chris, please answer your phone.

He knew who the missed calls would all be from then, so no need to check them. Hannah and him were over, and there was nothing she could say or do that would change that. Hopefully it wouldn't take long for her to get the message and stop calling him; he felt like an idiot thinking like that, but that was the only way to stop him hurting too.

Chris, hope you're okay? Don't worry about the case. Jen has got us all organised. Julie.

Good to know Jen had swooped in and taken over.

Then he noticed a second text from Julie.

Chris, Matt is in the wind.

Well, maybe Detective Garner wasn't that great then … no, he shouldn't think like that. He was a professional. He had been so busy looking at his phone he hadn't noticed another person appear at the staging area.

'Can I help you, sir?' The male wasn't in military uniform so he wasn't one of the bomb squad, and he wasn't someone he recognised as staff at the Arena.

'I'm fine. Just looking for something.' The mystery figure clearly didn't know who had spoken to him either because, as he turned round and looked at Chris, the colour completely drained from his face and Chris' heart started racing.

'Matt.'

'Detective Inspector Jackson.'

'Can … can I help you at all?'

'No, I was just looking for something that was left here,' Matt answered calmly as Chris debated whether Matt knew that the game was up and the Nottingham Special Ops team were looking for him.

'I'm afraid the military have cleared everything that was under the stage. Was there anything in particular you wanted?' Chris knew it was best to act calm and like this was all normal.

'No, it's fine,' Matt said, turning to leave suddenly.

'Matt, I know it was you.' Chris didn't know if Matt would break out into a run at that point and he sincerely hoped not, because running was the last thing he felt he could manage right now.

'Sorry?' Matt said.

'Why do you hate Carbon and Karl Jenkins so much? I admit I don't think very much of the guy myself, but still.'

'I'm sorry, Detective. I have a pub to run,' Matt said, striding off in the opposite direction.

'Matt, talk to me! Where did everything go so drastically wrong?' Chris asked as he tried to keep pace with him. He was increasingly conscious of the fact that he probably *was* going to have to run at some point.

'I don't know what you're talking about. Sorry, Detective.'

'Look, let me show you something on my phone,' Chris said, reaching into his pocket and hoping he could attempt to pocket dial someone for backup.

'I don't have time to look at anything, sorry.'

Chris had dropped back slightly so was able to dial and swiftly return the phone to his pocket.

Jen Garner

'Thank you for agreeing to talk to me, Mr Dale.'

'Detective, can you clarify before we begin why you want to speak to my father?' Danielle asked. She seemed to have been prepared for an interview scenario with her notebooks, some recording device and her mobile phone laid out on the table in front of them.

'We're hoping that he might be able to answer some questions for us, you know, just fill in some blanks?'

'Can you confirm that my father isn't under arrest and is free to leave at any time?'

'Of course. Like I said, I'm just hoping he can help us with some questions.'

'Okay, you may continue.'

Who the fuck does she think she's talking to? Jen thought.

'Mr Dale, I was wondering if you could confirm you have a part ownership in Carbon, the nightclub?'

'I do,' he replied, puffing out his chest.

'That seems like a bit of a strange arrangement, seeing as we've heard that you kicked Karl out of Dale's?'

'You don't have to answer that,' Danielle cut in sharply.

'Look, as I am sure you've heard by now, I caught Karl and my son in an … unsavoury position, and like any proud father would have done, I kicked Karl out and told him not to return. But, in my red mist of anger, I forgot that the only thing stopping Dale's being run into the ground was Karl's skills and his contacts.'

'Why make him leave in the first place?'

'I didn't want that nonce in Matt's life. Matt *isn't* gay, Detective. But he also hasn't got enough temerity to make Dale's a success by himself.' Mr Dale went silent for a moment. 'I was sitting at home and I noticed a derelict building had come up for sale and, trust me when I say this, it was too much of a good offer to resist. So … I contacted *that* man and made a deal with him that if he left my family alone, left quietly, I'd buy him a venue he could call his own.'

'Carbon,' Jen clarified.

'I'd also like to add that the arrangement between Mr Jenkins is all above board, Detective. My current firm were responsible for drawing up the legal papers,' Danielle cut in, which left Jen with very little confidence that the deal *was* above board.

'Does your son know about this little arrangement of yours?' she continued.

'Not at all. *That* was part of the arrangement.'

'Thank you, Mr Dale,' Jen said, standing and pushing her chair away. 'I suggest you both stay in the building till we find your son,' she said, walking out of the room and leaving troubled and confused faces in her wake.

'Well, Dale Senior pretty much confirms what we already knew: he's a nasty old homophobe who bought Carbon for Karl in return for leaving his family alone – although it was also because he realised that, despite Karl's personality, you can't deny the man's skills at running a music venue,' Jen summed up as she re-entered the office and noticed everyone typing away. 'But we still don't know where Matt Dale is!'

'We should've put a bloody tail on him when we originally suspected him,' Colin huffed.

'What after your little unarranged pub visit?' Jen knew she shouldn't have said what she'd said, and she was expecting Colin to bite back by telling her she wasn't the boss and that Chris should be here leading them all. But Jen knew in her heart that Chris wasn't in a great place right now and shouldn't even think about leading a team in a major case like this.

'Come on, you two,' Greg said, clearly trying to calm the situation. 'We're all worked up and have no clue where Matt is. We just need to sit down and take five and go back over everything again.'

'We've got units positioned at all the places we've been to; if he shows up, we'll know,' Trudie reassured them.

Suddenly, the theme tune to *Roobarb and Custard* erupted into the room, and everyone turned and looked at each other.

'Sorry, that's me,' Julie said, reaching into her bag. 'It's Chris' ring tone. Sort of an in joke,' she explained as her face reddened slightly. She answered the phone. 'Boss, is everything okay?'

Chapter Twenty-Eight

DI Chris Jackson

'Talk to me, Matt. I might be able to help. You never know?' Chris said as he managed to match the other man's pace again as he marched up the road away from the Arena.

'Since when has a detective inspector ever been able to help anyone?'

'Between me and you, mate, I might not have a job for much longer anyway, so where's the harm?'

'Did you know that my father, higher than almighty, *lied* to me about why Karl left Dale's?' Matt laughed bitterly. 'He bought him his own nightclub: Carbon.'

'Wait … I thought Karl Jenkins owned it?' And Chris really was telling the truth, because it was news to him.

'All this "I made my money working hard at the pub and we had tougher times than you're facing". Bullshit! He gets his money from the man he swore he hated and kicked out of Dale's just for being gay.'

'So you discovered your father had a stake in Carbon?'

'I'm talking about a *big* stake, so much so that Karl came running to my dad to try and work out how they were going to rescue the business after the explosions.'

'So that's how you found out about your dad's stake in Carbon?'

But it seemed Matt wasn't listening to him and kept ranting. 'I keep telling him this. Of course the books aren't looking great, every pub in the trade is in the same position, and then what happened to Carbon, well …'

'Well, what happened to Carbon will hopefully bring you more income again.'

'Yes. I mean no, I mean …' Matt was now starting to head towards Sneinton where Chris knew he didn't live, and Dale's was in the other direction. *Where are we going?*

'Does your father own part of the Nottingham Arena as well?'

'Well, if one music venue can't hold concerts, someone might as well take out the second.'

'Matt, we know it was you who blew up Carbon. You slipped up and we've got you in a photo.' Chris knew this was a huge risk, but hopefully Julie would be listening on the other end of the phone and arranging some sort of help.

‘I told your detective that I was supposed to be there. The door staff let me in.’

‘Even backstage?’

‘Well, obviously.’

‘So do you think the same person who targeted Carbon also went after Flavor too?’

‘Hell no, that was just some idiots messing around.’

‘So then … what happened at Carbon?’

‘Now you’re just confusing things.’

‘How so?’

‘You just are.’ That was when Matt broke out into a run.

Here goes nothing, Chris thought as he threw off his jacket and gave chase, past the windmill and up along Sneinton Dale. If the government hadn’t closed that police station there, perhaps he could have called for help, as he was no doubt going to be running past it soon.

‘Matt, there’s no point in running! I can tell you that now.’

‘I’ve not done anything.’

‘Well, stop and talk to me then.’

‘No can-do, Inspector.’

This wasn’t going well. He was beginning to feel dizzy and out of breath. He definitely needed a good night’s sleep, amongst all the other things his body was screaming at him about, but his mind, the part of him that was broken the most, was telling him to keep going.

Moments later, a car screeched to a halt as it came out of one of the side streets, and Matt practically flew over the top of the bonnet. Seeing his suspect dazed and lying on the other side of the car, Chris threw himself over the bonnet as the confused passengers climbed out, full of apologies.

‘Matt Dale, I am arresting you on the suspicion of *murdering* twenty-two people.’ He was out of breath and panting, but he knew the lines were etched upon his brain and no neurological illness was going to take them. That was when the cavalry arrived. Chris picked himself off the road as two uniformed officers rushed over to help restrain Matt.

‘No need for tactical support. I got this one the good old-fashioned way,’ Chris told the officers as they jumped out of the van, guns aimed at the ready. ‘And about bloody time too.’ He laughed, noticing Julie and the others diving out of various cars and Jen sprinting up the road in full runner mode.

'Just thank *Roobarb and Custard*.' Julie laughed. 'Or I'd have most probably rejected the call.

Jen Garner

So, here she was, waiting at the back of the police station, not only waiting to go home to her family but waiting for the arrival of a friend whose driving skills clearly hadn't improved as they screeched into a parking space.

'I got here as soon as I got your message. Where is he?'

'Sulking in his office'

'But you got the bad guy, right?'

'Yeah, he's getting comfortable in one of our interview rooms.'

'Brilliant! Thanks for calling me though. It was totally unexpected.'

'He told me what's going on … well sorta what's going on … and he needs someone right now. Unsurprisingly, you were the only person I could think of.'

'Thanks, Jen.' Hannah kissed her on the cheek.

'Do you know where you're going?' Jen asked.

'Of course, don't be silly,' Hannah laughed.

'Good because I've got a suspect sitting in an interview room and don't need you running around the station causing trouble.' Jen smiled as she followed Hannah back into the station.

Chapter Twenty-Nine

DI Chris Jackson

He had arrested the bad guy and it had all worked itself out. Karl had been released and, to everyone's surprise, had requested to be taken home to his partner. Who knew? Maybe now the truth was finally out about what happened with the Dales, he and his partner could start living together like a proper couple and Karl could be more open about his sexuality.

Chris also seemed to still have a job. Maybe with everything going on, Jen hadn't had the time to speak to the Superintendent. But then again, he was far too busy with all the media requests to deal with his failing detective inspector. Though Chris' hand was swollen, he didn't think he'd managed to break anything – although he'd be at the hospital for *that* appointment soon, so maybe he'd get it checked then.

So much for being left in peace, Chris thought as he heard a knock on his office door.

'It's open,' he said in the cheeriest voice he could muster after everything, but the sight that met him left him with his mouth gaping open. 'Hannah?'

'Chris, Jen called me—'

At that moment he didn't care, as he crossed the office and pulled her into an embrace, finally breaking down for the first time since he'd found out about his potential illness. Hannah stepped into his office, kicked the door closed and held him.

Jen Garner

'Sorry about that,' Jen said as she walked back into the interview room, armed with four polystyrene cups.

'I'll just restart the tape,' Greg said, reaching over and pressing record.

'Matt, I trust you've had chance to talk to your solicitor,' Jen said as she took her seat.

'I've advised that my client answers "no comment" to any further questions,' Danielle Dale said, closing her notebook.

'And I've told *you* I don't want anything to do with you,' Matt snarled at his sister.

'Mr Dale, it is totally your own choice who you use for your legal representation,' Greg reminded him.

'Oh, I want her here. It's about time she learns who Daddy Dearest really is.' Matt laughed a little wildly, tilting his head to the right as he did.

'Shall we start at the beginning then?' Jen questioned, hoping that this was going to be an easy confession. After all, they had the evidence that was being collected from Matt's house, the items he'd tried to remove from the Nottingham Arena while Chris was there, and the information Karl had provided previously about their relationship.

'Tell us about Karl Jenkins,' Greg prompted.

'What's there to tell? I'm sure you know it all anyway,' Matt said, still smirking.

'Enlighten me.' Jen looked at him intently as she picked up her drink.

'Well, it turns out he doesn't actually own Carbon. He isn't the self-made man he pretends to be. Daddy Dearest bought it for him instead of making him manager of Dale's. Though, as we all know, that place isn't going to be making either of them money anytime soon.'

'When did you find out your dad owned Carbon?' Greg asked.

'Do you want to know something really funny?' Matt asked, tilting his head again and making Jen wonder if they were going to try for an insanity plea. 'All those years of listening to my father, and him thinking he was better than me … I decided to follow his lead and do the responsible thing before I took over the pub fully: I wanted to make sure the deal was water tight. So I hired an accountant to look through the books and my father's finances.' It was now that Danielle turned and stared at her brother. 'And that's how I found the monthly payments coming into my father's business accounts. It took some investigation work, but you see Daddy Dearest isn't as clever as he thinks he is.'

'So you found out your father had a part ownership in Carbon?' Greg asked.

'Yup, and after all his "times were harder in my day, son",' Matt said mimicking his father's voice. 'He was a *liar*! He had money coming in from elsewhere.'

'I think we should take a break there, Officers, I'd like to talk to my client.'

'Shut up, Danielle,' Matt snapped at her, making her visibly sink back at his anger. Jen almost felt sorry for the girl and the unexpected situation she had now found herself in. It was clear that perhaps she hadn't been told everything about her father's stake in the nightclub.

'I asked my father face to face why he had bought Carbon for Karl when he hated him so much. And do you know what he said? He told me that he did it for me.' Silence fell in the interview room as Jen waited for Matt to elaborate further. 'And I laughed in his face. He said he wanted Karl out of our lives so I could concentrate on Dale's and having a proper family of my own.'

'Karl claims that you two were in a relationship?' Greg asked.

'I was his fuck buddy. He'd use and abuse me whenever he wanted a shag.'

Jen noticed Danielle wince.

'So why go to all the effort to frame Karl?' Greg continued.

'Oh, well, I couldn't frame Daddy Dearest that easily, and I always thought Karl needed bringing down a peg or two.'

'I think my client has said enough,' Danielle repeated, clearly trying to get her brother to stop speaking.

'Shut up! Will you just shut up? The only reason you're in this room is to try and save Dale's reputation, and I think you'll find it's too late for that,' Matt shouted. 'See, before I discovered that my father was involved with Carbon, I was getting really pissed off with that smug shit and his "wonderful venue",' Matt said making quotation marks in the air. 'It wasn't enough that the McDermitts had chosen to play there, he was now sweeping up the emerging talent as well. Who would want to play at Dale's? How was *I* going to make a name for myself?'

'So you decided to put a stop to it and frame Karl in the process?' Jen asked.

'It worked, didn't it?'

'Obviously not, seeing as you're sat here now.'

'Well, that's because I overreached myself, tried to be too clever, otherwise you'd have never suspected me. I'd set Karl up good and proper.'

'How did you do it Matt? Humour me.'

'Anyone can open a credit card account these days, especially with these internet companies, *and* with a credit rating as high as Karl's was. I used to know that man inside out so it wasn't hard to fake his signature, his whole identity!'

'So you've got the credit card and purchased the materials, now you need somewhere to manufacture the explosives.'

Danielle threw her pen on the table and moved her chair back slightly, clearly having given up trying to salvage anything from the mess unfolding in front of her.

'Now, that was a bit trickier, but then Mr Southyard doesn't exactly do things by the book. The staff he employs are young and are more than happy to take shortcuts to keep their boss happy.' Matt laughed bitterly. 'They never met "Karl".' Again, he made wild quotation marks in the air. 'But they spoke to "him" over the phone and accepted the documents I sent. They were more than happy to hand me the keys when I made some excuse about Karl not being able to get there.'

'But Mr Southyard identified Karl?' Greg questioned.

'That's funny … seeing as he's never met him.' This guy clearly wasn't as childish or stupid as they'd all been led to believe.

'What happened, today then? Why target the Arena?'

'I don't know, it seemed like a fun thing to do! I'd singlehandedly taken Carbon out, you guys seemed more interested in Karl Jenkins. I thought what the hell?'

'So you thought you'd kill more people for, I quote, the "fun" of it?' Jen could feel her fury mounting. He seemed to have no remorse for what he had done – in fact, he was proud that he'd taken out Carbon and his father's income stream. 'I am really struggling to understand your thought process in all of this, Matt.'

'Maybe you so-called detectives had it worked out all wrong.' Matt started laughing again.

'One more thing that's still bugging me, Matt … if you blew up Carbon, why barge into the press conference and make yourself centre of attention? Why not just quietly get on with your own life?'

'Because Daddy Dearest would have expected me to. "Back in his day", he mimicked again, '*he'd* have been demanding to know how other venues were being protected just like I did, no matter what he says. And come on, admit it, it was pretty funny too. The look on your DI's face …'

'Mummy, Mummy, we saw you on TV!' the kids echoed as she walked into the living room.

'I hope I looked okay?'

‘A bit, you know, stressed, but still …’ Melanie replied, always the first to dish out compliments.

‘We got Daddy to record it so we could show you,’ Alex told her excitedly.

‘Great. Where is Daddy anyway?’

‘In the garden, I think … something about wine,’ Melanie responded.

‘Okay, I’ll go and look for him.’

‘But you’ll come back and watch the news again with us?’ Alex almost begged.

‘Of course. I wouldn’t miss my starring role for the world.’

Jen left the living room in search of her husband and the hug she’d been craving since she’d left the station earlier. Walking into the kitchen, she found James coming back into the house with a bottle in his hand.

‘Honey, I’m home,’ she sang as James visibly jumped.

‘God, Jen. You scared the life out of me,’ James gasped. ‘I nearly dropped the wine as well.’

‘Something to celebrate, Mr Garner?’

‘Just you, always you,’ he said as he placed the wine safely down on the kitchen island and picked her up, spinning her around before pulling her close to him and finally planting that magical kiss on her forehead that made everything better.

Though so-called street policing was slower, the outcome of the Carbon case had surprised her. *Would Lisa Carter have really seen that coming?* Lisa had become part of the investigation in the end, whether Jen wanted her to or not. She just had to come to terms with the fact that she and Lisa were one and the same, and that her old life would always be a part of her. She didn’t need London or the undercover work; she had her new colleagues, and maybe things would end up being just as challenging and unexpected in her new role in Nottingham, as she tried to play “Super Cop” *and* “The Perfect Wife and Mum”.

DI Chris Jackson

So here it was: D-day. Chris was sitting and waiting for his consultant who was, unsurprisingly, already running at least thirty minutes late. But that was what you got when you had one of the top neurologists dealing with your case.

'Christopher Jackson,' his consultant shouted as he entered the waiting room. As Chris stood up, so did Hannah.

She took hold of his hand and squeezed it. 'Whatever happens today, we're in this together. Okay?'

Hannah followed him into the room, and he sat on the same chair he'd sat on so many times before, but this time was different because Hannah was sitting next to him; he wasn't alone in this. Chris's neurologist followed them in and closed the door.

'So, Chris, tell me how you've been …?'

Chris laughed his response. 'Busy.'

'Well, let's take a look at your latest MRI scans,' his neurologist said, clicking the mouse and pulling up the scans in front of him. Hannah reached for Chris' hand like the big, scary bit of the horror film was coming.

'As we can see, if we compare the scans from last year, there are further lesions on your brain,' his consultant said as he moved his screen to show Chris what he was looking at. 'The results of the lumbar puncture came back …'

'It's MS, isn't it?'

'Yes it is, but trust me when I say that it really *isn't* the end of the world …'

Chris momentarily closed his eyes and felt Hannah squeeze his hand, but the overwhelming emotion was something like relief. He'd done all the research, read up on the treatments, all he'd needed was the confirmation that his life was about to change. But then none of it really mattered, because Hannah was by his side, and he knew now that together they could face anything.

* The End *

Thank You

Hey,

Well, that was book three, which I really hoped you've enjoyed. This book for me personally has been the most challenging to write, because when you're married to a firefighter and ask his opinion on a fictional fire, I was constantly met with "That wouldn't happen in a real fire." In fact, he has requested that my next book be about insurance so he doesn't have to answer my questions… I can see that being a really exciting read: Jen, Chris and the team investigate insurance fraud.

And then there's Chris' illness and diagnosis. Having lived with MS "officially" for the past 12 years, I wanted to do this storyline justice. Though I don't lead a team of detectives (though, trust me, on a Monday morning when the kids can't find something for school, I feel like I am!), I have gone so dizzy that I know the floor is the only thing that's solid and doesn't move, and if you ask my work colleagues, I've also tripped a couple of times and probably should have been off work more times than I dare to count. Though no MS journey is ever the same, and at times it can be scary, there are some fantastic people and support groups out there meaning you're never alone.

More information on MS can be found at: www.mssociety.org.uk and www.mstrust.org.uk.

But what has really driven me on over the past weeks and months is logging on to Facebook and seeing your messages, and the emails I get send which I try and respond to, so please don't be scared about reaching out, because often these add bits of sparkle to my day.

I'm also continuously surprised when I log into some of the Facebook groups I'm part of and see someone has reviewed my book or taken a photo of it because they've purchased it from a bookshop. If you enjoyed *A Burning Lie*, I'd also be grateful if you could leave a review on the website you purchased it from – and tell your friends! Because it really does help us authors reach a larger audience.

Please feel free to reach out at any time.

Thank you so much.

Claire
x

About the Author

Claire lives in Nottingham with her family, a cat called Whiskers and a dog called Podrick.

She suffers from Multiple Sclerosis and as a result of the disease had to reduce her hours working in insurance for an Insolvency Insurer. This spare time enabled her to study a creative writing course which inspired her to write her debut, *Perfect Lie* and *A Silent Child* which followed.

When Claire isn't working she enjoys reading crime novels and listening to music – the band Jimmy Eat World is her biggest muse! Claire is also an avid reader and book blogger. The inspiration for her novels comes from the hours spent watching *The Bill* with her grandparents and auntie; then later, *Spooks* and other detective programmes like *Inspector Morse*, *A Touch of Frost* and *Midsomer Murders*.

To find out more about Claire, follow her on social media:

Twitter: @ClaireEESheldon

Facebook: @clairesheldonauthor

Blog: www.csheldonblog.wordpress.com

More Ruby Fiction
from
Claire Sheldon

Perfect Lie
Book 1 - Lisa Carter Files

What is 'perfect' trying to hide?
Jen Garner tries her best to be 'wife and mother of the year'. She helps organise school plays and accompanies her husband to company dinners, all with a big smile on her face.

But Jen has started to receive strange gifts in the post ... first flowers, then a sympathy card.

It could just be a joke; that's what she tells herself. But then the final 'gift' arrives, and Jen has to question why somebody is so intent on shattering her life into pieces ...?

Available as an eBook, audiobook and paperback.

Visit: www.rubyfiction.com for more details.

A Silent Child
Book 2 - Lisa Carter Files

The streets are no place for a child ...
After a traumatic event that almost ripped Jen Garner's family apart, life is finally starting to get back to normal. Then a woman's body is found in the river. Shortly afterwards, a young boy is discovered wandering the streets. He refuses to speak to anyone, just repeats one name over and over, to the confusion of most of the local authorities –but Jen knows exactly who he's asking for, and it's enough to make her blood run cold ...

Available as an eBook, audiobook and paperback.

Visit: www.rubyfiction.com for more details.

Introducing Ruby Fiction

Ruby Fiction is in imprint of Choc Lit Publishing.
We're an award-winning independent publisher, creating a delicious selection of fiction.

See our selection here:
www.rubyfiction.com

Ruby Fiction brings you stories that inspire emotions.

We'd love to hear how you enjoyed *A Burning Lie*. Please leave a review on the eBook store where you purchased this novel or visit www.rubyfiction.com and give your feedback.

Ruby novels are selected by genuine readers like yourself. We only publish stories our Tasting Panel want to see in print. Our reviews and awards speak for themselves.

Could you be a Star Selector and join our Tasting Panel?
Would you like to play a role in choosing which novels we decide to publish? Do you enjoy reading women's fiction? Then you could be perfect for our Tasting Panel.

Visit: http://www.rubyfiction.com/join-the-choc-lit-tasting-panel

Keep in touch:

Sign up for our newsletter for all the latest news and offers:
www.spread.choc-lit.com

Follow us on Twitter: @RubyFiction and
Facebook: @RubyFiction
Instagram: @Choclituk

Printed in Great Britain
by Amazon

61213242R00131